Case Files of an Angel

DENNIS GARVIN

WestBow
PRESS
A DIVISION OF THOMAS NELSON

Copyright © 2013 Dennis Garvin.

All rights reserved. No part of this book may be used or reproduced by any means, graphic, electronic, or mechanical, including photocopying, recording, taping or by any information storage retrieval system without the written permission of the publisher except in the case of brief quotations embodied in critical articles and reviews.

WestBow Press books may be ordered through booksellers or by contacting:

WestBow Press
A Division of Thomas Nelson
1663 Liberty Drive
Bloomington, IN 47403
www.westbowpress.com
1-(866) 928-1240

Because of the dynamic nature of the Internet, any web addresses or links contained in this book may have changed since publication and may no longer be valid. The views expressed in this work are solely those of the author and do not necessarily reflect the views of the publisher, and the publisher hereby disclaims any responsibility for them.

Any people depicted in stock imagery provided by Thinkstock are models, and such images are being used for illustrative purposes only.

Certain stock imagery © Thinkstock.

ISBN: 978-1-4908-0042-4 (sc)
ISBN: 978-1-4908-0043-1 (hc)
ISBN: 978-1-4908-0041-7 (e)

Library of Congress Control Number: 2013912084

Printed in the United States of America.

WestBow Press rev. date: 07/11/2013

This book is dedicated to Nancy, Emily, Alanah, and Mary, the ladies who own me. If humans could qualify as angels, I would nominate them—most days.

Preface

Because of the somewhat unorthodox nature of the viewpoint and content of this book, perhaps a little up-front information might be helpful. I am a physician, and I came to Jesus Christ at thirty-eight years of age. I really had no formal knowledge of Christ or Christians prior to this conversion experience. Because of my medical training, as well as my undergraduate degree in chemistry, I studied all facets of my new faith in a manner somewhat different from the norm. One point of scrutiny was the subject of angels. I realized that God created two categories of living, communicating beings: angels and humans. Thus, we have three divisions of conscious beings capable of communicating within and between those divisions: the divine, the human, and the angelic. When it comes to the written word, we have offerings from the human division (books, sermons, etc.) and the divine division (the Bible). Angels are portrayed in Scripture. Human portrayal of the angelic beings, however, is often in disagreement with Scripture and is even silly. Who has not seen a cartoon where a character has an angel on one shoulder and a devil on the other? It occurred to me that this third group, angels, despite their capacity for communication, had not produced a book that detailed their relationship with the divine and their relationship with humans. I conceived the idea of a fictional angel who is required to provide just such a book.

As I studied the Scriptures about angels and much of what has been written by humans about angels, my respect and fascination grew. Our modern secular society has produced fiction and fantasy in magazines, movies, video games, cartoons, and books. Our eyes and ears are challenged to fully grasp the scope of their imagery, a testament to the power of the artists and producers to both imagine such things and then to commit them to the powerful pictures and animations of our current technology. Yet these are only human creators working within the limits of human technology. God, as the Creator of angels, is under no such constraints. These beings, therefore, must dwarf humans' fantasy creations in their power, intent, warfare, and mere presence. Their warfare with the demons of Satan must necessarily exceed the human capacity to grasp, much less replicate. Our movies give us heroic cowboys, soldiers, and law enforcement officers. None can equal angels. Movies give us messengers, troubleshooters, and heroes bent on revenge. Angels, as creations of God, can exist out of time and out of physical bodies, and they act out of a love that surpasses a human capacity to understand. There is no movie tough guy who is tougher than an angel—and none so motivated.

I also found great disparity between the biblical portrayal of angels and those in secular books, movies, and video games. My angelic author will clearly have his work cut out for him if he is to clarify the proper nature of angels and their relationship to both the human and the divine. Bearing in mind that I must take the blame for any issues that arise from my humanity interfering with the angelic author of this work, I invite you to turn the pages and meet our angelic host.

Acknowledgments

In addition to the Lord, without whose help neither I nor this book would exist, I have received assistance from humans in the reviewing of this work, either as a completed manuscript or a manuscript in the making. Lucky Garvin, Lily Garvin, Richard Johnson, Tony and Sue Werner, I give you all thanks and no small credit for your comments and encouragement. Judy Goodwin, I give you special thanks for helping me out where I was confused. God bless you all.

I also thank Lily Garvin for the graphic art provided in this book. If there are computer angels, she is one!

Introduction

My name is Augie, and I am an angel. I am communicating with humans at the request of my superiors. Before we begin, I want to clarify two points of possible confusion.

1. My communication will be in the modern idiom or jargon. Angels have appeared on earth and had to speak in all languages and in all the ages of man, complete with geographical nuances. When you are carrying the message of God, it doesn't help to speak Middle English to a nineteenth-century Mandingo warrior or ancient French to a mid-twentieth-century Georgia cracker. It is hard enough to use English to communicate with English-speaking people, but I must start somewhere. This is why, for example, Caiaphas will consider Jesus to be a "clodhopper" (chapter 25).
2. This book is being dictated to a steno angel. In the celestial organization, actual writing is either a privilege (as in the case of a recording angel, such as the one found in Ezekiel 9:3-4, or the angel who writes in the Lamb's Book of Life)

or a chore (see Daniel 5:5). When it comes to steno angels, writing is a disciplinary assignment. For the purposes of full disclosure, I will mention that my current steno angel was assigned this task as penance for a celestial faux pas. Do you recall the first miracle that Jesus performed? It was the creation of wine out of water at a wedding. Jesus' mother approached him to help out. Do you recall Jesus' words? "Dear woman, why do you involve me? My time has not yet come." (John 2:4 NIV) He hadn't planned on doing any miracles yet. There are moments, however, when an angel has a little bit of trouble dealing with the physical body he inhabits (I will give more explanations in chapter 2). Such was the case here. When Jesus observed that the guardian angel responsible for the wine had actually consumed half of it himself, he covered for the scoundrel beautifully with a premature, unplanned miracle. Jesus got an early start on his miracle performing, and I got a stenographer, whose nickname, by the way, is Happy.

3. In these case files, I will refer to nonbelievers. I will use words like *atheist*, *secularist*, and *humanist*. These words are interchangeable. While these humans, usually intellectuals, would bridle at being lumped together, that is precisely what they do to humans of faith. So as an angel who is not compelled to turn the other cheek, I will return the favor. What unites them is the desperate search for a way to exclude God from his created universe without looking like imbeciles. Read on and you will learn how and why they fail.

I should begin by telling you why I am writing this book. The simple answer is that my superiors have requested it. They don't share with me their motivation, but I am free to speculate. I would imagine that it has to do with fundamental human foolishness. The last Bible I looked at contained over two thousand pages, and you humans managed to get yourselves kicked out of Paradise by page 5. That has to be some kind of record. Then let's look at the Old Testament. After the Lord set the rules for proper behavior in Exodus and Leviticus and pretty much repeated himself in Deuteronomy, the rest of the Old Testament covers the judges and the prophets either warning God's people about their misbehavior or cleaning up their messes after the fact—not a stellar observance of the rules. God then put on a human skin and came down to earth. Like Bill Russell when he was a player as well as coach for the Boston Celtics, Jesus got out on the court to *show* humans how to pass, dribble, and shoot the ball. How well did that work? Look at the last two millennia of human endeavor; it isn't encouraging. We angels often wonder why, of all the species he created, God decided to confer his love on humans. He would have had more luck with dogs or oysters. There was a human named Mark Twain who said, "Man is the only animal who blushes, or needs to." So my boss dropped this book project in my lap. I provide the view of a semi-disinterested third party who is neither human nor a member of the Trinity.

As to the content of the book, I have been asked to review my encounters with humans and publish them along with After-Action Summaries of each encounter. I include some older assignments where I was involved with biblical events. They are not organized in chronological order. There are also some encounters with humans that are either modern or of historic interest. I think my superiors want you to get to know angels better and, after learning how God uses us, perhaps to know yourselves a little better. Lord knows, you need help.

I will also be interspersing some brief chapters addressing FAQAAs (frequently asked questions about angels). This, again, is in the hope that lights might come on in the average humans' craniums and that they will correct their viewpoints about angels and what we do.

One other point needs explaining. In the case files themselves, God the Father is referred to as Papa. The main reason is that Jesus called him Papa, and we angels are following suit. In the King James Bible, the translators had a problem with the word *Abba*. There is no actual English equivalent for this word. A modern Israeli Jew would tell you the term embodies both intimacy and respect. It is still used today. The seventeenth-century King James translators must have felt that any word other than *Father* would have conveyed an emphasis on intimacy over reverence. In three places in Scripture, the translators left it as a compound word: *Abba-Father* (Mark 14:36; Romans 8:15; Galatians 4:6). Why use it in these situations? The commonality of all three Scriptures is that each one portrays a terrified child calling to his papa. There is only one place in Scripture where Jesus referred to the Father figure of the Trinity as anything other than Papa: when he was on the cross and the Father turned away from his sin-drenched son. Jesus quoted Psalm 22:1: "My God, my God." In that moment, he had no Papa. That was what Jesus had feared in Gethsemane. That was the true suffering of the cross. So we angels, like Jesus, refer to him as Papa. There are, no doubt, some humans who will feel that I lack reverence in using this word. That doesn't concern me greatly. I am tasked with writing the truth, not providing you with brain candy. You humans might want to consider calling him Papa. If you don't experience moments of fear like the ones described above, you haven't understood your world and its dangers. That is what Jesus invites you to do. Let his Papa become your Papa. His death purchased your right to that intimacy with his Father. Give it a try.

Chapter 1

Case File CW-3852-AD

Private Julius Gallagher, Twenty-Eighth Massachusetts Volunteer Infantry, is dying—and he knows it. It's June 3, 1864, and General Lee's right flank has turned the Union attackers into sausage meat. Thousands of men around him are dead or dying. The smoke across the battlefield obscures both the Union and Confederate lines, although they are only one hundred yards apart at this point. He hears men crying for their mothers—or just crying. The only distraction is the nearby rattle of muskets or the faraway boom of artillery firing canister to pin down some skirmishers.

Oh, mercy, is it hot! Moments ago, Private Gallagher's company charged beyond the abandoned Confederate earthworks until the mauling of the enemy howitzers stopped them. A minié ball, however, hit Gallagher, knocking him backward over the body of Lieutenant West. In the quirky world of the battlefield, Private Gallagher looked into the unseeing eyes of his lieutenant and said, "Beg your pardon, sir." Then the pain hit.

Like many men in his company, Gallagher carried a small Bible in his breast pocket, in the rather quaint hope it would protect him from a mortal bullet wound to the heart. The bullet entered his chest after tearing the Bible's cover. Now when he breathes out, blood spatters the exposed pages.

His Bible had been a gift from Becky Winter, the sweetheart who'd promised to wait for him. What a heady, intoxicating time that had been! Boston had simmered in martial fervor during those pro-secession demonstrations. Watching the new regiments drill on Boston Commons had struck a chord in Gallagher's heart. Almost before he knew it, Julius had run to a recruiting office and signed on for a three-year enlistment with the Twenty-Eighth. He was proud that he hadn't taken one of the bounties rich men paid to keep their sons out of the war. Private Julius Gallagher was no purchased replacement.

He'd been a little nervous about how to tell Ma he'd enlisted. The money he'd earned as a stevedore on Boston's docks wouldn't be matched by his army pay. Even so, it would go straight to Ma. Dad and his brother Logan would just have to find a way to make up the difference. The war effort had the docks crawling with activity, and extra shifts were easy to find. Little brother Freddie wouldn't be able to help much. Crippled from birth, he could barely help Ma with the laundry she took in to help make ends meet. Anyway, it had been too late to back down.

At nineteen, he'd lost his freedom to the army. Julius Gallagher—a soldier! He'd walked out of the recruiting offices and promptly added his heart to the things lost that day. She had bumped into him, mumbled an apology, and turned the most exquisite shade of red he'd ever seen. Never a smooth-talking dandy with the ladies, he had been tongue-tied to the point that he too had blushed. Suddenly aware of their shared affliction, they had both laughed.

"So are you going for a soldier?" she had asked.

"Yes. I feel I must," he had replied.

The look of adoration she had given him had become the cameo he kept in his memory. He had asked her name. *Becky.* The name itself had sounded in his ears like a whispered prayer. He had introduced himself and asked her to join him for some lemonade. She had said she had only a minute, because she was seeking thread for her seamstress mother. The minute had become an hour, which had then become a succession of encounters while Julius's time before regimental mobilization diminished.

At their final rendezvous, Becky had given him the Bible, and they had pledged their constancy to one another. Julius had been a stranger to kissing girls—a buss to Mother's cheek didn't count—but the look on Becky's face as they pulled apart had encouraged him that he hadn't done badly. She had even allowed a repeat performance. She had laughed when he promised to practice kissing her every chance he got when he came back, until he got it right. She had teased him about finding something wrong with every kiss, just to keep him practicing. The very thought had made him catch his breath.

His breath. He's having a hard time breathing as he lies there staring at the sky and thinking about Becky and Ma and his brothers and—there's a feeling of pressure inside his chest. He doesn't have much time. The day no longer feels hot, even though the sun hasn't set.

"Hello, Julius."

Julius turns his head and sees a man in civilian clothes, sitting on a low rock just a few feet away.

"What are you doing?" Gallagher tries to lift his head. "I didn't hear a cease-fire bugle. If you don't hunker down, someone's going to pick you off."

"Angels don't need to worry about such things."

"You're an angel?"

I nod. "Yes. God gave you humans the right to manage things on earth, and unfortunately, that included the option of killing each other. But here"—I place my hand on Gallagher's chest—"let's get you comfortable." The pain stops. "There. Now let's get a little water down your throat." I produce a flask and let a little water trickle down Gallagher's throat.

"Thank you. I'm dying, aren't I?"

"Yes, son, you are. I'm here to keep you company and to see you safely to God."

"So . . . I'm going to heaven?"

"I've watched you. Unlike a lot of men, you actually read that Bible in your pocket. You've believed and accepted God's offer. Yes, you have killed fellow humans, but your motives have been noble. It isn't the fault of you or any of these other young men that the political leaders were incapable of settling problems without bloodshed. So no, none of this keeps you out of heaven."

"But . . . Becky. And . . . and Freddie . . ."

"Don't fret, son. They'll grieve your loss, but they'll be comforted by the same God who loves you beyond all human understanding."

"What about all these others?"

"I've already escorted Lieutenant West. As for the others, take a look."

I lift Gallagher's head. He can see the carnage—bodies strewn about as though a doll factory has exploded. Figures move alongside each body. There are thousands of them, just like me—some male, some female in body, wearing civilian clothes. As he watches, a few of these civilians seem to fade away.

"Those are the ones whose boys have just died. We don't need our physical bodies to convey a person's spirit to the Lord."

Private Gallagher feels darkness settling in. "It's time, isn't it?"

"Yes, Julius. You have nothing to fear. I'll be with you all the way. You have no idea how much you are going to love where you are going."

Julius feels me taking his hand.

"Ready now, Julius? Okay, just breathe out slowly and let go . . ."

After-Action Summary

Angels inhabit battlefields. We are there in bloody foxholes. We are there in torture rooms, in prison cells, and on sinking ships. For anyone who, in agony or fear, calls out to God, we are his proxy. For those humans who have already given their hearts to God, it is not necessary to summon us. We never left them. Whenever human behavior manifests its most lamentable traits, angels are there.

For those humans who exclaim, when mankind's capacity for evil is unleashed, "Where was God?" I provide the following response: God was there. God doesn't violate free will even when humans abuse it. Take your American Civil War, for example. Both sides claimed a higher moral purpose, and both sides were astoundingly stupid. At that point in history, Brazil had more slaves than did the Southern United States. Their slavery ended without such an appalling loss of life. While racism exists wherever humans exist, the superheated racism of America following the Civil War was a natural consequence of that war. Ah, yes, the human capacity for evil—the gift that keeps on giving.

A critic might complain that since God refuses to stop human brutality, his presence in the midst of it is worthless. That critic should harken back to the story of Jesus feeding the multitudes with five loaves and two fish. Many humans pass over an important verse: "And the disciples picked up twelve baskets of broken pieces that were left over" (Luke 9:17). If God is conscientious about fragments of bread, how much more conscientious would he be in collecting the fragments of humanity left by mankind's misbehavior?

For those humans who are tormented by the thought that a loved one died alone or feeling abandoned, let me reassure you: no human spirit leaves a physical body unaccompanied. A spirit is far too precious to be left alone.

Chapter 2

FAQAAs (Frequently Asked Questions about Angels)

What are angels?

We are heavenly creations. We are sentient, and we have a degree of free will. Rather like Athena springing fully grown from the forehead of Zeus, angels simply exist. We are timeless and go through no birth, no growth, and no maturing process. That does not mean we cannot learn. For instance, we learn a great deal from observing humans—usually how *not* to do something.

What do angels look like?

Nothing and everything. Humans have a completely erroneous view of angels, mostly due to the Florentine Renaissance artists. The cute little childlike angels, the *putti*, do not exist. Ask a quantum physicist what a waveform is, and you will get a better idea. We normally exist only as light and are, therefore, invisible. As I will explain later on, light has been demonstrated, even by humans, to contain knowledge and awareness.

When we are on assignment, we may be called upon to collapse our waveform (again, consult your quantum physicist) and take on a particle (physical) form. One confusing aspect of quantum theory is that some forms of matter (solid stuff) are actually compressed packets of energy (stuff that is not solid but contains power). So an angel can travel in waveform (invisible, containing energy, like light) but arrive and work in particle form (solid stuff). That way, we are visible. We can assume any given age and either sex. It is true, however, that we tend to favor the same physical form most of the time, because we've already grown familiar with how that particular body happens to work, and we don't have to test-drive it.

For example, in my more modern assignments, I usually take on the form of a middle-aged white guy with a receding hairline and a beer belly. Having a name like Augie means I come across well with a Brooklyn accent, working as a taxi driver or bartender. When angels are working in a humanoid body, we refer to the experience as being *in the skin*.

As if the shifting from visible to invisible isn't enough, we exist out of time. Just like God, angels can be in the twenty-first century and then appear in the first century. Imagine trying to manage our itinerary.

What do angels do?

Here is where humans have it somewhat right. We are created with a love of God, and we do his bidding (Psalm 103:20-21). Angels have a degree of free will, as witnessed by the rebellion of

Satan against God. Normally, angels' free will is limited to the performance of our jobs. We are given an assignment, but we have latitude in how we accomplish it (Genesis 19:15-21). Occasionally, we will not carry out an assignment in the skin, but act as the voice of God (Judges 2:1). I once spoke out of an animal (Numbers 22:28). Balaam was asked to go to Moab to curse the Israelites. God opposed his going. Two angels worked that assignment. A guardian angel blocked the donkey's path to Moab, and the other angel—me—was inside the donkey. Speaking out of Balaam's ass made me feel almost human. And before you ask, yes, Happy was the visible angel standing in the road during that little activity. Guess who won the coin flip on that assignment?

How many angels are there, and are there different kinds?

There is a guardian angel for each human who is alive on the planet at any given time. After his or her physical death, a human doesn't need a guardian angel. There are other angels who help keep the universe working or handle celestial administration. Despite the first-millennium fantasies about cherubim, seraphim, powers, thrones, dominions, etc., there are only three types of angels.

1) **Seraphim**: These guys are appointed for eternity. Interestingly, when they are in the skin, they always have wings. Usually found around the throne of God (Isaiah 6), they are the caretakers of the throne.
2) **Cherubim**: These are the heavenly guardians. They guard Eden and the Tree of Life (Genesis 3:24). They guard the throne of God. When it was on earth, the throne was

guarded by cherubs until his glory departed from the earth (Ezekiel 10:18). The heavenly throne is likewise guarded (Revelations 4:6-8). Cherubim are somewhat the heavenly equivalent of the American Secret Service that guards the president. They have wings and eyes all over their bodies when they are in the skin. Why do they need to guard the throne of God? Look at Ephesians 6:12. Evil exists everywhere, even in the heavenly realms. Also, take a look at Isaiah 14:12-14, Ezekiel 28:16, and Revelations 12:7-9. Don't be surprised. After all, heaven is where Satan got his start. These cherubs can have four faces (cherub, man, lion, and eagle), and there isn't a single sense of humor behind any of those four faces. They can also choose to simply have one head with one face. I don't know why they switch like that. It doesn't improve their looks or their dispositions. These guys don't have any significant role on earth among the humans. Imagine trying to get through airport security with four faces.

3) **Archangels:** This is the final category. We are the regular Joes, the poor working stiffs. Like I said, we can be male (Ezekiel 9) or female (Zechariah 5:9). We are the guardian angels. We will be there for the end times (Daniel 12:1). We will be there for the second coming (1 Thessalonians 4:16). When you humans talk about the everyday angel, you are talking about us.

Do angels reproduce?

The answer is no. We are not born, do not grow, and do not need a maturing process. Hence, we are (thank the good Lord) not sexual creatures.

Are there bad angels?

No, for the simple reason that a bad angel is, by definition, a demon.

Can a human be an angel?

No. With apologies to songwriters and greeting-card companies, humans lack the requisite morality to ever qualify as angels.

Do angels love humans?

In a word, no. We have a love for human children because of their innocence (*human innocence* being defined as "unrealized capacity for error"), and we also love them for the suffering they put their parents through. That is the most godlike feeling a human can experience: being ignored by a rebellious child. Considering the assignments we are occasionally called upon to carry out, love of humans would be a liability. Look at Joshua 5:13. Joshua asked an angel to declare whether he was for the Jews or for the defense of Jericho. The angel declared that he was for neither and indicated that he was in the army of the Lord. The Lord was the commander of that angel, and he is our commander still. We favor no human on either side of any argument.

Examine 2 Samuel 24:15-17. The Lord ordered one of us to destroy seventy thousand people in Jerusalem. However, the Lord was so distressed by the sight that he ordered that angel to stop the killing. I suppose you might say that God has provided us with a sort of weary affection for humans. You may get this same feeling when your boss asks you to take care of his pet gerbil for the weekend and it gets out of its cage and pees on your rug. We act as guardians and protectors, yes, because that is part of our job. But God's will trumps any other consideration. Let me give you an example. In the USA, the Secret Service protects the president. Agents of the Secret Service also protect the president's family with the same zeal, even to the point of risking their own lives. What if the agent who guards the president's son observes the son pulling a knife to attack the president? That agent gives Junior a ventilated skull and saves the president—no ambiguity.

All this may seem to contradict Luke 2:10-13, where an angel proclaimed good news about the physical birth of Jesus and a group of angels happily sang about the arrival on earth of the Savior. We were happy, but not because of the coming redemption of humanity. We somehow thought his arrival would lighten our workload. Don't forget, the New Testament hadn't been written, and angels don't have foreknowledge of earthly events (1 Peter 1:12). Had we angels known that Jesus' redemptive sacrifice would only marginally improve human earthly conduct, we probably would have been a little bit less joyful.

Hebrews 1:14 tells you that angels are sent to minister to those who will inherit the earth. Does that cause angels to be bitter or jealous of humans? Again, the answer is an unqualified no. Humans love to indulge in anthropomorphism. Envy and jealousy are uniquely human sins that are simply not present in angels—except in Satan. That brings us to the next question:

How do angels feel about Satan?

Angels will never slander Satan (Jude 1:9). That is God's prerogative. The answer is complex. For free will to exist, humans must have a choice between good and evil. God can command evil spirits (1 Samuel 16:14), but it was easier to put the dispensing of all evil under the authority of one angel. Satan was put in charge of evil and dispensed it, even on one occasion in consultation with God (Job 1:8-12). Satan, however, had no foreknowledge of God's intent whenever evil was permitted. If you ask an angel why Satan rebelled, he would probably say that Satan got infected by the evil he administered, causing him to feel anger at God when that evil was thwarted and to feel pleasure from inflicting pain upon humanity—the ultimate *schadenfreude*. Did God intend for Satan to rebel? The answer to that is above this angel's pay grade. I can only say that Satan's love of evil is the most humanlike thing about him. Unlike humans, however, he doesn't like evil for evil's sake or for the pleasure it brings. He really doesn't care if a human is a sinner. He only cares that you are lost and dead. Sin is simply the cheapest bait. Satan is not nice. You humans have a phrase for such as he: with friends like him, who needs enemas?

Interestingly, Satan might unwittingly push humans into seeking God. This is how it works: Some humans who first doubt the existence of God are then subjected to an overdose of evil. Those humans become convinced that pure evil exists as a separate entity. Once convinced of the existence of pure evil, they then seek that which balances it—God, who is perfect goodness.

Do heaven and hell exist?

Yes. They are not my area of involvement, so I have been to neither one. I can tell you where they are. Let's let modern physics again give us a little help. String theory is propounded in an attempt to explain the behavior of subatomic particles. The entirety of string theory is not germane to understanding heaven and hell. One axiom of string theory, however, is germane. To make string theory work, there must be multiple dimensions beyond the visual and quantifiable capacity of humans. Angels find it amusing that human scientists will gleefully theorize multiple dimensions yet bridle at the very idea of a place called heaven, whose existence is neither more nor less conceivable than the dimensions of string theory. Perhaps some particle physicists might even accept this possibility. If so, their silence on the topic might stem from their fear of secular excommunication by campus liberals (see chapter 11).

I can tell you what heaven is not. It is not the human perception of a simple place, rather like a church where humans wear robes and endlessly sing hymns. Deep-space probes have exposed the immensity and complexity of the universe. Linear accelerators are helping humans understand the complexity of the subatomic foundation of that universe. Since the architect of the universe is the same one who designed heaven, how can humans infer that heaven is less complex? At the second coming, a whole new universe will exist (Revelations 21:1)—again, same architect. Remember John 14:2: "In my Father's house there are many mansions." Haven't you ever scratched your head over that one? How can a house hold a bunch of mansions? Do yourself a favor: keep scratching. Let me assure you, heaven is not, and will not be, boring. It is, and will be, complex.

Chapter 3

Case File A-30JC

Wilderness is a euphemism for this place; *pitiless desert* is more apt. A merciless sun makes molten waves of the near horizon. Birds of prey rise on thermals coming off the barren cliffs to the south. People coming here to fast need not worry about the temptation to drink water, because there isn't any water. Our shadows expand and contract on the irregular terrain as we pass; the only sound is the sibilance of our wings.

This is the wilderness of David, of Elijah. They fled here to escape evil. He walked here to confront it. Speaking of him, there he is, half covered by the shade of a rocky outcropping.

We land and run to him. There is dust on his hair and beard. He is not conscious, and his breathing is shallow. His pulse is rapid and weak. His lips are swollen and cracked. We drag him into the shade and strip away his outer clothes. We begin to bathe him with our tepid water. With his eyes closed, he looks pretty average—a typical Jewish face framed by dark, wavy hair and beard. Taking after his earthly father, he has worked in stone and wood, and his body bears the stigmata of a builder's life. He is muscular, and his hands are densely calloused. I pause in the bathing to let some water trickle over his lips and into his mouth. He swallows. Good. I soak his hair with water to draw off more of his body heat.

Slowly, over a day, he regains consciousness. Night brings a relief of sorts, and an insubstantial wind frets the dust around our camp.

"Hello, Augie," he says.

"My Lord, Jesus."

"No, Augie, just Jesus for now. I haven't yet announced, much less fulfilled, my ministry."

"All right, 'Just Jesus'—whatever you say. It's simply that I remember where you were and who you were before you put on that human skin."

"Augie, as usual, you have a question in your eyes."

"Yes, Jesus—actually, two questions. One for each eye. First, would you like to try some food?"

Jesus nods.

"Great. Paulie, hand me the bread. I'll make a fire; you go kill something, and I'll roast the meat you bring back." Paulie is the other angel assigned to this trip.

Jesus is looking at me, smiling. "Next question, Augie."

"Yes, Lor—sorry, Jesus, why did you pick this place and this time of year? It's so hot here that your Papa could close down hell and just bring the damned here. Save on energy outlay."

"Augie, it had to be done." Jesus munches slowly on the flat bread. "I had to test this body and my spirit. A less hostile environment would have meant a lesser test; a lesser test would mean less confidence in my fitness to ransom mankind."

The fire sends tendrils of orange light up into a leavening darkness. Paulie brings a deer carcass, slices strips of meat, skewers them, and roasts them over the flames.

I turn to Jesus. "So did he come to tempt you?"

"Yes, just as expected. Just in those last days, when I was barely conscious. He doesn't attack humans when they are strong. Why should he treat me differently? He is never interested in a fair contest, strength against strength. Augie, have you ever noticed that the humans who do his bidding are spiritually weak? They are the ones who succumb to his temptation, sometimes even before a wilderness experience. They have a counterfeit strength in which they have confidence, whether it be money, intellect, or great physical talent. You have to look beneath that outward power to glimpse the spiritual emptiness."

"Don't I know it? I was here with Elijah. He did some great things; then he folded when Jezebel started after him." I test the venison and move it away from the flames. Sparks fly upward as the dry wood crackles in the consuming fire.

"But, Augie, all that did was expose his humanity. What patriarch failed to expose his fallen human nature either before or after doing a great work for Papa? Elijah didn't flee Jezebel out of fear of her evil. He had done miraculous things, yet Ahab and Jezebel still were in control. You think he ran because he feared for his life, yet he wanted Papa to end his life? A coward who fears for his life does not offer that life up to God, and he certainly doesn't expose that life to the perils of this wilderness. No, Satan attacked Elijah with fear and doubt. He was trying to prevent Elijah from performing his next fulfillment, that of apprenticing Elisha and passing on the mantle of prophet."

"After which, Papa gives Elijah a free chariot ride, and Jezebel becomes puppy chow. I get it, Jesus; I need to be a little less harsh in my view of humans. After all, you and your Papa love them."

Jesus smiles. He accepts some roast venison with a steady hand. The night breeze freshens and modestly cools the heat radiating off the surrounding rock. Eventually, he falls into a healing sleep. Paulie and I nod off.

By morning, Jesus is back in his strength. I stand behind him and pour a measure of oil on his head, finger combing his hair and working out the tangles.

"Are you anointing me to mark the start of my ministry, Augie?"

"No, I'm trying to clean you up so you won't scare any children when you get back. Right now, you look like a hungover centurion."

Jesus laughs.

"There. At least the dogs won't chase you away when you get to Nazareth. That is where you are going, isn't it?"

"Eventually, Augie, yes. I have to tell them that Isaiah predicted my coming and his prophecy is fulfilled." He wipes away a little of the oil that is tracking down his forehead.

We start to break camp, and I help Paulie scatter the remaining embers from the fire and fold up our blankets. "And that is what really starts everything off?"

"Yes." Jesus combs his beard with his fingers and then takes a sip of water from our water skin.

"Will he stay away from you for a while?" I look up with my spirit eyes into the lightening sky. There are dark smudges up there, like flies on a blue corpse. "He still has his idiots hanging around up there." Even though they are far away from us, the demons set my teeth on edge, and I have to be satisfied with clenching my fists and not heading up there to bust up a few demons.

"His demons will keep their distance. He himself has already gone ahead to Nazareth to poison their hearts."

"So, Jesus, can we carry you back to the so-called civilized world?"

Jesus puts a gentle hand on my shoulder, somehow intuiting that I want to go break up a few demons for him. "No, thank you. A wilderness experience includes the long walk back. I will keep your bread and water, though."

"Okay, Jesus, but you know that I'll be around."

"Augie, tell Papa that I love him. I talk to him all the time, but he'll still appreciate hearing it from you." He pauses as his heavy, calloused hands grasp the water and the food bundles. "Oh, and, Augie?"

"Yes?"

He looks at me with a smile that turns the sinews of my physical body to oatmeal. "I love you, Augie."

"I love you too, and you'll never be 'just Jesus' to me."

Later, after Jesus has risen from the grave, he will ascend into heaven to prepare a place for mankind. In an odd reverse preview of the ascension, it is Paulie and I who ascend, leaving Jesus there in the wilderness. He remains on the earth and will refuse to leave it until he has redeemed its inhabitants.

After-Action Summary

Before his wilderness trip, Jesus submitted to baptism. By "fulfilling all righteousness" (Matthew 3:15), Jesus the man signaled his physical readiness to embark on his ministry. The Holy Spirit descended like a dove. Son of God and Son of Man became one. (Matthew 3:16) Then he was a ripe target for Satan, who never lacks for arrogance, because Jesus was the last Adam. He was a target for Satan because of his humanity. He was a target because he was only the second man created in sinlessness, but the first and only man to whom sin had to be accorded in order for mankind to be cleansed. He was a target because he was the Son of God, and Satan was going to do the same thing that had gotten him ejected from heaven—attempt to usurp God's sovereignty.

Why the wilderness, and why the fasting? I must use a modern metaphor. In the early days of NASCAR, the drivers would weld a frame into the interior of their cars to protect them during crashes and rollovers. To test the strength of the welds, they would hit them with sledgehammers. A frame that could not withstand a sledgehammer would not withstand a wreck. Jesus had to do the same thing with his physical body in order to know that it would be up to the rigors of temptation and the abuse of his final physical hours.

The wilderness temptations were standard satanic claptrap: he asked Jesus to turn the rocks into food. He was tempting Jesus to break his fast, to meet the need of his physical body at the expense of fulfilling his spiritual challenge. He invited Jesus to put God to the test, just as he encourages humans to demean their God by daring him to prove himself. Satan then offered the whole world to Jesus in exchange for repudiating the sovereignty of God. Humans really should hold out for an offer like this. Most humans turn away from God simply for the privilege of deluding themselves into thinking that they are the masters of their own destiny. Jesus, Son of God and Son of Man, proclaimed his subservience to the Father figure of the Trinity. If Jesus had to do this, how much more must humans need to do it?

The greater, unwritten temptation was to give up his mission. How easy would it have been for the weakened Son of Man to turn his back on God and his destiny? He didn't do it, choosing instead to preach and then bleed and die for those he loved. This is why many Bibles have the words of Jesus written in red, the color of blood. It is the color of your redemption.

Chapter 4
(Luke 4:14-30)

Case File A-29-JC

"**B**astard!"
    The man walking next to me is getting louder, his companions muttering their agreement with every curse he screams.

He and his friends were there, in the synagogue, but they have somehow begun to fortify themselves with wine during the walk up the hill. The crowd is pushing Jesus up the hill, although no one has actually grabbed him since he was first thrown out of the synagogue. I too was in the synagogue, in the skin. I heard him read from Isaiah, essentially announcing his ministry. At first, the crowd loved his calm self-assurance and his voice. Jesus, however, had warned us that there would be demons. It didn't take long for them to fire up the crowd. One man reminded the crowd that this was Jesus, son of a working-class family. Neither Pharisee nor Sadducee, and certainly not wealthy, Joseph's family was definitely in the lower strata of Nazareth society. The crowd began to jeer.

Jesus quietly reminded them that the Jews had a bad habit of missing those prophets born into their midst. He then reminded them of two major prophets who had gone to, and been accepted by, Gentiles. The implication was clear: God's favor was neither reserved solely for Jews nor an automatic reward simply for having been born Jewish. Galilean Jews, living in an area of heavy Gentile infiltration, didn't want to hear this. They erupted in rage, further stoked by the demons within them.

I ask him, "Why do you call him 'bastard'?"

"Because that's what we call someone whose mother gets pregnant before she gets married."

"Oh, really? I thought a bastard was someone born to an unmarried woman."

"Doesn't matter to us. His mother was still a trollop. Say, what's your name?"

"My name is Augie."

"What kind of name is that?"

"I'm from Jerusalem."

"Oh, one of those big-city boy names, eh?" he says with all the curious arrogance of the small-minded, small-town bigot.

We are almost to the cliff. The crowd's violence has not abated. The demons are doing their job. At the edge of the cliff, Jesus turns and looks at the crowd. *Oh, heavenly Father, I love this!* He is giving them the Look. There is only one thing that can stop a lynch mob: the absolute guarantee that they themselves will feel pain. The murmuring stops. As Scripture will reveal, Jesus "walk[s] through the crowd and [goes] on his way."(Luke 4:30 NIV) The Scripture is correct, but I feel constrained to use the human expression "ya had to be there." This is delicious! Jesus slowly walks up to each man and looks in his eyes. No one can meet his gaze. Heads go down, and men drop rocks as they turn away, some showing shame but most showing fear. As Jesus heads my way, I see, out of the corner of my eye, a larger shadow disappearing into the forehead of the idiot standing next to me. He still holds his rock.

I realize that he now has a demon within him too strong for me to simply wrestle down. I need a distraction.

I bark at him, "Hey, you!"

The man turns to face me. I grab his jaw, jerk his mouth open, and rip his tongue out. When an angel does this maneuver right, there is remarkably little blood, but the pain is a reasonable distraction. The man and his rock both take a quick seat on the ground.

Jesus comes up to me, and love replaces the severity that had been in his eyes just moments before.

"Thank you, Augie, but that wasn't necessary." He takes the tongue from my hand and gently replaces it in the man's mouth. The man looks up at me and curses me softly as Jesus walks away.

"Okay, you're all better now, but you are still stupid. Do yourself a favor and stay down until we are gone." I hurry after Jesus.

"You didn't get Papa's permission to come here, did you, Augie?"

"Well, not exactly, but you should have seen the size of the demon that—"

"It's okay." He shakes his head and gives an indulgent grin. "I'm sure it's not the last body part I will need to reattach, at least as long as you are around."

"Uh, Jesus, you're not going to tell Papa that I—"

"Augie, you asked that question as though you aren't aware that he already knows everything. Don't worry. Just please be more careful with the humans. When I have completed my work here on earth, things will change, and angels won't be doing the things they did before. You will have to adjust." He cups my neck with his hand and draws me near, into that mesmeric gaze.

I ask, "Adjust to what?"

"You'll be working with humans who are saved."

"Saved? What does that mean?"

"Just keep watching, Augie—just keep watching."

After-Action Summary

Okay, so it was me and not Happy who prompted the first unplanned miracle that Jesus performed, but nobody else saw the tongue reattachment, and it didn't get recorded. No harm, no foul. When Jesus reattached that servant's ear in Gethsemane (Luke 22:50-51), he was no doubt thinking of me, grateful for the practice opportunity I had provided.

On a serious note, Jesus went to the synagogue as the final step in declaring his ministry. Step one was cleansing (baptism), step two was testing (wilderness temptation), and step three was announcing his mission statement. His job, according to Isaiah, was to announce the following, as written in Luke 4:18-19:

> The Spirit of the Lord is on me,
> Because he has anointed me
> To preach good news to the poor.
> He has sent me to proclaim freedom for the prisoners
> And recovery of sight to the blind,
> To release the oppressed,
> To proclaim the year of the Lord's favor. (NIV)

In over two thousand years, Jesus' mission, as passed on to his followers, has not changed one jot or one tittle. Sadly, the reaction of nonbelievers has, likewise, not changed. What could possibly be offensive about the above proclamation? Nevertheless, people are still getting angry and throwing Jesus out of their mental synagogue. In Jesus' case, they sought to disparage his message by observing that, though his words were marvelous, they were uttered by a blue-collar redneck of questionable parentage. People were enraged when Jesus suggested that their faith, as practiced, would not assure them of heaven.

Today, human Christians face the same confrontation. The usual way nonbelievers attack evangelical Christians is to disdain their lack of intellectualism. The nonbelievers then follow up their attacks with anger that their own goodness would be insufficient to gain them entry into heaven. This is what Christianity teaches, that personal goodness does not gain them admission into heaven. The nonbeliever maintains that his morality is unimpeachable and sufficient for heaven. True Jewish and Christian morality has never changed. Human morality, however, is changeable with time and place. In history, it has been, at various times, moral to own slaves and to load Jews into boxcars, or for children to report their parents for infractions of Communist doctrine. Regarding regional morality, the modern world still has countries where it is righteous to murder a sister or daughter who violates religious protocol or has the misfortune to be raped and therefore guilty of extramarital sex.

It is sad that these humans ignore Jesus' offer to redeem them. For them, the admission that they cannot achieve heavenly acceptability by their own efforts is simply too great a price to pay.

Chapter 5

FAQAAs, Part 2

How do angels feel about the cross?

Angels consider the sacrifice of Jesus Christ an excessive expenditure on God's part to ransom a species of questionable value. The degree to which we committed angels exercise some free will is mostly in our assessment of God's plans. The only place there is some uncertainty is in the realm of God's choice of species for his love. We place a higher value on Jesus Christ than humans can imagine. Hence, we feel his value, surrendered in sacrifice, should be for a worthy species. We love God in all his manifest forms, but we have some doubt about the creation that he loves. Consequently, an angel views the cross as a totem commemorating the heavenly equivalent of a man who has purchased the Brooklyn Bridge. Jesus is well aware of angels' dim view of humanity and treats us mostly with an indulgent smile. I think, however, even he shares our despair at people who wear the cross as an adornment yet act as though they had no need of salvation. (Do you know what Satan calls a crucifix worn by a nonbeliever? A bulls-eye.) It is worse when one is worn by a misbehaving believer. I know it grieves Jesus to see this. It makes me want to take on physical form just so I can bite myself. We should make up T-shirts that read "Don't wear the cross unless you know who's Boss." Ask any angel and he will tell you how much a crucifix on a misbehaving believer resembles the crosshairs on the scope of a sniper rifle.

How do angels feel about prayer?

Prayer is the fossil fuel of an angel's motor. It is power at the quantum level. It is impossible to overemphasize. Conventional physics teaches that nothing travels faster than the speed of light. This is laughable in the heavenly realm, where everything is light and travels at that speed or greater. However, that notion is simply untrue even in the earthly realm. Humans know, from studies where calcite prisms are used to split light, that something can travel at supraluminal speed (faster than the speed of light). What is it? Information and instruction, including the power to accomplish that instruction. Thus, prayer can travel from a believer to God and from God to the human who is being prayed for and at faster than the speed of light. Or it can travel to the angel guarding that particular human. Clearly, God could provide angels with sufficient power to accomplish all prayer petitions. Judaism and Christianity, however, are relational faiths. God wants to relate to humans and wants humans to relate to him and to their fellow humans. Romans 5:5 indicates that the love of God is shed abroad in human hearts by the Holy Spirit. That love is not to be kept but to be shared. It should permit humans to glimpse the depth of God's love for them and, by extension, to perceive their fellow humans with the same degree of love. That should then prompt compassion for the needs of others. That prompts, among other things, prayer (James 5:16). This isn't really all that hard, is it? You would think that even a humanities professor at a liberal university could understand it.

How do angels view praise?

Some academically challenged humans say that God is narcissistic, always requiring praise, singing, and worship. They note that the Bible portrays the throne of God as surrounded by angels singing hosannas. From this, they conclude that God, if he even exists, must be like a Hollywood prima donna. In truth, the throne of God *is* surrounded by angels singing hosannas. There are two purposes. The first concerns us angels. Angels can suffer burnout. After all, consider the species with whom we interact. We periodically return to the throne of God for a transfusion of reality. It helps us recall that the redemption of mankind doesn't depend on us angels. Sometimes we lose sight of that. A visit back to the throne also reminds us of the One who loves us and that he is in charge. All this helps to remove a self-imposed burden from our backs. It isn't sinful, but it is an impediment to our effectiveness. These deficiencies, among numerous others, are what separate us from the divine. The second purpose of heavenly praise is to protect us angels. Self-congratulation and pride are toxic both to angels and to human spirits. You have only to look at Satan to see what they can do to an angel. Praising God is the best antidote to a prideful spirit. It replaces pride with gratitude. You then feel gratitude to the One who loves you beyond all human comprehension. Can that be bad? Only when you are in the grasp of the Enemy.

God neither needs nor benefits from the praise of men or angels. Again, it is for our benefit. If it were merely a matter of wanting praise, God could have made different arrangements. Luke 19:40 tells us, "If these were silent, the very stones would cry out." Personally, having listened to the singing of some humans, I would prefer to be serenaded by a rock.

How do angels view the Trinity?

I will paraphrase a human, Robert South: "as he that denies it [i.e., the Trinity] may lose his soul; so also he that tries too much to understand it may lose his mind." Modern physics again comes to rescue you. The big bang theory of the universe corresponds to God's declaration "Let there be light."(Genesis 1:3NIV) God preexisted light. The Koran also maintains that creation was preceded by knowledge, or intelligence. The Bible, the Koran, and the big bangers all have it right. Part of God's essence became measurable light. Light proceeded to the condensation of subatomic particles and thus to the visible universe. God continues to exist in what humans could best grasp as light. Remember when we addressed this earlier in the FAQAAs? This is known as waveform, having no mass, impossible to see or touch. There is an accepted quantum physics principle known as the collapse of the waveform, whereby invisible waveform light can become particulate matter. (I know, I know. You are saying, "Here Augie goes again with that esoteric garbage.") This is another source of angelic chuckling. A four-year-old child can grasp this concept, but adult humans need a PhD in theoretical physics in order to keep their heads from exploding. That is why humans fall back on old science—it is wrong, but they prefer it because they can understand it and it comforts them. Wrong but predictably human. Maybe this is where the Yiddish term *oy vey* came into being—if God had a forehead, it would be red from slapping it all the time while saying, "I can't believe those humans think that." God, in complete consistency with established physics, can exist in invisible or physical form. How hard would it be for a portion of God's essence to collapse its waveform and become physical man? Jesus. In fact, I would have little use for a God who was incapable of doing this. Jesus even gave you a hint of this blending of light and physical man in the transfiguration (Matthew 17:2): "There he was transfigured before them. His face shone like the sun and his clothes became as white as the light."

Muslims are correct in assuming that God had no son in the conventional biological way. Physical human male did not mate with physical human female. In Scripture, Jesus is portrayed as a son because it reflects the intimacy between a heavenly being (Father) and an earthly portion of that heavenly being (Son). In modern physics, the term *phase entanglement* refers to the idea that any entity (wave or particle) that ever existed in a quantum relationship with another wave or particle will continue to have a communication with that wave or particle. Are Father, Son, and Holy Spirit separate? Yes. Are they so strongly unified as to be inseparable by human means or understanding? Again, yes. Is Jesus the Son of God? Yes. This is not schizophrenia. This is human quantum physics.

Chapter 6

Case File M-49-AD

This is Lupe's time of year and Lupe's town. During the Christmas shopping season, New York City has an otherworldly magic, an energy distilled from the confluence of tourists, natives, money, power, advertising, and the holidays. Lupe is anonymous in the weather, bundled in a hooded coat, with a scarf shielding the lower half of her face from the sharp wind that blows snow horizontally down the valley of Fifth Avenue. As she makes the turn onto Forty-Ninth Street, the wind relents and compels Lupe forward. What an exhilarating time! The smells of diesel and hot-dog vendors pull at her nose while festive decorations pull at her eyes in a diffuse night glow. People walk, bump, laugh, and say, "Merry Christmas." Lupe loves it—her city, her time of year. Now she arrives at her place: 30 Rockefeller Plaza, GE building—home of NBC studios, NYC. While the Statue of Liberty invites nations to "send us your huddled masses," Manhattan prefers the huddled masses that have credit cards. Most such tourists end up, tempest tossed, visiting the Radio City area.

Lupe goes through a private entrance away from the tourists. Lupe would never escape their notice if she entered 30 Rock by the main entrance. To them, she is Lupe, one of those rarified company whose celebrity is compressed into a single name. There have been Cher, Madonna, Oprah, and even Rosie. Now there is Lupe.

There is a hiss as the security module recognizes her thumb print and the door opens, exorcising the cold with blasts of hot air from the overhead blowers. The production crew, like acolytes who have forgotten how to genuflect, signal their reverence by shutting off their iPads and iPhones. They silently surround her, unsurprised by being ignored. They are rather like remora fish, necessary accompaniments of the shark to which they are attached, as she navigates the marble-and-granite grotto of this highly select ocean. A fragrance of her expensive perfume touches the air as Lupe's entourage clatters down the uncarpeted hallway.

Hers is an American success story. She was born Guadalupe Montcrief to her father, a Cajun from Iberia Parish, Louisiana, and her mother, a former illegal alien from Guadalajara, Mexico. Her father retired from the army at Fort Rucker, Alabama, and settled in the area as a civilian contract mechanic for the helicopters. That was where Lupe grew up. She attended Troy State on scholarship. Majoring in communications, Lupe rose to the top of her department with her intelligence, to the point of brilliance, and her beauty. The TV camera loved her appearance, and that love deepened into obsession when she opened her mouth to speak. She spoke with a deep, purring voice, the Hispanic and southern cadences of her heritage charmingly apparent. After graduation, she was hired by KXAN, the NBC affiliate in Austin, Texas. She went from news reporter to news anchor to host of her own local nonsyndicated show. Lupe was one of those rare beings who could be one of us while somehow being better than us.

Within two years, she was called to NBC, NYC, the mother ship. Beginning as a fill-in for the morning news program, Lupe leapfrogged unpredictably into hosting her own show. It was a tremendous success. Lupe knew that much of her success was attributable to her Baptist upbringing. Coupled with her brains and beauty, she possessed a kindness, humility, and transparency that lit up the television screen and elevated her to TV sainthood.

Along the way in New York, she learned that a faith anchored in Jesus Christ was an impediment. The studio suits would gently chide her. Advertisers were concerned about a host with an inflexible morality. The worst part was her new social set. They didn't reject or taunt her. These rich and famous illuminati gathered her to their bosoms and treated her with the indulgent affection one reserves for an idiot child. They would smile knowingly as though waiting for her epiphany—the moment she could grasp and inculcate their mantra into her soul: "There are many ways to heaven, if heaven exists at all; every person gets to God in his or her own way. It should be enough for God, if he exists, that you are a good person."

Lupe has now advanced to the point where she and her guests embrace a sophisticated God, all discussions larded with abstract banalities accompanied by throaty, knowing chuckles and an odd, supercilious reverence. Lupe now only feels a mild unease about turning away from Jesus.

The ratings, however, seemed to flatten and then decline a bit. No one, of course, thought it could be because of her departure from the faith of her childhood and her embrace of 'do-it-yourself religion.' The advertisers thought it was due to her on-the-fly style. No one was sure where Lupe would end up on a show. One time, Lupe began a segment about bulimia and ended up discussing rap music with her guests. It was cute, and Lupe pulled it off, as only she could. The advertisers, however, wanted predictability and consistency. They knew Lupe would land on her feet. They just couldn't ever be sure where those feet would be. So pressure was brought to bear, and the approach became formulaic.

Tonight, the director, Greta Shores, has landed a beaut. Sally Clarke, a hugely famous fiction author, has declared that she is a lesbian. She has been savaged by the Baptist folk of her hometown and essentially publicly disowned by her parents. She has written a book describing her suffering and her repudiation of a Christian faith that could justify such attacks upon her. The book is a current best seller. She is scheduled to appear alongside a Christian fundamentalist to debate whether homosexuality is a sin. Greta knows that these shows don't reflect the morality of the majority of viewers. They alter morality. With someone as beautiful and winsome as Lupe defending homosexuality, the insecure viewer at home will feel vaguely uneasy in their opposition.

The last thing Greta wants is a free interchange of ideas. That leaves too much to chance, risks violating the formula. To ensure a predictable outcome, the formula demands that they invite an unappealing fool to embrace the opposing viewpoint—in this case, the Reverend Lister. Lister has been carefully selected. An excellent author and old-style preacher, he does well working from notes. He is, however, only a marginal extemporaneous speaker. In debate, he is a disaster. Frequently confused and tongue-tied, he will lash out. In short, he is perfect. If it appears that he is making headway, he will be interrupted or they will cut to a commercial. When all else fails, editing the prerecorded segment will achieve the desired balance.

But tonight there is an issue. While Lupe is in makeup, Greta gives her the bad news.

"It seems our Christian had a small accident. Cab ran over his foot. He won't be here."

Lupe glances up from the prepared interview questions that are bullet-pointed on her iPad. "What are your suggestions?" She tilts her head slightly so that the makeup artist can brush her jawline.

"I say we cancel." Greta is chewing on a pencil that is ever present, although she never uses it to write.

"No. Sally is already here and pumped for a confrontation. This religious issue is hot and current. But a simple interview is sure to crash. We need a Christian idiot to fight with her. Oh crap! Why did our idiot have to get injured?" Lupe thinks awhile. "Greta, let's go back and wing it one last time."

"What do you mean?" Greta looks a little apprehensive at the departure from the producer's formula.

"I let the audience know what happened to the reverend and then tell them we are just going to relax, let our hair down, and ask for a volunteer to come up from the audience to debate Sally. I'll say it will just be fun and won't be recorded or aired."

"But you won't really mean that last part, right? We will record, right?"

"Of course. Don't swallow your pencil. Maybe we'll hit some luck and get a good volunteer. If Sally hits it out of the park and the opponent doesn't look like a complete disaster, we can edit it and air it."

A young lady with a short, spiky hairdo comes up to the stage microphone, and the murmuring of the audience stops.

"Good morning, folks. My name is Marla. I am what is known as a production assistant. For you folks who are visiting from England, over there I would be called a dogsbody. Welcome to *The Lupe Show!* We are ready to start the program. As you know, it usually is recorded this time of morning and aired at the regular afternoon slot, so you can ignore everything else Manhattan has to offer and hurry back to your home or hotel room and watch *The Lupe Show*. You can see yourselves in the audience. Make our advertisers happy, right? Today, however, there will be an exciting twist, and Lupe can't wait to tell you about it. Sally Clarke is backstage, getting her makeup applied. Unfortunately, Reverend Lister won't be joining us today. He had a minor accident. But not to worry. You know our Lupe. She has come up with something a little bit daring, a little bit innovative. Maybe just a little audience participation, okay? All right, before Lupe comes out, let's find out a little about our audience."

As Marla goes through the routine of setting up the audience and stoking them for the show, Lupe and Greta huddle backstage, going over final details. Lupe begins to feel a peculiar restiveness. It isn't stage fright, and it isn't self-doubt. Lupe is far beyond those things. She can't grasp it, but she doesn't have the time to wrestle further. Showtime.

The theme music blends with audience reaction as Lupe comes onstage. There is no need to hit the Applause Now lights, as the people leave their seats with a uniform chant of "Lupe, Lupe, Lupe."

"Hi, everybody. I'm Lupe."

Applause fills the room.

"We have a great guest with us today. Welcome Sally Clarke!"

There is more applause as Sally walks out onto the set. She gives a fluid bow, a wave, and a smile to the audience before sitting on a guest stool. She has long blonde hair and a soft complexion. She is attractive in a conventional way, her face devoid of rancor or bitterness. She is neither leggy nor busty. Her appearance, plus her lesbianism, is such that the women in the audience will feel neither jealous nor insecure. They will be on her side.

"Now for the surprise. As you know, Reverend Lister was to be our other guest for a debate on free sexual expression and the role of the church. However, we have learned that, earlier this morning, Reverend Lister's foot already lost a debate with a New York taxi."

Laughter erupts from the audience; there are bright eyes all around. Lupe already has them tuned in.

"So this won't be a recorded segment, but we don't want to lose this wonderful opportunity to hear Sally Clarke tell about her challenges and her heroism. So this is going to be a chance for someone from the audience to come up and speak for the religious side of the debate. That's right! It will all be in good fun. Who wants to join us up here?"

At this point, the plant is supposed to get up. A production intern from NYU has been drafted to sit with the audience and stand up to play the role of punching bag for Sally Clarke. No one moves. Lupe glances over at the intern and sees, to her surprise, that he is fast asleep in his seat.

"Yeah, I'll do it."

"Sir? Ah, okay, well, just come on down."

I come down from the low risers and walk onto the set. I look to be in my midforties, middle height and moderately overweight. I am bald except for a horseshoe of grizzled gray hair behind my ears. I am dressed in a short-sleeved polo shirt and khakis, clean but slightly wrinkled.

"Hello. What is your name?"

"Augie."

"What's your last name?"

"Augie'll do. Last name is unpronounceable."

"Okay, Augie. I can tell from your accent that you aren't a visitor to our city, right?"

"You got it. Brooklyn born and bred."

"So, Augie, what sort of work do you do?"

"I drive a taxi."

"Aha. You didn't, by chance, have an encounter earlier today with Reverend Lister's foot, did you?"

"You never know, ya know? Bad as the streets are, you could run over a foot and never know it."

The audience laughs. They like me. The debate is going to work. Just then, Lupe notices my eyes. They are a deep, fathomless green, almost glowing with internal light. You don't have to be handsome to get a lady to look twice at you if you capture her with your eyes. Very slowly and deliberately, I wink at her. I didn't hurt Lister's foot that badly.

Slightly nonplussed, Lupe says, "Okay, well, let's get started. Augie, meet Sally."

"Hello, Sally. I read your books. Great stuff."

"Thank you, Augie." Sally extends her hand to shake and looks into my face. At that moment, her smile first falters and then returns. Now, however, her face betrays some comfortable bewilderment, rather like the face of a child being gently teased by a loved one.

Lupe begins, "Okay, Sally, you have had a rough time of it. It's sad that it still takes courage to declare your sexual preferences. I know you were risking your reputation and, let's face it, book sales by this marvelous act of courage. I know it has endowed many men and women with the courage to do likewise. But it came at a cost. Tell us about that."

Sally describes how her parents attacked and condemned her, ordering her to leave their house, the $5 million home she had purchased for them. As she recounts the television interview in which her parents publicly disowned her, she makes eye contact with Lupe and the audience but still darts curious glances at me. Lupe notices that I am leaning back comfortably, hands resting on my paunch. I know that my face carries a sympathy and, what is it, a glow? Lupe still can't get a handle on me. Sally finishes with a description of the book burning in her small hometown. Again, she is perfect. She is drained, and her shoulders sag. There is no animosity. She doesn't cry, but it wouldn't take much. Lupe allows for a deliberate, silent pause. Then she says, "Okay, Augie, do you say homosexuality is a sin?"

"Nope."

Lupe frowns. "You said you were on the religious side of the debate."

"I am, but you asked me if *I* said homosexuality is a sin. I don't say it; the Bible says it. Leviticus 20:13 and Romans 1:26-28."

Lupe is back on firm ground but seems a little surprised that this cabbie is quoting specific Scripture. At least, she realizes, he has staked out a biblical position. Still, she bites her lower lip, a habit she has when things don't add up completely.

A little bit hesitantly, she asks, "So do you believe the Bible is the Word of God?"

"Let's just say I know it is."

Lupe seems to feel better about this inflexible position. "So based on your acceptance of the Bible, do you consider homosexuality a sin?"

"Lupe, I'm only gonna answer you if you will permit me to define that term and explain a few things."

"Okay."

"All right. Let's say, for example, Reverend Lister was jaywalking. Maybe that's how he got his foot run over. So, anyway, he gets to the curb, and I tell him that he broke the law. I don't write the law; I don't enforce the law. I don't even call the cops on him. I'm just letting him know there is an authority who takes issue with that kind of stuff. So I'm kinda saying, 'Hey, pal, keep up the jaywalking and there might be a problem for you.' Friendly like."

"So, Augie, does God punish homosexuals?" Lupe is leaning forward, looking for an answer that Sally can spike over the net.

"Lupe, we gotta get away from this whole 'angry God' routine. Let me explain. Homosexuality is a sexual sin, yes. But look at Matthew 5:28. Jesus is sayin' that 'if a man looks at a woman with lust, he has committed adultery with her in his heart.' Sexual sin! Just by lookin'! Somebody might say that homosexuality is described in the Bible as detestable and an abomination, so it must be a worse sexual sin than simple lust. I would have to reply that the Ten Commandments, which God took the time to carve in stone tablets, mention adultery but not homosexuality. So maybe adultery is even higher on God's list. So let's just agree that these are equal, okay? May I continue?"

Lupe nods. Sally is leaning forward, looking on intently. The audience is stone silent. The sound engineers, however, are noticing something strange. The resonance and depth of the voice is increasing, the pattern on the monitors no longer resembling a common human voice pattern. It sounds somehow three-dimensional in their headsets. Even the Brooklyn patois seems to be falling away.

"God is not a cosmic bad guy looking for reasons to smack us on the nose with a rolled-up newspaper. Look at television. There is no way a man could go through one night of prime-time shows without lust. Advertising depends on it. When was the last time you saw a shaving-cream commercial that didn't have a mostly naked woman in the bathroom with the guy? To buy their stuff, they appeal to our capacity for lust. And you, ladies, sorry, but you have the occasional lustful thought too, don't you?" The grin on my face is matched by the smiles of many of the ladies in the audience.

"So, Augie, are we all sexual sinners?"

"Lupe, every person is a sinner, period. Sexual sin is just the one that grabs the headlines. A sin is nothing more than a thought or behavior that God would like for us to avoid. At the same time, he knows it is in our nature to sin."

It's time for me to focus on Sally. I turn to her, noting that she is unaware that I have moved our chairs close together without anyone picking up on it. "You know, Sally, whenever a committed Christian looks down on you or judges you or condemns you for any sin, you are watching a Christian who is getting himself in a whole lot of trouble. A judgmental spirit is a dangerous sin, mostly because folks don't even realize it is a sin. Jesus himself reserved his harshest words not for sinners but for the self-righteous religious folks who looked down on other sinners. Look at Luke 18:9-14. Sally, you should feel sorry for your parents and the folks in your hometown."

I know that now Lupe is beginning to flash back to the country baptisms back in Alabama—people gathered on the mud bank of the Choctawhatchie River, people coming out of the water to let the world know they have acknowledged the need for God's help in their circumstance. Lupe hears herself ask a question she has not consciously constructed. "Augie, as a Christian, what message do you have for Sally and, for that matter, for us?"

I again turn back to Sally. I know her heart is opening, letting her separate the Jesus of her upbringing from the foolishness of his misguided believers back in her hometown. "Sally, you have a Papa who won't turn from you, ever. He loves you. He misses your voice and the sound of your laughter in his house. He knows that, like everyone else, you have bumped up against the world and come away bruised. He has a special medicine, made from blood, that takes those bruises away. As for your sins, you and he can work on that together. It is absolutely nobody's business but yours and God's. Ignore the self-righteous children of God—he clearly has a lot of work to do with them as well. What do you say—are you still his daughter?"

Sally gives a small sob and slips from the stool onto her knees. As she bows her head, I join her, murmuring in her ear. Lupe, too astonished to speak, looks down at her knees, which are shaking as though they want to bend of their own volition. Resolutely, she locks her knees and then turns in response to an unfamiliar sound. At least half of the audience is approaching the stage and going down on their knees. Someone begins to sing "Amazing Grace," and almost all the audience members join in. Greta, off camera, gives Lupe a "What is going on?" look. Lupe gives a small shrug. The song ends, and the folks get off their knees, some saying, "Praise God." They begin to hug one another. Sally is among them, crying and laughing. The crowd envelops Lupe. She eventually breaks free and looks for me. She can't spot me, because I am no longer visible. I have done what I came to do.

Marla and Greta reach Lupe at the same time.

"I can't believe it! A real revival on *The Lupe Show!*" Marla bubbles. "The sound technicians can't believe how Augie's voice registered on their monitors!"

"Marla, you have it all recorded?"

"Lupe, we got it all. There is even one natural pause where we could cut to commercial if you want. Otherwise, nothing to edit. Perfect!"

Greta and Lupe look at each other. Greta raises an eyebrow in question. Lupe makes her decision and shakes her head at Greta.

Greta turns to Marla. "Marla, erase every recording of that segment."

"What?"

"You heard me. Instruct every crew member to forget what happened here. Nobody talks to the press either."

Lupe nods and walks away. Greta notices the stricken look on Lupe's face.

"Greta, I don't understand. This is great television."

"Marla, Lupe is not going to commit social and commercial suicide for one splashy segment of questionable taste. Just clear the set and follow these orders. Where is Sally?"

"She invited some audience folks back to her dressing room—a man and wife just back from a mission trip. I think she'll be okay."

"Yeah, I expect she'll be more okay than she has been in quite a while." Greta looks over at Lupe, closing her dressing room door behind her. "I don't know about Lupe. She looks like she just sold her soul or something."

After-Action Summary

In this assignment, I confronted two people who had fallen from their faith. Sally had not been seduced away by lesbianism. She had been driven away by judgmental spirits manifest in people who should know better. I think all humans who presume to publicly condemn a fellow Christian should preface their comments with a confession of their own major sin. That would shut a lot of mouths.

Lupe is a different story. Seduced away from the faith of her upbringing, she has joined the intellectual elite. This is the crowd that, if they acknowledge God at all, insists that he be a sophisticated God. The God of Scripture does not tickle the IQ. He can be understood and accepted by the simplest intellect. Such a God does not resonate with humans who submit their entire worldview to the power of their mind. Rejecting the truth, they proceed to construct their own God and endow him with only those attributes that pass the sniff test of their own idiosyncrasies—sort of a theological Mr. Potato Head. Such a God is convenient because he yields to modification. Personally, were I human, I would have no interest in a God who was no better than my capacity to imagine.

Lupe wishes to remain acceptable to these intellectual elitists. Just like Satan, who, in the skin, is beautiful (2 Corinthians

11:14), these people have wealth, beauty, power, and intelligence (2 Corinthians 11:15). Lupe wants to be with them, to *be* them. I gave her a chance to embrace her faith again. Or she could simply have aired the recording and allowed her program to be associated with a startling television event that might have served nonbelievers in the viewing audience. She rejected all this.

Because nothing is impossible with God, she may receive another chance. If she rejects that, she may find herself on the list of the ten most beautiful people in hell.

Chapter 7

FAQAAs, Part 3

Are there only Christians in heaven?

Again I must plead that heaven is not my realm of responsibility, and I have never been there, but the answer to this question is manifestly no.

There are four nice Jewish boys in the Old Testament whom you must account for.

a. Enoch (Genesis 5:24) walked with God until God took him up.
b. Moses died a physical death (Deuteronomy 34:5) yet was present at the transfiguration of Christ.
c. Elijah did not experience a physical death but was taken up in a whirlwind (2 Kings 2:11). Both Moses and Elijah were present with Jesus at the transfiguration (Mark 9:4: "and there appeared with them Moses and Elijah"). Where do we believe Moses and Elijah existed before their return to earth to be visible with Jesus? Did Jesus drop by hell to

pick them up? The only logical conclusion is that they were, and are, inhabitants of heaven.

d. Abraham was a righteous man, and in Romans 4:3 (see also Genesis 15:6), Paul alludes to God attributing righteousness to Abraham because of his steadfast faith in God. In fact, Jesus himself (Luke 16:22-31) describes Father Abraham at the gate of heaven. While some might argue that this is a parable, how likely is it that Jesus would construct a parable with an inaccurate description of heaven?

I believe it is safe to assume that these four righteous Jews are residents of heaven. Additionally, there is the question of Melchezidek, Prince of Salem (Genesis 14:18-20, Psalm 110:4, Hebrews 7:15-17). Melchezidek was neither Jew nor Christian, but a Jebusite. He was righteous enough that Abram gave a tithe to him. You may look at Hebrews 7 to see the implications of that act. Also, Hebrews 7:16 refers to Melchezidek having an indestructible life. Does that imply a heavenly existence? I don't know, but the author of Hebrews used this Prince of Salem as a forerunner and example of the priesthood that resides in Jesus. Sounds like a pretty heavenly pedigree. With the exception of Elijah, the commonality of these men is that they preexisted the law, and their acceptability was based on righteousness.

These men lived before the sacrifice of Christ. So we now have an issue with the people who came after the covenant of Jesus' atoning blood. There are some humans who feel that Romans 2:14-16 provides a back door into heaven:

> Indeed, when Gentiles, who do not have the law, do
> by nature things required by the law, they are a law
> for themselves, even though they do not have the law,

since they show that the requirements of the law are written on their hearts, their consciences also bearing witness, and their thoughts now accusing, now even defending them. This will take place on the day when God will judge men's secrets through Jesus Christ, as my gospel declares.

To these people we must add the more modern, sophisticated, spiritual secularist who feels that his own standard of goodness should be sufficient to purchase him entry into heaven. Elsewhere in these case files, I have referred to the expedient morality of modern people and modern nations that have lauded behaviors expressly condemned in Scripture (for example, lust, murder, slander, and theft, just to name a few). These same people explode at the counterargument that such moral codes are neither sufficient for heaven nor even acceptable on earth.

Let's examine what a man, on his own, can do about heaven. A man can purchase a toxic-waste dump and put up a sign declaring it to be heaven. He can then move in and be in heaven without having first suffered a physical death. He can even be proud that his heaven, just like his moral code, is of his own construction and is independent of any deity. Alternatively, he can conduct his earthly life according to his own standards and, after death, let's imagine that he gets escorted into one of those dimensions theorized by quantum physicists. He can also declare that his new dimension is heaven, and by his own estimation, he is indeed in heaven. He can ignore the smell of sulfur and enjoy eternity there. Neither of these fantasies equates to the heaven of Scripture. Heaven is not a reward but a place where rewards are found (Matthew 6:20: "store up for yourselves treasures in heaven").

Imagine the arrogance of a human who appears before the State Bar association and demands that he be admitted as an attorney with full rights and privileges. In response to a question about his qualifications, he responds that he is a good person, obeys the law, and watches lots of lawyer programs on TV. In his own opinion, he is perfectly fit for admission into this entity. The modern good person who assumes that his self-assessed adequacy should get him into heaven is doing much the same thing. He substitutes his own list of acceptable behavior for the unchanging demands of Scripture. The heaven of Scripture is a place one enters as a result of fulfilling a series of acts, obligations, and repentances. A moral code of your own devising will only get you into a heaven of your own devising.

If you wish to attain biblical heaven by some other means than the atoning blood of Jesus, you are welcome to try. That is part of free will. Those who trust in their own definition of goodness are doomed to failure. Those who, as in Romans 2:14, attempt to live a life of goodness consistent with scriptural law but without the intercession of Jesus have to live a life equivalent to that of Enoch, Elijah, Moses, or Abraham. Good luck with that. And it is not just a life of outward righteousness but a heart and mind that must be judged blameless. Can such a human exist? The good news is yes; the sad news is that there has only been one, and his name is Jesus, the last Adam, Son of Man.

What about hell?

If a human excludes God from his earthly life, God reasonably should conclude that this human also doesn't want God to be a part of his eternal life. Hell is where the atheist's wishes come true—not only is there no God to offend his intellectual autonomy, but there are also none of God's pleasurable creations to remind the atheist of God's existence. On earth, the pleasures of God are conferred on all humans (Matthew 5:45). This must be pure agony for a true atheist. Lest that atheist complain that God is also intruding in hell, God has removed love and joy from that dimension. Remorse, however, is thought permissible. While hell is, indeed, warm, it is not fully the inferno of human imagination. The type of heat that humans imagine would cause third-degree burns (yes, humans will inhabit bodies after physical death—2 Corinthians 5). Third-degree burns kill the nerves, and there is no pain. Where is the suffering in that? If you want to understand the burning experience in hell, try to recall a time when you were embarrassed or humiliated. You had a blushing, burning face, but you also had an internal burning. Now imagine that feeling magnified a thousandfold for all eternity. What could cause that degree of humiliation? Perhaps it comes when a human dies and begins day one of eternal life only to learn that he was an imbecile to disregard God in his earthly life. Were I capable of embarrassment, I would imagine that such a revelation would prompt some pretty robust humiliation. Not to worry. Out of regard for your sensibilities, hell is constructed (so I am told) so that no one will be there to laugh at you. No one at all. You will be alone. For all eternity. Enjoy.

How do angels view the humans doing separation of church and state?

This is an odd question, but Happy, my steno angel, thought I should address it because it really is an example of Satan at the top of his game. Let's focus on the United States, since that is where this fantasy is most bizarre. Virtually all angels agree with separation of church and state. Incorrectly, however, most fire-breathing liberals and secular witch hunters interpret this doctrine to mean rooting out all vestiges of Christianity from both the government and all human organizations that suckle on the federal nipple. They would consider it secular heresy to actually remove the government from all church endeavors. Reasonably, however, humans should expel government from institutions that are, by time and tradition, the purview of the church before the enforcement of this separateness. Let's take a few examples.

A. Marriage: Marriage is a sacrament. It clearly originated in the church. The government should honor its own commitment to separation of church and state by getting out of marriage altogether, including enforcement of marital law and divorce.
B. Health Care: The earliest hospitals were in ancient Greece and dedicated to Asclepius, the god of healing. Aside from increasing the cost, what has government intrusion into health care accomplished? Certainly, the tradition of medicine and religion should mandate an exclusion of government from health care.
C. Charity: The earliest definition of charity held that it was agape, or universal, love. This was a Christian concept. With the advent of government and secular organizations, charity became benevolent giving but still primarily through church organizations. Welfare (now designated SSI) is the government's replacement for charity, and it works no better than any other government program. The administrative cost is far higher than in faith-based groups and is often given to undeserving people. The meeting of legitimate temporary needs has now become the provision of so-called entitlements in a permanent lifestyle where the recipient is never given the chance to achieve self-respect. Humans should take charitable work away from the

government and give it back to the traditional faith-based organizations. They can hardly do worse.

Human governments should return to the things that they do best: collecting taxes, making war, and lying to constituents.

Chapter 8

Case File M-23-AD

It's springtime, and the earth is renewing itself. The robins have already built their nests, and the river is running high from the snowmelt up in the mountains. It's a light-jacket morning, and Rita Dulaney looks over the playground. The children are playing with the mania of inmates released from winter confinement—all except her Lily. Lily had played for a while and then taken her customary place on the bench on the other side of the playground, kicking her legs and shaking her long black hair from side to side. Once a friendly, effervescent girl, Lily now rarely smiles and never laughs. Rita watches her, knowing she will stay there awhile before rejoining her mother. The anemones and bluebells have replaced the daffodils at the park's edge, and Lily scrutinizes them while talking to her imaginary friend. Since losing her father, Lily seems to prefer imaginary friends to real ones.

Rita sighs. It has been just over a year since her husband, Sergeant Kyle Dulaney, was killed in Afghanistan. Rita had stopped work to be a full-time mom, the family getting along on military pay plus some royalties Rita received from a few mildly successful country songs she had written. Survivor benefits, however, aren't that great, and she needs to get back to work. The words, however, won't come. She can't even capture her grief in cathartic poetry. Maybe it's the time of year. Nearly seven years ago to the day, she had met Kyle in Charleston, on the battery overlooking Fort Sumter. It had been love at first sight. She had written lyrics about such occurrences but had been somewhat cynical about such easy love. Kyle had purchased a cross on a chain for her, to commemorate their first date. When Kyle's unit left for Afghanistan, she had put the cross around his neck and prayed that it would keep him safe. An IED had left no identifiable remains. The prayer now seemed naïve.

"Hello, Lily."
"Hello. Who are you?"
"My name is Augie."
"Mommy says I shouldn't talk to strangers."
"I don't think she'll mind since she is right close by. Besides, she can't see me. Only you can see me."
"How can you do that?"
"I'm an angel."
"You don't look like an angel. Where are your wings?"
"I only use wings when I need them. Otherwise, they're invisible. But watch close." Lily watches as wings sprout out of my back.
"Wow! Okay, you're an angel, even if you don't look like one."
"Why don't I look like an angel?"
"Well, you're bald and real old and a little chubby."
"A lot of little children think I look charming."
"Well, I guess you are a little cute."
"Thank you very much."
"Kind of like Daffy Duck on television."

"Hmmmm."

"Do you know my daddy? He's dead."

"Yes, Lily, I did have a chance to meet him."

"Is he in heaven?"

"Yes, he is."

"Why did God take him away from me?"

"Oh, sweetheart, I don't know why God does the things he does. I just know that God loves you and your mommy and doesn't want you to be sad. Let me sit next to you." I retract my wings so that I can sit back on the bench.

Lily giggles. "Can you make your nose disappear, too?"

"I can make all of me disappear." I vanish and pop right back.

Lily laughs and claps her hands.

"Lily, your daddy is fine and wants you and your mommy to be fine. You always have him in your heart, and there will be a time when we are all together."

"Even you?"

"Even me. But for now, your daddy wanted me to tell you something and to give you something. Then I need to go do something."

Rita is dumbfounded. Lily is animated, laughing and kicking her feet as she talks to the air beside her. She reaches out her hand as though to grasp something. Then Lily is staring intently at Rita. Rita feels a warm breeze that seems to bump up against her for a second. Lily giggles again and runs over to her. "Mommy, Mommy! I just met an angel who knows Daddy! The angel's name is Augie."

"Lily, that's wonderful." She hugs her daughter. "It's so nice to hear you laugh again."

"Guess what, Mommy? Guess what?"

"What, sweetheart?"

"Augie said Daddy wants us to do something."

"Okay, what does he want us to do?"

"First, he wants you to take me to Charleston, where he met you."

Rita freezes. She has never told Lily how and where her parents met. "Lily, I—"

"Oh yeah, Mommy, and something else. He wanted me to give you this." Lily holds up a necklace with a cross. "Daddy told Augie it helped God find him when he died, 'cause he was wearing it."

Rita feels her peripheral vision start to darken, and her legs feel rubbery. "How did he give this to you?" she whispers.

"He had it in his hand, silly Mommy."

"But I didn't see anyone."

"I know, Mommy. He made himself so only I could see him. Did you feel it when he touched you?" Lily giggles again. "He kissed his fingers and put them on your head."

"Oh . . . Lily, we'd better go home. Mommy's feeling a little funny."

"Okay, Mommy." Lily takes Rita's hand, and they start walking to the car. Lily begins to sing softly.

Another shock. Lily has not sung in a year. "What are you singing, sweetheart?"

"Oh yes, I forgot to tell you. That's the song Daddy wants me to help you write."

Silhouettes of Love
Music and lyrics by Rita and Lily Dulaney

I remember Momma standin' near my
Bedroom door at night.
She could see her darlin' daughter
With the help of a hallway light.
She was always there when I had dreams

That I was frightened of.
It was more than Momma standin' there;
It was a silhouette of love.

Grandma kept her rocker on the porch,
Where we would play.
She would rock and stroke my hair in her
Old lovin' Grandma way.
Though she is gone, the chair remains,
And if I'm there long enough,
The breeze still sets it creakin',
A rockin' silhouette of love.

Silhouettes may be shadows imitating art,
But silhouettes of love you have to look for with your heart.

My satin gown now brushes up against
My handsome groom.
As he holds me, twirling, dancing
In the darkened, firelit room.
He kisses me, and I now see what my
Heart's been dreaming of,
Our shadows dancing gently there
In a silhouette of love.

Silhouettes may be shadows imitating art,
But silhouettes of love you have to look for with your heart.

It's my turn now to stand beside
A window late at night,

To look down on my baby
In her crib of pink and white.
Through the window just behind me comes
Some moonlight from above.
As my shadow falls upon her,
It's a silhouette of love.

Silhouettes may be shadows imitating art,
But silhouettes of love you have to look for with your heart.

And when it comes my time to leave
This world I know so well,
I'll go to meet my Maker at the tolling of the bell.
The sun will shine and cast the sweetest
Shadow from above.
It's the cross that brings salvation,
Heaven's silhouette of love.

Silhouettes may be shadows imitating art,
But silhouettes of love you have to look for with your heart.

After-Action Summary

No one is truly lost to you when you know where they are. While Christians grieve at the loss of a loved one, something distinguishes them from other humans: "For we do not grieve as those who have no hope" (1 Thessalonians 4:13). Rita and Lily can recover from grief in the certain promise of reunion.

Humans who doubt God's love or his existence may suffer from highly selective amnesia. They point out terrible events and say that if there is a God, how could he allow such things to happen? The answer is because he is the God of the Bible. He gave us free will, along with all its consequences. When mankind decides to schedule a war, the resultant suffering of innocent people is not God's fault. The deaths of people in a recent tsunami have also been blamed on God. The nearby island inhabitants and the domestic animals had the instinct to seek higher ground. Tourists, lacking the instinct necessary to live in that high-risk area, were at the mercy of their own inexperience and of a government that elected not to install an early warning system for tsunami detection. Again, a close examination will often find a human agency involved in the terrible events. In the New Orleans flood, the deaths have been used to accuse God of being unloving or nonexistent. The problem in New Orleans was that people had been encouraged to put their faith in an all-providing government. Had those people known that their government would leave them to their own devices in case of flood, do you honestly think those people would have stayed at a below-sea-level place? Instinct alone would have prompted them to make the journey to higher ground, even if it meant a very long walk. God gave you legs, common sense, and instinct. In this case, man-made government failed to deliver on its promises, and people who otherwise would have known better died as a result of misplaced trust.

Still, there are many cases where blame cannot be easily attributed to human failing. What about a child stricken with cancer or a young person dying in a no-fault accident? Here again, God is the God of the Bible. If you read Job, you will see that God makes no apology but simply points out that human reasoning is wholly insufficient to understand his actions (Job 38-41). Also, see Isaiah 55:8-9, where God declares that human thought and divine thought are not equal. Free will then permits you to accept his authority over you or to rail against it. One thing I might caution you humans about: death is *your* artificial end point, not God's. In the view of God and the angels, physical death is simply the dividing line between your physical life and your eternal life. If an innocent child, for example, suffers and dies in the physical realm, that child is welcomed and loved in the spirit world. That child is given an eternal life that more than compensates for the suffering they experienced on earth. That a death must occur in every human life is the consequence of the first man's abuse of free will. Make no mistake: Satan did not introduce sin. He introduced temptation, but it was Adam who sinned. Adam decided to sin. Of course, a human who rejects God must necessarily reject his Bible, so this argument is foolishness to him. That is also free will, with all its consequences.

By the way, when I kissed my fingers and placed them on Rita's forehead, that was the final part of my assignment. God wanted me to remove a small cancer from her breast that would have gone undetected and killed her within five years. God sends angels to remove a multitude of cancers every year, in believers and nonbelievers. I don't know why he chooses whom he chooses for healing. I cannot fully explain what I myself cannot understand. Rita's cancer was not known and, therefore, had not been the subject of prayer. God's sovereignty permits him to heal whom he will heal. For you humans who wonder when God doesn't heal in response to fervent prayer, I am sorry that I don't have a good answer. A cancer death is rarely pleasant or pain free, but the happiness and joy imparted by heaven are not diminished by the manner in which someone arrives there.

Many cancers that humans previously blamed on God have subsequently been found to be due to human behavior: tobacco consumption, toxic environments, radiation, or lack of basic health care. God has also designed man and his world so that, with proper study, man can discover the cures for additional cancers and better avoid natural catastrophes. When mankind makes these breakthroughs, it is rare to hear any humans thanking God. They restrict themselves to thanking the scientists rather than the God who provided the intelligence used in those discoveries. Humans. You make me crazy.

Chapter 9

FAQAAs, Part 4

How do angels view atheists?

Speaking as an everyday angel, I miss the old atheists. Whether they were outright rebellious or mentally challenged, they shook their fists in the face of heaven and declared they wanted no part of God, extant or not, involved in their lives. Their belief was not corrupted by, as Abraham Lincoln would say (about despotism), "the base alloy of hypocrisy." Atheism changed with Isaac Newton and Charles Darwin. While neither man committed to atheism, Newton and Darwin gave atheism its first sniff of intellectual and scientific respectability. Newtonian physics proclaimed that all workings of the universe had to conform to the laws of nature that he and others propounded. This left no room for divine intervention. Darwinian evolution suggested a progressive development of species from basic to more complex forms, supposedly repudiating the biblical creation of life. It didn't matter that neither man addressed the origin of the universe itself. Deism offered a compromise, maintaining that God created the universe and then left it alone. The pure atheists, however, wanted God totally out of the equation. Less than seventy-five years after Darwin posited his theory, the atheists had a landmark victory. The Scopes trial of 1925 challenged the law that prevented the teaching of evolution in government schools. Creationism was forced to allow evolution an equal seat at the table. Evolutionists crowed that they had broken the narrow-minded absolutist control of education by creationists. Then, with the help of the doctrine of separation of church and state, evolutionists and atheists imposed their own narrow-minded absolutist control of education. Today, you cannot even suggest intelligent design in a public-school dialogue. How can scientific inquiry and experimentation be free when its overseers demand that there is one conclusion that must never be reached, for fear of offending the random sensitive atheist? Thankfully, there are private endeavors within the United States, as well as a host of universities outside the United States, who refuse to be so intellectually hamstrung.

Angels are amused by these modern atheists. They claim that science supports the nonexistence of God, a fifteen-billion-year-old universe, and a self-created species development of staggering complexity. To do so, they must rely on outdated physics and ignore quantum physics in general, Einstein's theory of time dilation in particular. I refer you to standard physics textbooks, preferably those published in the last one hundred years. They point out that many of the problems of Newtonian physics led to the development of quantum physics and quantum physics resolved those problems. It is one thing to be a victim of poor scholarship but quite another to be proud of it. When you come right down to it, it takes less faith to believe in God than it does to believe in a self-created universe. I must bear in mind that God loves these humans despite their foolishness. Thankfully, as an angel, I am not compelled to.

What do angels think about the Bible?

There are no Bibles in heaven. No need. The Bible is the owner's manual for any human being who drives around in a physical body. As with an automobile owner's manual, you are free to ignore it, but it is the best source for maintenance information. Sadly, it is usually read, as with an automobile manual, after the problem develops.

The Bible is inerrant. But there are problems with this assertion. First, even Satan can quote Scripture (Matthew 4:6), and you will note that Satan deliberately misquotes it (compare the verse from Matthew with Psalm 91:11-12) for his own purpose. Humans can misquote Scripture either accidentally or on purpose. How can you introduce error into the Bible? Have a human open it. The moment he reads it, the Bible becomes weighted down with his biases and expectations. How else, for example, could the Bible have been used to justify the American system of slavery or the British concept of empire?

Critics of the Bible point out that it was written by men. To use a modern slang expression, "Well, duh." Is God supposed to grow a pair of hands and personally emblazon the Scriptures on the insides of your eyelids? God chose men to whom he dictated the books of the Bible. The use of a stenographer doesn't negate the authority of the source, nor does it call into question the validity of the communication. These same critics also question the assembling of the canon, the final collection of books of the Bible. At the Council of Carthage, AD 397, a list of books of the Bible was promulgated. The same Holy Spirit who guided the original authors of those books worked to ensure their proper assembly. I know, because I was there. Happy says he was there as well. That might explain the wine shortage that occurred.

Maybe it would help you humans if you realize that the Bible is a collection of love letters sent to you by your Papa. It is simply not possible to read the Bible and not come away convinced that he exists and that his love is boundless. Get to know him. Read his words. Permit yourself to simply *feel* his love.

Chapter 10
Case File M-398-AD

Walter Livesy, MD, is a man on a mission—a mission he doesn't want. He is a short, compact man with eyes that dance with delight at the slightest provocation. Now, however, there is no cause for happiness. For years, he has provided free health care at a clinic just on the border between Haiti and the Dominican Republic. Initially, starting his practice was simply a matter of learning to speak Spanish and Creole, then cobbling together a network of donors to provide funding. Dr. Livesy has been content to stay at the clinic and take care of sick folks. A deeply spiritual man and committed Christian, he prays with his patients. He delivers their babies and their souls. He ministers to bodies and spirits. He never fails to impress upon his patients that it is Christ's love of mankind that animates the Livesy Clinic. Thus it would have continued until Livesy's death or retirement, except that Livesy showed up on the radar screen of Gaspar Killian.

Killian is a journalist with the *New York Times*. A self-proclaimed iconoclast, Killian specializes in ripping what he calls "the Christian Establishment." With a skillful blend of innuendo and quotes from unnamed sources, Killian routinely skewers Christian endeavors that the heretofore-unenlightened reader might have deemed beneficial to the public. With all the fervor of a truly anointed secularist, Killian never concerns himself with the plight of those people left helpless after he has destroyed their humanitarian agency. In researching a series aimed at Christian foreign missionary work, Killian happened upon the clinic. In a brutal article, Killian identified the Livesy Clinic as "representative of all that is wrong with Christian medical proselytizing overseas."

He wrote, "Dr. Walter Livesy preys upon the sick and uneducated, infecting them with an antiquated belief structure that urges them to embrace a childish fairy tale instead of relying on their own common sense." He added that "persuading innocent people that their health is linked to their reliance on God is the lowest form of emotional extortion." It didn't matter that Livesy never promised health in return for faith. Killian's allegiance to accurate quotes, never strong on even neutral subjects, becomes nonexistent in articles on religion.

The impact was, at first, gradual. A few nonreligious philanthropic groups withdrew their support of the clinic. A follow-up article that promised a listing of all organizations supporting the "repressive cult of Mr. Jesus'" opened the gate. The faith-based support groups, long accustomed to the toxic vapor of men like Gaspar Killian, held their ground. Because of the loss of the other groups' support, Dr. Livesy is now back in the States, trying to attract individual donors. Livesy is thinking, *What in the world am I doing here?* His morning had begun weirdly and gotten weirder. He had awakened to find a man in his hotel room.

"Who are you?"

"My name is Augie. I sorta came with the room. Think of me as the two-hundred-pound mint on your pillow."

"Why don't I believe you?"

"Ya got me, Doc. The truth is, I'm an angel."

"I think your mint story sounds more reasonable. You should stick with that."

"I get that all the time. What's my problem, Doc? People just don't buy it when I tell them I'm an angel."

"Well, Augie, you sure don't fit the stereotype."

"Okay, let's try this." I direct my eyes skyward, letting my face assume a simpering piety. The air shimmers above my head, and I get a glowing halo to appear, suffusing my face with a beatific radiance. "How am I doin', Doc? Feelin' celestial yet?"

"Uh, yes. How about . . . how about some heavenly music?"

"Naw, my iPod's not charged up. Besides, I left it in another dimension. I hope you're convinced that I'm an angel, 'cause we've gotta get on the road. My taxi's just outside." This seems a good time to burp, so I do. Feels good.

"Taxi. Of course."

So now he's in a taxi driven by a most unlikely angel, heading for Long Island. "Augie, forgive me, but this is a little peculiar. I'm going to a garden party in a taxi driven by an angel who looks like he belongs in a bowling alley."

I let the good doctor sit in the shotgun seat so that we can chat face-to-face—or maybe that's profile-to-profile. "Wow, Doc, you are good. Turns out, I am on a bowling team back upstairs."

"Back upstairs?"

Doctor Livesy seems only a little bemused. For a human who is having a first contact with an angel, he is handling it pretty well. Maybe my style is improving. After six thousand years, it ought to.

"Yeah, that's in-crowd slang for where us angels hang out."

"Heaven?" Livesy is holding on to the dashboard, more bothered by my driving than my angelic status.

"Nope, not us working guys. We have our own watering hole, complete with a bowling alley." I slow the cab to take a curve with all four wheels on the ground.

"Can't all of you just do miracle stuff and always score three hundred?"

"Not allowed. Straight-up bowling. The last angel who tried something tricky—we turned him into a bowling ball and rolled him down the alley. Had migraines for a week."

"Ouch. So what are we doing at this garden party?"

The sun is coming through the tunnel of the trees to dapple the windshield. "We're gonna meet Sam Rutherford. His house, his party. He's a philanthropist, and he doesn't give a rip about public opinion."

"So Mr. Rutherford is the man you want me to meet?"

"Uh. Well, yeah. Him, too."

"Augie, are angels always this vague, or maybe you're practicing to be a politician?" Livesy smiles and seems to have gotten over some of his misgivings.

"Hey, Doc, that's a good one. After all, maybe a politician is nothin' more than an angel who has had a moral lobotomy—you do that kind of procedure at your clinic?"

"Nice try, changing the subject. But I'm afraid we won't be doing much of anything at my clinic if I can't raise the support. I've never asked for money. I don't know how to do this." The uncertainty is back on his face.

I give a sigh. I must be losing my touch. "You won't need to do *this*. You just be ole Dr. Livesy. Everything else will fall into place. Let's just say I've got faith. And speaking of *place*, we are here."

I turn the car into a long driveway. The electronic gate is open. Security will be up near the house. We pull into a circle in front of a Victorian monstrosity. A valet hovers near to drive the car away after a security check. We exit the taxi. A muscular bratwurst with an obligatory shaved head, earplug, and sidearm bulge in his coat comes to check us out. "Invitation, please." I hand him a blank three-by-five-inch card. As the man glances at it, his eyes glaze over, and he says "Ah, yes, Professor Augie. Everything is in order. Welcome to the party. You and your wife can go on in." He steps back and talks vacantly into a lapel transmitter, and the door opens in response.

As we enter the foyer, Livesy hisses at me, "What was that all about?"

"Oh yeah, the 'Professor' part? I like bein' a professor sometimes. Just havin' a little fun."

"No, the part about him calling me your wife!"

I look at him with my most sincerely apologetic expression. "Sorry, Doc, it's the only way I could be sure he was, you know, pixilated. Completely out of it."

"Thanks for trying to lighten my mood, Augie."

"Is it workin'?"

"No." Livesy has a tousle of grayish-brown hair over an unwrinkled brow that he keeps fidgeting with. His gray eyes take in the beautiful family room as we go through some French doors onto an immense deck.

"Ah, there's the host. But first, hey, look! Some of the folks brought their kids along. Let's look." I steer Dr. Livesy to the side of the yard where a group of little children are playing. There is a face painter and a balloon twister. The main attraction, however, is an inflatable castle with slides and a bouncing room. "Cute kids, huh, Doc?"

I look over and smile, seeing that the doctor is paying me no attention. Livesy's attention is fixed on a little girl who is with a group of breathless children coming down the slide and then running back to get another turn. The little girl, a darling brunette perhaps six or seven years old, runs from the slide and then abruptly stops. She is totally still until another child runs into her, knocking her down. They both get up laughing and then run back to mount the stairs to the slide. They run up to the top, where the little girl stops again, her eyes unfocused. Her friend goes down the slide, and after a bit, the little girl follows her down. Dr. Livesy observes her for a few more minutes and then turns to me.

"Augie, I need to talk with that little girl's parents."

"Well, Doc, here's the man who would know 'em." A handsome, friendly man is approaching, smiling and extending his hand. He is bluff and hearty, with thick iron-gray hair. I say, "Mr. Rutherford, you probably don't remember me. My name is Augie. This is my buddy Walter. Thanks for inviting us."

"Well, Augie, they say that if a man knows everybody at his party, he hasn't invited enough people."

The doctor says, "Mr. Rutherford, is there any way you can introduce me to the parents of that little girl over there? I know it seems peculiar, but it really is important."

"Well, sure. In fact, it's only the dad, and he's right over here. Let's go introduce you. By the way, what is your full name?"

"Walter Livesy."

"Okay." Rutherford stops abruptly and spins around. "Did you say Walter Livesy? Is this some kind of joke?"

"No, sir. What do you mean?"

Rutherford gives the doctor a close look while I stand off to the side with a small smile on my lips. "Okay, Walter. I believe you; let's introduce you and Augie to Katie's father. This should be interesting."

We walk over to a man in his midthirties who has longish brown hair and an executive stubble. He has a pleasant face and is trying to look interested as a heavy dowager wearing too much makeup is explaining her travails with a flatulent corgi. He looks relieved when Rutherford touches the lady's arm and asks permission to steal the man away. "Thanks, Sam. I owe you one."

"No problem, Gas. Actually, this gentleman wanted to meet you. Walter Livesy, meet Gaspar Killian."

As each man hears his adversary's name, his facial expression goes from surprised to feral. Sam and I seem to shrink into the background.

Dr. Livesy's expression is the first to soften, his face again becoming congenial. "Mr. Killian, I must apologize. When I asked Mr. Rutherford to introduce me to Katie's father, I didn't know it would be you."

Killian's expression goes from feral to confused to suspicious. "Katie? What do you mean?"

Livesy now smiles as though he has found the answer to a riddle. He glances over at me with a knowing look and then turns back to the journalist. "I know what you must be thinking, Mr. Killian. Walter Livesy has recognized you and has asked to be introduced so he could provoke a confrontation. Right so far?"

"Yes. Go on." Killian's face has reassumed its original confusion.

"Then you daughter's name is mentioned, and your parental hackles go up, right? Good. Please let me clarify. Had I known you were at this party, I would not have come. I surely would not have approached you about your articles. You are an expert in words, while I am not. I wouldn't presume to cross verbal swords with you. Are we okay on that?"

"All right, Doctor. I'll buy that for now. But how does all this involve my daughter?" Killian's jaw recedes a bit, and his hands cease to look like talons.

"If you'll bear with me, let's put all the missionary stuff and the newspaper stuff behind us for now and just talk like what we are—a doctor and a parent. Still okay?"

"I'm listening."

"Fair enough. When we wandered past the children, I noticed one little girl, Katie, who exhibited some interesting behavior." Livesy pauses to point over to the children playing in the castle. "I wished to speak with her parent about that behavior, and here we are."

"What behavior?" Killian now has a genuine look of curiosity and actually seems to be leaning closer to the doctor.

Livesy says, "The stopping and starting of play while she's running around with the others. Is that something you have observed before?"

Killian nods.

"I know it runs contrary to a journalist's nature, but may I first question you regarding your daughter and then let you interview me regarding my thoughts?"

"Okay, Dr. Livesy, ask away."

"Is your daughter on any medication?"

"No."

"Does she have any health issues?"

"Not really, no."

"Does she have any learning or attention disorders?"

"Yes, she does. We have had her tested. She isn't hyperactive but can't seem to stay focused. Just seems to zone out, get lost in her own private world. She has some dyslexia, but the teachers are helping with that." Killian pauses and then says, "I have taken her to the best pediatricians and learning experts in the city. I have another appointment for her this week with a pediatrician who is an expert in learning and attention disorders."

Livesy's face has a frown of deep concentration. He tilts his head and then seems to come to a conclusion. "Forgive me, Mr. Killian, but you wouldn't be having that appointment if you were happy with the reports you have received thus far."

Killian sighs. "You are correct."

"Let me ask one more thing: Does Katie have nightmares?"

Killian steps back with a shocked look on his face. "Yes, in fact, she does. Terrible nightmares. No one has asked that before."

"Are the nightmares terrible to the point that you would call them night terrors? Where she remains fearful even after she wakes up?"

"How could you know?" Killian whispers. He is clearly stunned to be hearing questions never before asked of him. Unconsciously, he reaches over to touch Livesy on the shoulder.

"Let me do one small experiment. Would you call Katie over?"

"Katie, sweetheart! Come over here for a sec." Killian turns to look at Livesy with a glance of trust, a facial expression most unfamiliar to him.

Katie walks over with a skip to her step, smiling. "Hi, Daddy. We've been on the slide!"

"Katie, this man is a doctor, and he wants you to do something."

"Hello, Katie. Actually, I want both you and your daddy to play a little game." Livesy pulls over a lawn chair and has Killian sit in it so that he is at eye level with his daughter. "Now, Katie and Daddy, I want you to look each other in the eye. Good. Now I want you each to touch your right ear with your right hand; then put that hand down and touch your left ear with your left hand. Good. Now just keep doing that over and over. Look at each other and keep touching ears with hands, and don't stop for any reason, okay?"

Katie giggles a little and then settles in, watching her father as she alternates touching her right ear and then her left ear, her father doing the same.

"Okay, Katie and Daddy, now I want you to take deep breaths, in and out, in and out, as fast as you can."

Katie and her father begin the hyperventilation. Within seconds, Katie's breathing slows, and her hands stop moving. She begins to blink her eyes rapidly and smack her lips. Killian is alarmed. "She's never done that before. What's wrong?"

"Don't be alarmed. Just keep moving your hands. She'll come back in a little bit." Sure enough, after thirty seconds, Katie focuses back on her father and begins to touch her ears again.

"Okay," says Dr. Livesy, "you can stop now. Katie, you did very well. Tell me, from the time I told you to start touching your ears and then to stop just now, did you stop doing it on your own?"

"No, sir."

"Excellent. You are a wonderful patient. You can go along now. I see they are bringing out some hot dogs for the children." Katie walks over to join the other children.

"Dr. Livesy, what did I just see?" Killian has ceased to be an adversary after seeing the bizarre changes his daughter showed in the game. He is now simply an agonized parent. Sam Rutherford and I, who have been watching silently, draw closer.

"Mr. Killian, the hyperventilation blows off carbon dioxide, and it provoked in your daughter an underlying issue that the French call an 'absence.' You might know it better as a petit mal seizure."

"You mean epilepsy?" Killian whispers the word as if to lessen his fear of it, rising from the chair with his hands clinched at his side.

"Yes, but you don't need to be afraid." Doctor Livesy smiles reassuringly and puts his arm around the shoulders of a worried father. "Many such seizure disorders resolve with time. You need to get a pediatric neurologist to confirm the diagnosis with an EEG. With medication, you will probably see a great deal of the learning, attending, and nightmare issues go away. Epilepsy certainly doesn't carry the stigma it did in years past."

"Dr. Livesy, I . . . I don't know what to say. Here I have attacked you in my newspaper, and look at what you do in return. You . . . you give me answers to things that have been frightening me. I don't understand."

"These are separate issues. To me, you are a concerned father, and I am able to help you. As far as the issue of the editorials is concerned, we are blessed to live in a country where men like you maintain a cynical scrutiny on the activities of other men. I hope we never lose people like you. But yours is a terrible burden, because you hold sway over many folks' opinions. Whatever you label as good or bad, many of your readers will simply accept it because they believe in you. Your conscience must always prevent you from making mistakes." Livesy pauses as Killian looks down at his shoes. "In many respects, we are alike. I must always be careful that the medical or spiritual care I dispense is accurate, because my patients will believe me. I was happy to help you and Katie, because that is what I do, what I believe God has called me to do. I thought I was coming here today for one purpose, but what God really wanted me to do was to meet Katie."

"Dr. Livesy, I am in your debt. I don't know how to thank you."

"You can repay me, perhaps, by accepting an invitation to my clinic. Bring Katie. That way, you can expand your body of information on faith-based medical missions. Some of them may, in fact, be bogus and deserve censure. You know, I should actually be thanking you. When your articles came out and donors began to desert us, I lost my focus and began to fear, instead of leaving it in God's hands. So now I am doing what I should have done at the beginning: invite you down. Come look at what we are doing. If you still think we need to be attacked, then attack us. If God wants us to thrive, nothing you do will destroy the clinic. Parenthetically, if God wants the clinic to go away, there is nothing you can do to preserve it. Maybe God wants some changes to which I am blind, so perhaps you will be his agent of change. In any event, you will be welcome."

"Dr. Livesy, for the first time ever, words have deserted me. I am relieved, ashamed—I don't know—grateful, confused. I think I might well come visit you but not before I get my own goals and motivations straight. It truly was a pleasure to meet you."

They shake hands, and Killian departs. Sam Rutherford says, "Dr. Livesy, I share Gaspar's astonishment. With simple observation and—what, a provocative test?—you make a diagnosis that has eluded some pretty smart doctors."

"I simply had the opportunity of watching her run and play. Playing is what provoked what we call a stop-and-stare episode. Maybe we doctors should add simple playing to our diagnostic testing."

"Sure would be a cheap test," I say.

Sam Rutherford draws closer and hands Livesy a card. "Dr. Livesy, have your administrator call my foundation. I will see to it that you will never have to hunt for donations. We need you back practicing medicine. And yes, practicing your gospel."

"Sam, you are a good man," I remark.

"Thank you, Augie. Tell me, though. You and I—we really never have met before, have we?"

"Not in this world, Sam."

"And you didn't really know anyone at this party, did you?"

"Not a soul."

"Well, Augie, Dr. Livesy, in that case, I am, I guess you call it, *blessed* to have you here."

"Great choice of words, Sam. I've got to get the doc back to his hotel. We both have other places to be."

"Will I ever see you again, Augie?"

I give him my thousand-watt angel smile. "You never know, Sam—you never know."

After-Action Summary

To humans, forgiving someone who has wronged them is counterintuitive and counterinstinctual. If you read many popular books and watch TV or movies, you will see that forgiveness is certainly countercultural. To repay an injury with kindness is viewed as "countersanity."

Nevertheless, forgiveness is foundational to a human's relationship with God. God repays humanity's repeated transgressions with forgiveness and salvation. When a human doesn't manifest a similar behavior toward his own transgressors, God could reasonably wonder whether that person got the memo: God's best way of knowing that a human has yielded to divine guidance is to see that human emulate the behavior of Christ. The ultimate manifestation of hero worship is imitation of that hero's behavior.

It makes me crazy that so many humans recite the Lord's Prayer without considering what they are saying: "forgive us our trespasses as we forgive those who trespass against us." You are essentially saying, "Okay, God, watch how I forgive people who have wronged me, and then forgive me for my wrongs against you in the same manner." You are tying God's hands, as it were, and telling him to be as forgiving (or unforgiving) as you have been. Be careful what you pray for.

Forgiving others makes sense for several reasons. First, failure to forgive may lead to a desire for revenge. Revenge may lead to sin. There is an old human proverb: he who sets out for revenge must first dig two graves. Also, forgiveness is healthy. Bitterness and a desire for revenge disrupt sleep and gnaw at you when you recall the offense. So you are losing sleep and eroding your stomach lining while the transgressor is probably in the best of health. As long as you permit the memory of the offense to affect you physically, you are essentially giving that person control over your life. You are effectively volunteering for ongoing offense.

If you have trouble forgiving someone with God's love in your heart, at least try some revenge forgiveness. You simply say, out loud, in private, "I forgive you because it is best for me and because you simply are not important enough to distract me." However, understand that this is not the forgiveness that God teaches. It is a first step. It must be accompanied by a prayer: "God, please teach me how to want to forgive properly and then how to do it." Because it is not in your human nature to forgive, it requires God's help. Ask him.

Humans also need to understand what forgiveness is and what it is not. Fundamentally, forgiveness is a decision to not seek revenge for having been wronged. It does not mean that a woman whose husband beats her should remain in an abusive relationship, nor does it mean remaining passive in the face of physical threats to you or your loved ones. From this angel's perspective, it is amusing to see how often humans quote that Scripture about turning the other cheek, especially atheists who get dismayed when their Christian victim fails to remain passive. (It is a strange bully who feels the need to remind his victim to behave like a victim.) There are at least an equal number of verses encouraging definitive self-protection. For example, "Praise be to the Lord, my rock, who trains my hands for war (Psalm 144:1 NIV). Also, "But now, if you have a purse, take it, and also a bag; and if you don't have a sword, sell your cloak and buy one" (Luke 22:36 NIV).

There is a difference between the insult of a slap (Matthew 5:29) and an assault with a deadly weapon. Nowhere in Scripture are you encouraged to be an idiot. Nowhere, however, are you given permission to repay bad treatment with your own brand of bad treatment. A final reason I would ask humans to avoid repaying evil for evil is that God uses his angels to avenge in his time and at his pleasure. Don't put me out of a job.

The forgiveness that Doctor Livesy exhibited to Gaspar Killian was of the highest order of Christian love: he overlooked an attack that was baseless, yet insulted both his motives and the purity of his faith. Livesy repaid it with love. Jesus asks you to mirror such forgiveness.

Chapter 11

Case File S-50-AD

There are few places more beautiful than Cape Cod in June. The night chill lifts off Nauset Marsh, and the rising sun draws the mist from the channels of tidal water. Hiram Stratton breathes in the brackish air like a connoisseur. Professor Stratton loves the marsh and is eager for another day of bird-watching. The migratory season is over, but there are terns, herons, and dozens of other bird species. The only drawback is the need to share this wealth with average people who have neither the education nor the perspicacity to appreciate the splendor of the Cape Cod National Seashore. He steers his one-man kayak up his favorite unmarked channel. *Oh no!* There is a cluster of kayaks ahead. As Stratton paddles past them, he is disgusted when he hears the kayakers proclaiming the beauty of God's creation. *Good grief, a Christian tour group, with all that smarmy gratitude drivel,* Stratton thinks. *I am not going to let those religious fools spoil my day on the water. I can go farther up the channel away from them. Maybe if they're unfamiliar with the tidal shifts, they'll get stuck at low tide and* have to hoof it back through the mud, dragging their kayaks. See how much they praise the Lord when that happens.

Hiram Stratton, PhD, is a full professor of sociology at Harvard University. He earned his undergraduate and master's degrees from Princeton and his doctorate from Columbia University with his thesis "Hispaniola: American and European Abuse throughout History." Like most PhDs in the humanities, Stratton takes pride in being, according to his peers, an expert in a given area, conveniently ignoring the insignificance of his area of expertise. After all, hadn't he been an adviser to a Senate subcommittee on Central American and Caribbean policy during the enlightened Clinton years? That Colonel Cedras deposed the duly elected president of Haiti in a military coup with the connivance of the CIA during the Clinton administration was not the fault of the American liberals or of his committee. No, this had to have occurred despite President Clinton, not as a result of his authorization. The fact that President Aristede was a guest of President Clinton when the coup occurred? Pure coincidence.

Tenured professorship was initially designed to protect academic freedom and to permit a professor to follow truth wherever it led, without fear of censure or dismissal. In Professor Stratton's case, it is a license for intolerance. He embraces all the requisite positions mandated by his stature and by secular orthodoxy: he is a vegetarian and supporter of PETA, and he is rabidly pro-choice and supports partial birth abortion. Proud of his lack of racism, he supports open borders. Of course, he wants to disarm all Americans. While he is a deep green ecologist and fervently believes in global warming, he has had no problem siding with the Kennedys and the Cronkites against windmills on Cape Cod. Let them be placed elsewhere, he figures, where they are not a threat to his birds or to the view from his kayak. Or to land value.

Like most liberals, the professor considers himself open-minded yet hates the free expression of opinions that disagree with him. Those dissenters who cannot be defeated by logic or dismissed with derision must be exiled or silenced. He strongly supports efforts by the FCC to silence conservative radio talk show hosts, believing that the majority of the radio audience are intellectually unequipped to resist the toxic oratory of conservatives. Stratton, as one of the liberal cognoscenti, believes that theirs is the burdensome job of determining which philosophies should be permitted into public discourse. For example, in the case of stem cell research, Stratton and his enlightened friends don't care that the majority of Americans are against tax dollars being used for embryonic stem cell research. They ignore the science that shows totipotent cells can derive from adult stem cells, making embryonic stem cells unnecessary. Science should not be hamstrung by people who worry that advances based on fetal stem cells will lead to baby farms meeting the stem cell demand by unethical means. The will of the majority should only prevail when it has been found to coincide with the conclusions of really smart people, people like ... well ... like Professor Stratton.

Stratton, however, reserves his most potent vitriol for Christians. He finds their mere existence invidious. It is not enough that they believe their own nonsense; they feel compelled to export it into other vulnerable intellects. While Stratton does the same thing with his philosophy, the very truth of it justifies his spouting it abroad. Stratton has proudly proclaimed to his colleagues that he is a predatory atheist. Early in his career, Stratton frequently had innocent Christians appearing in his classroom. With greater public enlightenment, however, that is becoming increasingly rare, certainly in Ivy League schools. While espousing an open mind, Stratton shouts down any class discussion that places Christianity in a positive light. He rants about the transgressions of the Catholic Church in particular or the Christian community in general.

Students soon learn that any thesis or term paper that reveals any positive impact by Christianity on the world will receive a failing grade. He does not view Muslims the same way. While he dresses this exemption in self-laudatory prose, the truth is that Stratton, like most members of either liberal academia or liberal media, is a coward. Muslims don't turn the other cheek. Muslims might shove a bomb up your nose. Bullies don't pick on people who might actually fight back. Stratton sticks with the safety of assaulting any Christian who wanders into his hunting sector.

As a faculty adviser, he has the chance to exert a more personal influence. Amy, for example, had been an unqualified success. Amy had been a scholarship student, an underprivileged minority child who had been adopted and raised by poor, fundamentalist Neanderthal parents. Her need for acceptance by her classmates and her hero worship of Stratton made short work of her faith. With Stratton's encouragement, she "expanded her horizons," "dared to live," and "took life by the horns." Predictably, this led to a pregnancy. Stratton convinced her to go to Planned Parenthood, even taking it upon himself to accompany her. When she hesitated in considering an abortion, he reminded her that she had her whole life to live and that carrying a child to term would effectively cancel out a least one semester. It would also, he said, bring unwanted attention to her on campus. She had an abortion and bled to death afterward. Who would have guessed that she had Glanzman's thrombasthenia, some weird clotting disorder not picked up on standard preoperative testing? Stratton comforted himself with the thought that he missed her and, therefore, was himself suffering. At least, he thought, he had helped her such that when she, unfortunately, died, she wasn't burdened by any of that Christian crap about guilt or eternity.

Stratton reaches another unmarked channel in the refuge and paddles to an expanse of open water that, even at low tide, is many fathoms deep. He stops paddling, allowing the kayak to drift toward a bank covered with a raucous crowd of birds. Suddenly, the kayak stops drifting. At the same time, the bird noises cease.

"Wow, looks too deep here for us to be stuck on a sandbar. Whatta ya think, Professor?"

Stratton, startled, twists around to look back at the source of the voice. Unaccountably, his one-man kayak has become a two-man kayak, and occupying the rear seat is a man—me. I am middle aged and slightly paunchy, wearing a California Angels ball cap over my grizzled gray hair. There is a smile on my face that doesn't seem to occupy my eyes, eyes that are green, cold, and empty.

"Who are you?"

"My name is Augie."

"What are you doing in my kayak? What did you do to my—"

"Easy, Professor. The front half is still your kayak. I sorta modified the back half so I would have a place to sit."

"This is freaking insane! What is happening?"

"Well, let's just say that your activities here on earth have not gone unnoticed."

"Here on earth? Are you crazy?" Stratton has been unable to get his eyebrows unstuck from his forehead. His eyes dart from me to the birds to the water, as if looking for enlightenment.

"Me, crazy? I'm not the one who came out here in a one-man kayak and is turning around to talk to the back half of his boat. Get a grip, and I'll explain."

Stratton relaxes just a bit. "Okay, there has to be a rational explanation for this. I never dropped LSD or had a seizure. Did somebody spike my water bottle, or do you have some aerosolized hallucinogen, or was it hypnosis or what?"

I chuckle. "No, nothing that simple. I'm an angel."

"Right. And I'm the Easter bunny. You were with that bunch of Bible thumpers I passed, and now you . . ."

Stratton is starting to hyperventilate, and his professorial control is wavering, so I raise a finger, and the professor is unable to speak.

"Sorry, Professor, but I just hit your mute button. There are some things you need to listen to. Despite your protests to the contrary, there is a God, and I am one of his angels. That's the good news. All the rest of the news, for you, is bad."

Stratton strains to speak and cannot. When he tries to gesture, he finds that he can't raise his hands. I feel my voice slide into deeper registers and take on a sinister softness. The accent fades, and the words become a physical force. Even the birds, silent on the banks, seem unable to look away.

"Even by human standards, Professor, you are not a nice person. It isn't enough for you to embrace the stupidity of atheism; you think you ennoble yourself by destroying the faith of innocent people. In history, there were Muslims and Christians who forced conversions onto Jews or anybody else who wasn't of their faith. You, no doubt, condemn that sort of thing, but what you do is far worse. You are a soul killer. No doubt you would say that you were 'liberating people by tearing down the shibboleths of an antiquated religious fantasy,'" I say with a whiny, nasally upper-class accent, "when in fact, these people's lives are little more than scalps on your philosophical belt." I reach down and lift up a rope that extends over the side of the kayak.

"Professor, can you guess what's on the end of this rope? Well, it isn't a millstone. Millstones are hard to find, and this assignment was a last-minute sort of thing. Didn't give me much time to prepare." I pull up forty feet of rope, at the end of which a footlocker is tied. The professor's eyes widen as more of the rope becomes coiled in the kayak. His mouth continues to contort, making him looked like a beached guppy.

"What's in here, Professor, is a collection of books. All written by virulent atheists like yourself. We've mixed a few old turkeys like Nietzsche and Feuerbach in with some modern turkeys like Dawkins, Hitchins, and Harris. Their works are weighty, but only in the avoirdupois sense being dead weight. Still, altogether, they make a good substitute for a millstone."

I make a loop in the rope and toss it around Stratton's neck. "Professor, without knowing it, you have been looking into an abyss. Let me quote your atheist Nietzsche: 'when you look long into an abyss, the abyss also looks into you.'" I let go of the footlocker, and it plunges down, jerking Stratton out of the kayak by his neck, deep into the salt water.

"Vaya con Diablo, mi amigo."

After-Action Summary

As mentioned, I couldn't find a millstone, but I thought a trunkful of atheist garbage quite apposite. Improvisation! "But if anyone causes one of these little ones who believe in me to sin, it would be better for him to have a large millstone hung around his neck and to be drowned in the depths of the sea" (Matthew 18:6 NIV).

Whenever Jesus is quoted in three of the four gospels (Matthew 18:6; Mark 9:42; Luke 17:2), chances are that the Holy Spirit thought it deserved emphasis. Don't be led into assuming that "little ones" refers to children. It refers to spiritual children—those who, despite their chronological age, are young in their faith and, therefore, vulnerable. To use a covert ops term, Professor Stratton was "terminated with extreme prejudice." While Scripture makes clear that it is Papa's will that all people be saved (1 Timothy 2:4), it is equally clear that certain people are expendable (for example, Simon Magus, and Ananias and Sapphira). The decision regarding

Stratton came down from my superiors, but I confess to a little satisfaction in ushering such an intellectually sanctimonious twit into his hereafter.

New England has long been inhabited by some curious humans. They proclaim that the earliest settlers came seeking religious freedom. The truth is that they came seeking the freedom to be intolerant. These are the same pleasant folk who tried to get Shakespearian plays banned in England. In that sense, they were forerunners of the modern American liberal: it wasn't enough that they personally could choose to avoid watching Shakespeare. They wanted to prevent everyone from watching anything that violated the puritan concept of acceptability.

Along the way, the New England universities got rid of the religion but kept the intolerance. While extolling the veneer of open-mindedness, they manifest a staggering myopia and a willingness to levy secular excommunication on anyone possessed of the temerity to deviate from liberal orthodoxy. The very fact that their core beliefs align precisely with Hollywood liberalism informs you that it is based neither on intelligence nor access to factual data.

Why, then, this disconnect with regard to faith? Perhaps it is because it is faith. Let us consider the Renaissance man. This was the ideal of the enlightened individual who sought to excel in the three disciplines of mind, body, and spirit. Most professors of higher education would love to be perceived as Renaissance people. In fact, many do excel in matters of the mind, such as intellectual and artistic pursuits. In the discipline of the body, they seek proper diet and exercise. Stratton, as an intellectual, vegetarian, and avid kayaker, was a classic example.

The problem occurs in matters of the spirit. Most intellectuals who claim to be spiritual are usually simply subjecting religious topics to their mind. To a degree, this is understandable, because this is the faculty with which they are most comfortable—rather like an infant who evaluates everything by shoving it in his mouth. The intellect is no more capable of spiritual searching than your elbow is capable of inflating a balloon. You are welcome to try, but don't expect a sterling result. Look at it this way: if there is a God responsible for the universe and everything in it, the chances are that his intelligence far exceeds that of any mortal, finite human. It is the ultimate hubris to assume that any human intellect could appreciate such a creator. If there is a creator, he is also the one who provided a mind, body, and spirit, so doesn't it seem reasonable to use all three faculties to seek him? The God of Scripture makes the issue fairly clear. Consider the following verses: "Without faith, it is impossible to please God" (Hebrews 11:6 NIV); "God chose the foolish things of the world to shame the wise" (1 Corinthians 1:27 NIV); and "For the message of the cross is foolishness to those who are perishing" (1 Corinthians 1:18 NIV).

The best-kept secret of all intellectuals is a fear that is common to all of them. They fear being perceived as intellectually unsophisticated. It is a form of intellectual insulation when one repudiates the nonintellectual message of Scripture. The problem with this approach, however, is that it requires one to selectively overlook modern physics and its capacity to destroy the fairy-tale label attached to religion over a century ago. I suspect, however, that there is a more sinister power working here. Using one's intellect to deny the existence of a God that can be found only by faith is adolescent rebellion writ large. Such individuals' thought processes go something like this: *If I deny the existence of God, I can deny any authority above myself. Over the years, I will resolutely refuse to reexamine my conclusions as new evidence appears that might challenge my presuppositions. I will claim to remain open to debate or study while, in fact, all I do is continue to accept or reject new viewpoints based on their consistency with my longstanding bias.* Scripture explains such people as follows: "Hear this you foolish and senseless people, who have eyes but do not see, who have ears but do not hear" (Jeremiah 5:21 NIV).

The best Renaissance people on earth are children. Their minds are open, their spirits are receptive, and their bodies are vehicles for play. They are not self-conscious in the use of any human faculty. Compare the average child to Professor Stratton. Who has the greater freedom, the greater receptiveness to their world? What happened to Professor Stratton between childhood and adulthood? Was he better as a result? Perhaps this is why Scripture says "unless you change and become like little children, you will never enter the Kingdom of Heaven" (Matthew 18:3 NIV). You are to become childlike, not childish. You are to become Renaissance people—God's Renaissance people.

Chapter 12

Case File M-673-AD

Gert Bastop doesn't like quandaries. A quandary promotes uncertainty. *Uncertain* is not an adjective that anyone would apply to Gert. "Whenever you're uncertain," Gert would tell anybody, "just find your answer in Scripture." Gert herself rarely searches the Scriptures, having already memorized the verses most convenient to the conduct of her life. Gert and her husband, Joe, live in a small city in the southern Midwest, from which their two children fled to raise their families elsewhere. Gert doesn't agree with all the migratory trends of the modern American family. Gert has never understood that the children's short visits home are even further abbreviated by Gert's unsolicited and unending advice on childrearing (firm), clothing (modest), and topics suitable for discussion (the Bible, preferably the Old Testament). Gert doesn't truly mind the shortened visits. It is so hard to constantly bite her tongue at the frequent mistakes made by young parents who are not fully versed in Scripture. The observations that Gert feels compelled to make simply escape her lips because she cannot contain them. Despite their poor reception,

Gert is persuaded that she has planted seeds that will ultimately guide their recipients in proper decorum. Her only frustration is that Joe never shares her enthusiasm for the admonition of folks who are insufficiently schooled in the Bible, the Bible according to Gert. No, Joe just smiles and says, "Yes, dear," whenever Gert illuminates the deficiencies of her fellow man. Joe just smiles and hugs her, hugs their children, hugs everybody. Joe knows a lot of Scripture but seems to think that a hug and sympathy are more beneficial to a person than the two-edged sword of the inspired Word. Everybody loves Joe. Gert doesn't need people's affection; she is focused on their proper instruction. Gert has long concluded that theirs is the perfect partnership. In her mind, Joe provides the hugs while she does the heavy lifting of perfecting the saints.

Her ripest field of exhortation had been taken from her by her mandatory retirement from the insurance company where she had been the administrative supervisor and resident blowhard. She had maintained a proper dress code and a prohibition against alcohol at office parties, and she had ensured that personal pictures on desks were family only and nonprovocative. Because the prettier girls were at greatest risk for sin, Gert had concentrated her advice on them. Her only compromise had been allowing Christian music to be replaced by nondescript elevator music. Joe had gently suggested that a steady diet of gospel music to the uncommitted would only alienate them. Gert had reluctantly agreed, but had drawn the line at country and pop songs. Her flexibility was only so great. It had been heartwarming, however, to see how truly happy and affectionate the staff had been at her retirement party. They had hugged her and reassured her that the office would never be the same after her departure. Gert still considers her mission work at the insurance office to be a monument to her spiritual commitment.

Still, Gert doesn't like quandaries. The last quandary she confronted had been resolved to perfection. Should Gert sit in the front pew, where the preacher could receive her nonverbal feedback by watching her face during the sermon? All the folks behind her could watch her head nod whenever she felt the preacher had made a point that merited her approval. The only problem was that by sitting in the front row, she would be unable to scan the congregation for signs of inattention to the service or infractions of apparel. The quandary was resolved when, in the pastor's absence, the associate pastor gave a sermon on AIDS. When he suggested that saying that one should "hate the sin and love the sinner" was both meaningless and inadequate, Gert was sufficiently scandalized and decided never again to endorse the associate pastor's sermon by sitting in the front pew.

On Sundays when the associate pastor preaches, Gert joins her friend Loretta in the back pew, where she can critique the reverence of her fellow churchgoers. The location also helps project her singing voice for all to hear. She likes to describe her voice as powerful. In truth, her voice can peel the crust off the communion bread and turn the wine into vinegar. Had she sung off-key, it would have been funny. However, her perfect pitch makes the sound merely painful. Sitting in the back also sends a subtle message to the associate pastor that his sermons aren't up to Gert's exacting standards. She is slightly miffed by the fact that her absence never seems to trouble him. On occasions when the senior pastor preaches, her role as his *éminence grise* mandates her presence in the front pew. On those front-pew Sundays, Gert has Loretta posted in the back pew, tabulating the visible sins of the congregation. Loretta is a quiet, mousy sort who basks in Gert's formidable shadow and leaves to Gert the onerous task of advising her fellow congregants of the features of their appearance or behavior that must surely offend a righteous deity. Hemlines too short, bodices too low, children too unruly—nothing escapes the scrutiny of the spiritually vigilant duo. Whenever someone takes umbrage at her gentle remonstrations,

Gert comforts herself that, according to 2 Timothy 3:12, "those who desire to live Godly in Christ Jesus will suffer persecution." She further comforts herself by spreading the word about those people whose responses are insufficiently repentant. This is not gossip, for gossip is wrong. Gert is simply providing object lessons for her fellow Christians. In short, Gert never has doubts about her role in promulgating scriptural behavior, never a quandary—which makes her current situation all the more vexatious.

It is Saturday, and Gert has come to the sanctuary to ensure that the ladies have arranged the altar flowers with due reverence. She loves this part of her ministry. The sanctuary is vacant, and she can take her time looking for insects, dead plants, or clashing colors. But this Saturday, the sanctuary is not vacant. Right there in the front pew—in *her* seat, no less—is a man.

"May I ask what you are doing here, sir?" Gert is peering slit-eyed down her nose at the interloper.

"Hello. I'm just sittin' here, enjoyin' the quiet."

"Well, the church is closed to the public. You will have to leave." She is brisk and businesslike, flapping her hands as if to sweep the problem out the church door.

"If it's closed, why are you here?"

"I'm a member of the church."

"So what you're sayin' is that the church is not open to those people who need it?"

"Don't be tedious. You will have to leave. Now." Gert applies her favorite we-are-not-amused look to her face.

"Okay. I'm thinkin' of bringin' some friends with me to your church. One is a drunk, one is a jailbird, one tried to pimp his wife to a politician, and one is a homeless guy with no job."

"We don't need your kind of people around here." The very thought brings scandal and resistance to her face. "There is a rescue mission downtown for you and your friends."

"I'll bet your pastor is comforted by the fact that he has such a committed guardian at his gate. Now, surely you gotta have somebody helpin' you with all this, it bein' such a job to act as a self-appointed church policeman."

"Sir, I don't need your insults. Do I need to call the real police?" Gert has always prided herself on her forbearance in the presence of those less perfect than herself, but this situation is getting away from her.

"No need to call the police. Your phone won't work anyway. By the way, the friends I referred to are Noah, Saul of Tarsus, Abraham, and Jesus Christ. You gotta admit, there's something peculiar about a Christian who won't have anything to do with people who were completely acceptable to God."

"Fiddlesticks. What do you mean my phone won't work?"

"Try it."

Gert's phone is dead. Now her irritation is becoming tinged with a bit of uncertainty. "All right, Mr. Wise Guy, so you've got some signal-blocking thingy in your pocket. Are you here to rob the church or what?"

"No, Gert. You have done a masterful job of robbing this church already." My voice modulates and becomes formal. "You have picked it clean of joy and spontaneity."

"I don't take criticism from the likes of you. How do you know my name?"

"My name is Augie, and I am an angel. I have some good news for you and some bad news. The good news is that all of heaven knows about you. The bad news is that all of heaven knows about you."

For the first time in her life, Gert's well-used vocal musculature seizes up. Her eyes bulge with incredulity.

"Gert, I know how you hate quandaries. On the one hand, Scripture makes clear that angels exist. On the other hand, your common sense argues against accepting that there is an angel standing in front of you. Plus, I have been told that I don't look very angelic. Right so far?"

Numb, Gert only nods.

"Gert, I am here because your enthusiasm for rooting out unrighteousness is counterproductive." I point my finger, and the altar flowers rise up and scatter across the floor. I watch as Gert's glance seems magnetically drawn to the floral mess I have made.

"Uhhhh . . ." Gert shakes her head as though to clear either her vision or her reality.

"Some of us angels are concerned about your judgmental spirit. Personally, I think that if you had been in that crowd around the adulterous woman when Jesus said, 'Let him among you who is without sin cast the first stone,' you'd have brained her with a split-finger fastball." I leave the flowers on the floor and turn back to her.

I know that I have moved the discussion to an area of comfortable familiarity to Gert. She is able to find her voice. She tosses her head back proudly. "It doesn't have a thing to do with me. Yes, I would have stoned her. The Old Testament called for exactly that punishment for exactly that sin. Here you are, an angel—or so you claim—and you are telling me to ignore the commands of the Old Testament?" Gert seems so fully restored to self-righteousness that I regret having to pull her theological pants down for her.

"I have a newsflash for you, Gert. While you weren't looking, someone added a New Testament. It talks about, among other things, taking care to remove the log from your own eye before addressing the speck in your neighbor's eye."

"I have no logs in my eyes, and I *am* speaking spiritually. I'm serving the Lord by helping his children behave better. That's all. Where is the sin in that?"

"Who is the worst sinner you know, Gert?"

"That's a ridiculous question. I know lots of sinners. Bad sinners."

"But you don't number yourself among them, do you?"

"Of course not."

"Gert, if every Christian doesn't consider himself to be the worst sinner he knows, he hasn't grasped the essence of Christ's sacrifice."

"Ridiculous. I've never heard such tripe." She gets up from where she had slumped just minutes before. Again, she makes shooing gestures with her hands.

"Exactly. To you, it's tripe precisely because you haven't heard it. When Jesus talked about people having ears but not hearing, he was talking about Gert Bastrop."

"This conversation is becoming boring. Are you leaving or not?"

"Since you accepted Christ, have you ever told a lie? Have you ever coveted anything belonging to someone else? Don't bother to deny it. Since you're the one who brought up Old Testament rules, we can be virtually certain that you are a covetous liar and, despite salvation, you continue to violate those two of the Ten Commandments. But I'll wager that you don't agree that Christ's death on the cross needs to continue to atone for your ongoing sin. When Jesus asked his Father to forgive 'them, for they know not what they do,' don't you know that he included all humans present and future in that prayer to his Father?

"When evangelicals talk to a nonbeliever, they sometimes say that if the nonbeliever were the only person on earth, Jesus would still have gone to the cross for him or her. That is true. If any of you humans were the only one on earth, Jesus would have died to redeem you. What you seem to miss, Gert, is that even if you had been the only human on earth, Jesus would have *needed* to go to the cross to redeem you. You seem to think his sacrifice pertains only to the sins of others. How about 'judge not lest you be judged'? Maybe your Bible had a typographical error and that verse got left out."

"I'll be damned if I'll stand here and listen to your condemnation." Gert heads for the side door.

"You might be damned if you don't listen." I am left staring at the slammed door. "Okay. Plan B."

The next morning is Sunday. Gert has almost completely convinced herself that her encounter the day before was the product of overwork and excessive zeal. Nevertheless, she is relieved to enter the sanctuary and find the stranger is absent. Today is the associate pastor's turn to preach, so she settles into the last pew with Loretta.

"Gert," Loretta whispers, "those flowers on the floor are a scandal. You must not have had time to come by last night."

Gert looks up and sees that Loretta is right. So upset by our encounter, Gert had not remembered to clean up after me. The mess is simply unacceptable. Gert opens her mouth to speak and hears a loud oink escape.

"What did you say, Gert? Oh, never mind. Look at Jessica over there. No one should wear a red dress in church. She looks like a tart."

Gert looks at Jessica and gives another loud oink.

"Gert, what is wrong with you?"

"Oink. Ernnnkkk."

Loretta shrinks away at the loud expostulation. People turn their heads to look at Gert. Gert has always felt it improper for anyone in church—except her, of course—to pay any attention to distractions. Despite the fact that she is the distraction, Gert feels her disapproval kick in and is horrified to hear a loud "Oinnnnnnnnkkkkkkkk! Errnnnnnnnnnkkkkkk! Snort!" emanate from her face. She is up on her feet, hearing herself responding to solicitous voices with a rhapsody of porcine utterances. Her face a flaming red, she brushes past her husband, Joe, who is standing by the exit with a bemused expression on his face. Fleeing the church, Gert races to her car. She locks herself in and buries her face in her hands.

"Having a bad day, are we?"

Gert looks in the rearview mirror and sees me sitting comfortably in the backseat. "Oh, for the love of the sweet Lord in heaven, why are you here?"

"Just to remind you that God admonishes those whom he loves. So somewhat to my surprise, he hasn't given up on you. You, however, will continue to sound like a pig whenever you judge or condemn someone. This will hopefully help you curb your tongue. When it comes to curbing your brain, I think you will need to ask God for help."

After-Action Summary

I chose a pig to inhabit Gert's larynx. According to Old Testament dietary laws, the pig is unclean; it is unwelcome, therefore, at the Lord's table as either a guest or as a side dish. In the New Testament, pigs were used as a garbage receptacle for exorcised demons (Matthew 8:32). Additionally, while talking with Gert, I was reminded of Matthew 7:6. I was definitely casting pearls before swine. The choice of animal was, therefore, quite scriptural.

One of the criticisms of Christianity is that it is a judgmental religion. While Christianity most certainly is not judgmental, many of its practitioners are. Just as every village has its idiot, every church has its Gert Bastrop. While a mature Christian might regard them simply as buffoons, their impact on church attendance and upon spiritually vulnerable people is malignant. People who come to church seeking grace go home with a virulent dose of religion. That these judges can justify themselves with Scripture makes them all the more lethal. The Gert Bastrops of your world are people who let their own religion get in the way of other people's faith. Recall that Jesus was not angered by generic sin, but he directed his undiluted rage at religiously self-righteous humans during his physical time on earth. Does anyone think that his anger toward such behavior has been somehow stopped? It still angers him. For whose kingdom do the Gerts of this world labor?

The Academy Award-winning movie *The Bridge over the River K'wai* illustrates a similar issue. In this film, a British army engineer, Colonel Bogey, is the quintessential English patriot—ramrod straight, a stickler for discipline, and never a question of loyalty to God, king, and country. In the dramatic conclusion, Bogey realizes that he has been manipulated by a brilliant enemy into working for the destruction of his own military forces. In the same way, Satan encourages Christians to work for him. Gert Bastrop is not an agent of light, and her work is not for the kingdom of God.

When reading Jesus' words in John 12:47—"I do not come to judge the world, but to save it"—the Gert Bastrops of the world assume that Jesus has left vacant the post of Magistrate to the World. And as luck would have it, they themselves are just the persons to fill that vacancy. I have suggested to Papa that he arrange for humans to be born with lights in their foreheads. When they are judgmental, the light would glow red; when they are jealous, it would glow green; and so forth for every nasty little habit the Gerts of the world cherish. They would have a hard time judging other people while displaying their own sin on their forehead. Perhaps that would curb such behavior.

The pastor of a church afflicted with one or more Gerts usually receives the subtle message that he should emphasize only those sins that are mostly alien to his congregation. He feels obligated to keep everything focused on sex, drugs, and rock 'n' roll and to walk softly around issues of gossip, slander, backbiting, envy, sloth, and gluttony. It is a brave preacher who ignores these prohibitions.

A final note on the associate pastor when he alienated Gert by addressing the AIDS question. Many humans say that AIDS is God's judgment on homosexuals. If that were true, why do heterosexual drug abusers and transfusion recipients contract it? Why is it rare among lesbians, who, last time I checked, are also homosexual? Be advised that we angels think that AIDS is God's challenge to the church, not a judgment on homosexuals. God will judge homosexuals in his perfect time, just as he will judge all of you. Christians, however, will be called to account for their response to AIDS victims. The associate pastor was right: "hating the sin but loving the sinner" is a vapid phrase if it is not accompanied by active compassion. Jesus also said, "[W]hatsoever you do unto the least of these, you do also unto me."(Matthew 25:40) When Gert Bastrop, or your local Christian magistrate, condemns an AIDS victim, he or she condemns Jesus Christ *in absentia*.

Chapter 13

Case File M-582-AD

Rebecca is thinking of getting a drink. No, she is thinking about getting drunk. She never drinks alcohol, but now her liver is calling out for a dose of abuse. Why? *Small wonder*, she thinks. *My other remedies haven't worked.*

It's late evening in Atlanta, and Rebecca is taking in the night air. While Atlanta can experience insufferable summer heat, the springtime can be beautiful, as it is tonight. Rebecca, however, hardly notices the pleasant evening as her boot heels click a staccato rhythm on the sidewalk, the hemline of her skirt keeping metronome time.

Rebecca Salem is a successful singer. With two biblical names like Rebecca and Salem, it's almost obligatory that her genre would be Christian pop. A few nights ago, she had received the ultimate accolade in her business: Christian Female Vocalist of the Year, the Dove Award, presented at the old Fox Theatre. She'd had a series of hits, but her latest song, "Silhouettes of Love" by Lily and Rita Dulaney, had raced to the top of the charts and even crossed over into the secular audience. By the end of the evening, she had dared to hope that the burden on her heart would lift. It hadn't. The award was no more therapeutic than music, being with friends, or even praying. So why not try some booze?

She goes into her hotel and spots a sandwich-board sign advertising a bar on the second floor. *Why not?* She goes upstairs and enters the bar. Except for the bartender, the place is deserted.

"Wait, don't tell me," Rebecca says. "You serve moonshine, and all your other patrons are dead, right?"

"Nah, the Hawks and the Braves are both playin' tonight, and my cable connection is on the fritz. So my regulars are drinkin' where they can watch TV. So it's you and me. What'll you have, ma'am?"

"Oh please, my mother is a 'ma'am.' The name is Rebecca."

"Augie is my name. What can I get you?"

"I'm not sure. What's the beer that sounds like the first book in the Bible?"

"Hmmmm, sounds like Genesis? You must mean Guinness."

"That's the stuff."

"Okay, Rebecca, but you seem a little, ah, uninitiated. I gotta warn you that Guinness is a bit of an acquired taste."

"That's okay. It's not the taste I'm looking for."

"Okay, young lady, a pint of Genesis Stout comin' up." I go to the tap, give it a long pull, and then scoop the foam off with a knife.

I hand Rebecca the beer, and she takes a healthy swallow. For a second, I am afraid her face will implode. Finally, her beautiful face comes out from behind the Guinness face that had hit her. "Whew, well, Augie, if you're missing some rat poison, I think I just located it."

"Like I said, an acquired taste."

"No, Augie, cannibalism is an acquired taste. I think this stuff could remove my fingernail polish. Maybe take my fingers with it."

"Want to try somethin' else? Ya know, your eyes are kinda pretty when they aren't crossed. Maybe your eyeballs don't approve of this beer." I move as though to take her glass.

"No, this is good. I'm feeling a little masochistic." Her brown hair has a sable glow in the low light of the bar. She leans forward to rest her elbow on the arm of her barstool.

"Hard day?"

"Hard month."

"Care to share?"

"Augie, I know that bartenders are traditionally sympathetic and nonjudgmental, but I don't want to burden you."

"Well, look around. It isn't like I'm swamped or anything."

Rebecca has a fleeting image of a little boy, her little brother, following her around, calling, "Recca, Recca." She thinks about how she mothered him, calling him Mikoo in loving mimicry of how he had first pronounced his own name. She begins to talk. With occasional lubricating sips of Guinness, she shares her sorrow with Augie. Mike Salem, all grown up and a committed Christian, had delayed college so that he could join the army and serve his country.

His first week in Afghanistan, his platoon had acted on a tip about a Taliban cell and approached an abandoned Kabul apartment building. It's one thing to be told that the Taliban will strap explosives to the bodies of children and send them at you; it's quite another to actually see a seven-year-old boy coming at you wearing a Semtex vest, tears streaming down his frightened face. It's one thing to be told to take out the child before he can wipe out your platoon; it's quite another to actually do it. Mike's buddy hesitated; Mike did not. Had they fired at the same time, they could have both deluded themselves into thinking they had missed while their partner had not. There was no question it was Mike's kill.

He had saved his platoon, and all it cost him was his mind. Mike was soon back stateside, in and out of a series of military hospitals, in and out of a variety of drug regimens and support groups. His church friends rallied and kept him almost constant company. Nothing worked. The image of that little boy must have been on the inside of Mike's eyelids, for it never left him and only became more vivid when he tried to sleep. As he recounted the incident to Rebecca, even she could feel the horror of it: a quick look around the corner of a cinder-block wall, a view of the boy ten meters away, zombie-walking in Mike's direction. A snap decision and a signal to his buddy. Then a snap shot. Rebecca had replied that the child had been effectively sentenced to death by the terrorists the moment they strapped the explosives to him. "Death is still death, whether by bullet or by bomb, but the bullet functioned to save other lives," she told him. "The bomb would have added to the body count."

Mike wasn't hearing. He mused about whether Allah considered such a child to be a martyr and, therefore, suitable for paradise. What good would a bunch of virgins in paradise be to a seven-year-old boy? The sad and morbid preoccupation persisted. Mike stopped attending church and, by his own admission, seemed to stop talking with God. Mike blew his brains out on the second anniversary of the little boy's death.

"Oh man, Rebecca, I am so sorry."

"Believe it or not, that wasn't the worst part. At his funeral, we had a childhood friend preside. He is a pretty standard product of a Baptist seminary. He gave me no heads-up on what he was going to say. The gist of his message was that suicide is self-murder and not forgivable. He said he was grieved that Mike had lost his eternal life, his entry into heaven."

"You are kiddin', right?"

Rebecca blinks away a few tears. "Augie, up to that point, I was incredibly sad but at least comforted that Mike was in heaven. Now I just don't know. It's as though the preacher stole my certainty and left me with doubt. I'd do anything to get back the assurance that I felt before the funeral."

"Well, the guy, bein' a friend of yours, must have been pretty convinced of his facts. It can't have made him very happy to have said what he said." Even though I know all about this, it is hard to keep the anger out of my voice. I distract myself by wiping the counter with my rag.

"No, he wasn't happy. That just makes it worse. If he had been an arrogant jerk, I could have dismissed him. But he wasn't, so I can't."

I am silent for a while. "His theology sounds more Catholic than Baptist. All that stuff about sin that hasn't been confessed to a priest. Suicide victims not bein' buried in hallowed ground. All that."

"Do you believe that?"

"No, I don't accept any theology that shrinks God, puts him in a box. I don't believe there is any situation where God *can't* do something according to some human interpretation of Scripture. Plus, once you start talkin' about suicide, you have so many reasons. How about the man who throws himself on a grenade to save his buddies? Somewhere in the book of John it says that 'no greater love has a man than that he would give up his life for his brother.' And then, what about the guy with wrecked lungs who continues to smoke or the diabetic who keeps on pigging out? They're just shooting themselves with a slow-movin' bullet."

"I see what you mean, but the intent is what counts. Your soldier is a hero for diving on the grenade; your smoker and your diabetic are just foolish. Mike wanted to end his life." Rebecca is staring off over my shoulder, her grief a pallid mantle over her heart, seeming to fend off any incursion by grace. I know I need to drill through it to get to her.

I say, "Maybe not. Some suicide survivors will tell you that all they wanted was for the thoughts and memories to go away. People like Mike may not necessarily want to die; they just want to stop the torment. They feel like their emotions are being beaten to death and that there will never be an end. In their despair, they let go of God's hand. They don't stop loving him or believing in him; they just lose track of him."

Rebecca gives a sad smile. "Augie, you almost have me persuaded." But she is leaning toward me, and her deep brown eyes take on an entreaty that invites more of the truth.

I move closer so that I can whisper and capture her with my eyes. Her pain is almost palpable. "Sweetheart, the most famous suicide of all time was that of Jesus Christ. He knew the Sanhedrin wanted him dead, but he went to Jerusalem. He knew Judas would betray him, but he stayed in Gethsemane. He knew the trials would lead to a death sentence, but he neither ran nor defended himself. He committed suicide in order to save people like Mike. When Mike ended his physical life, he couldn't have canceled Jesus' sacrifice. No human is strong enough, and no act is bad enough to accomplish that. So forget the Scripture Nazis when they try to tell you what God *can't* do. Remember Romans 8:38? 'For I am persuaded that neither death nor life, neither angels nor demons, neither the present nor the future, nor any powers, neither height nor depth, nor anything else in all creation, will be able to separate us from the love of God that is in Christ Jesus our Lord.' Don't forget, St. Paul was a lawyer, and he was covering all the bases in his list. I think that you'll find suicide buried somewhere in that list."

Rebecca is smiling and crying at the same time. "Thank you, Augie. You are such an angel."

"Well, it's about time somebody recognized my true calling. Lean over here." Rebecca leans over, and I kiss two fingers and place them on her forehead. "That's to give you a good night's sleep. Why don't you head on up to your room?"

"How did you know I was staying at this hotel?"

"Like you said, I'm an angel. We know many things."

"Good night, Augie."

"Good night, Rebecca. God will bless you."

Rebecca awakens after her first good night's sleep in a long time. She enjoys a cup of coffee as she dresses. She jots a quick thank-you note to Augie and goes to the second floor, thinking she'll slip her note under the bar door. When she gets there, the sign is gone. She opens the door, and there is no bar. It's a storage room, a little dusty from disuse, filled with stacked chairs. Shocked and perplexed, Rebecca spots a single chair in the middle of the room with a piece of paper on it. She walks over and sees that it's a note addressed to her. As she reads, a smile of understanding comes to her lips.

Rebecca,

I checked last night after you went to bed. Mike is in heaven. So is the little boy who died in Afghanistan. Mike said to tell you, "Recca, it is beautiful here. I have no sorrow. Keep your faith. Mikoo loves you."

Rebecca, get Lily and Rita Dulaney to tell you about Augie the angel.

In his love,
Augie

After-Action Summary

The Catholic Church has taken a lot of well-deserved criticism lately. But all humanity needs to recall the enormous debt owed to the Catholic Church. For over a millennium, it was the Catholic Church that sustained Christianity and insisted on accurate and precise preservation of God's Word. I might also add, as an erstwhile bartender, that without Catholicism, there would be no Ireland. Without Ireland, there would be no Guinness.

The Catholics produced a few interesting problems, at least for angels. They have a pope, and they call him a pontiff. The word *pontiff* is Latin for "bridge builder," as though the pope is the intermediary between man and God. As an angel, I view the true bridge builder as Jesus Christ, and *pontiff* shouldn't be in any human's job description. Not a big issue, just an oddity.

Most angels, however, think the more vexing issue is the confession to a priest. Scripture says humans are to confess to God and "confess our sins one to another" (James 5:16). For a Catholic, confession must be done before a priest; penance is prescribed and absolution given. For a sin of suicide, the sinful action leads to death, which renders moot the opportunity for confession and absolution. To their credit, however, the catechism of the Catholic Church includes a reassurance that humans shouldn't despair for the souls of suicide victims. The mind of God is beyond human understanding, and the mystery of God could well have provision for just such souls. Certain Protestant denominations would do well to incorporate this catechism.

What does suicide prove? It proves that while Satan is not the intellectual equal of God, he is smarter and more powerful than any human. Temptation is not his strongest weapon. Despair is. A committed Christian succumbing to the onslaught of despair and taking his life is nothing more than verification of the resolve and the evil of the Adversary. It is not an occasion to place strictures on a loving God. Those who assert that God cannot allow a self-murderer into heaven justify their position by saying that God, while loving, is also righteous and cannot accept any mitigation of this sin. I would be happy to send some of my fellow angels to those of you who hold this position. They can provide you with a day or two of despair equal to that of a suicide victim, and we'll see how well your theology holds up. To paraphrase an old line: never judge a man until you have walked a mile in his misery.

On a final point, let's take a gunshot suicide, like that of Mike. The muzzle velocity of the average handgun allows only milliseconds between the trigger pull and loss of life. While that is an unimaginably small amount of time to a human, its brevity is of no consequence to a deity who exists at the speed of light. It gives God ample time to weigh the heart of this person. It is more than enough time for Jesus to say, "Papa, he is one of mine." It is more than enough time for Satan to rage at finding that the physical life he so carefully ended has been replaced by an eternal life.

Chapter 14

Interlude

This chapter is not a case file. My boss is reviewing the progress of this little pastiche, and she feels that it is not a complete reflection of angels in general. I am sure she thinks she is being diplomatic when she refers to me as a curmudgeon. Of course, when a cherub calls you a curmudgeon, that is like a toad calling a human being ugly.

So I have fetched around and decided to bring you, gentle reader, into what we call our "zip shop." From time to time, angels need to gather. There are debriefings, coordination of plans, and reviews of new assignments. These are done with the bosses. There is a separate chamber, however, where tradition permits only working angels to enter. No bosses. This is where we meet old friends, relax, and get some maintenance work done on our physical bodies. Most angels like to stay in the skin while maintenance is being performed on us. That way, we can sip a little wine while the mechanics work their magic.

Welcome, therefore, to the zip shop: it's a combination men's locker room and neighborhood tavern. It's like the barroom scene in

Star Wars but without the charm. A word of preparation: because we are angels, we exist out of time, which means that what a human would categorize as vastly different time periods—ancient history, present day, and the future—all occur in the same time frame for God and for his angels. This is hard for humans to understand, but read to the end of this chapter and you will see how even an angel can get confused about the era he is looking for. *If you still don't understand, find a theoretical physicist and slap him around.*

I am back at the zip shop. I have just finished occupying the body of Balaam's donkey (Numbers 22), giving him a voice. It must have irritated the donkey to have an angel highjack his little donkey brain. When I popped out of him and back into my normal body, he bit off three of my fingers. Because angels can feel pain inflicted on their physical bodies, it was most unpleasant. You remember that Happy was with me? Well, he tried to correct the problem, and I ended up with a finger coming out of each nostril and one finger in a place that modesty forbids my identifying. So I finished the debriefing, with my boss sniggering at my appearance, and then came to the zip shop to have my anatomical furniture properly rearranged.

"Yo, Augie!"

"Yo, Sid!" Sid is the zip-shop bartender. He used to be a working angel. He was a guardian angel to Jews during the Holocaust and then to the Chinese during Chairman Mao's Great Leap Forward. No guardian angel ever had so many of his humans destroyed in such a short period. He never questioned why his bosses didn't let him intervene, but he asked for retirement from earthly assignments, and the higher-ups said okay. Sid is the only angel who doesn't tell war stories. Interestingly, Sid, unlike me, has an unreserved affection for humans. Go figure. Sid changes the zip-room decor frequently and whimsically; today it has a look of American Southwest meets Spanish Inquisition.

"So, Augie, are you ready to try some wine from a blue state?"

"The usual, Sid," I say as I sit down where Frankie, the mechanic angel, can work on me. "And give me a straw I can use until Frankie here can get these fingers out of my nose." Sid loves to tease me about blue-state wines. The way I figure it, blue-state wines come from grapes grown out of blue-state soil. They bury too many liberals in blue-state soil, and it's bound to influence the wine. If I drink blue-state wine, I'm afraid I might start singing John Lennon's "Imagine" and getting my eyebrows waxed. So I stick with Virginia wine, which, fortunately, is equal to any California vintage.

Frankie gets the fingers out of my nostrils and puts them back on properly. I have to stand up for him to get to the last misplaced finger.

"So, Augie, has Happy finished his debrief?"

"He'll probably be a few minutes, Sid. The bosses are trying to figure out whether the thing he did with my fingers was a mistake or deliberate."

"Well, if Happy is coming in, I'd better lock the wine cabinet," Sid says with a laugh.

"He'll just pick the lock."

"Augie, I still remember a few tricks from my earth assignments. That donkey isn't the only one who knows how to remove fingers."

The door opens, but it isn't Happy. It's Raya. She is a gorgeous angel, soft spoken, with a specialty in guardianship of children. She's the only angel I know who seems to love humans to a degree approaching that of Jesus and Papa. I guess dealing exclusively with children might have that effect.

"Hi, guys."

"Yo, Raya. Where's Herb?" Herb is a dour angel who favors a Scottish accent. He tries to maintain what he thinks is a serious demeanor, but somehow he just comes off looking constipated. He is Raya's partner. Raya has always had one charming problem when she is in the skin. Just as Happy can't always control his body's fondness for wine, Raya can never control her facial blood flow, the result being that she blushes with the slightest provocation. Right now, she is crimson. While she is pondering her response, two more angels, Happy and Paulie, come through the door.

"Herb is still in debriefing," she says. "Uh, guys, you'll need to cut Herb a little slack when he gets here. We were guarding a children's field trip to a zoo, and"—she is blushing furiously—"well, he blocked a demon from letting the lions loose from their cage. Herb wasn't expecting the demon to play a trick on him." If Raya's face gets any redder, Sid is going to use the fire extinguisher on her.

Just then, the door opens, and in comes Herb. Only it isn't Herb. Well, sort of. It's Herb's face, but the face is topped by a huge Dolly Parton-style blonde wig, and the body is distinctly female, from the stiletto heels and fishnet stockings to the hyperbolic bosom jammed into a spandex tube top. Herb, as usual, is not smiling.

The zip room is stone silent. Then Paulie breaks the silence with a decompensating howl of laughter. Sid joins in. Happy adds his high-pitched giggles. And yes, I confess to a little bit of a chortle.

"Churls. Laugh if ye must." Herb's speech reverts to Middle English whenever he starts to lose his cool. Raya tries mounting a sympathetic look on her face, but it becomes clear that her blushing came from fighting her laughter. She now dissolves into unangelic screeches of mirth. Herb fixes her with a frown of disapproval, which only makes us all lose what little control we had. Laughter is now punctuated by gasps for air. Even Happy has stopped looking at the wine cabinet.

Herb tries for wounded dignity. "Never mind. I simply need Frankie to sort this all out and get me back into a proper skin. Where is he?"

Weakly, I manage to squeak, "He was just here with me." I turn around. No Frankie. Then I look down. Frankie is on the floor, convulsing with silent laughter, beating his fist on the carpet. "Frankie, get it together, bro. Herb needs some help," I manage to say. "We really shouldn't laugh at him."

Frankie catches his breath and gets off the floor. "Sorry, Herb. I wasn't laughing at you." Frankie bites his lip and looks down. I think his face might fracture.

"Well, what are you laughing at?" Herb says.

"Herb, that's a switched body. Your demon must have borrowed it from some poor innocent hooker. I was thinking that right now, that poor tart is trying to sell *your* body to her clientele." That is it. Frankie is back on the floor, fighting for air. I must look about as unhinged as Frankie. Herb needs Frankie to help him get back into a proper skin, but he doesn't need me. So it is me he goes after.

"Frankie, I will be here waiting for your jocularity to end. As for you, Augie, at least my predicament is the result of demonic revenge, not my own poor sense of time and direction."

My humor flees. The others go silent and look at me. Then the shrieking laughter begins again, now at my expense as they recall what has become known as Augie's Odyssey. Remember Genesis 14? Isaac gets invited out of King Abimelech's land. He goes elsewhere in Gerar and opens some wells to water his sheep and cows. He gets thrown off of that land. He has to dig two more wells before he is no longer forced to move. It's a perfect lesson in persistence and patience. The only problem is that it wasn't supposed to be that way. An angel was supposed to see that he only had to dig one new well, not three. That angel was me, and it was my first solo flight. Somehow, instead of the Middle East in 2000

BC, I ended up in America in AD 2000—Las Vegas. I was so disoriented that I actually stopped a lady of the night and asked her where I could find Isaac, a guy with a lot of sheep. I guess she had a problem with the sheep; she called me a pervert and beat me up.

Papa is eternal. Jesus is eternal. Angels are eternal. Saved humans have eternal life. That's the good news. The bad news is that some stories also have eternal life. You just learned mine. I hope the boss is happy.

Chapter 15

Case File M-267-AD

She has a way of half closing her eyes and gently touching his face during a kiss. *How can a kiss actually have a taste?* he wonders. She darts her tongue against his lips and then pulls back, giving him that quirky smile that reminds him of Cameron Diaz. "You're running late, Wal," she says. "Head out, and give me a call when it's over."

"Yes, crosstown traffic is going to be a bear. You know I would only tolerate it for a chance to be with you. I'll be in touch." He enters the cab. Wallace Fitzgerald may run a bit late. Rush hour across Manhattan is horrific, but a stop for afternoon delight with Cherie is worth it. Their intimate friendship goes back years. Their living in different cities places a limit on their assignations that keeps the relationship simple and uncomplicated.

Uncomplicated—that's how Fitzgerald likes his life. He gave up a busy OB-GYN practice to perform gynecology exclusively, relieving himself of those inconvenient deliveries at all hours. For the past twenty years, he has avoided all night-call work, all hospital-committee work and, indeed, all hospital staff membership with its myriad complications. He is a TOP—termination of pregnancy, or abortion—doc.

A super-restricted practice, it normally isn't lucrative. Although he received a silver-spoon inheritance from his parents, Fitzgerald is a good businessman. He hired a New York interior designer to redecorate his office. He renamed it Empowered Women's Clinic. He began to support feminist initiatives and insinuated himself into the power circle of women's groups.

Fitzgerald is vocal in his support of the contention that a fetus feels no pain during an abortion, and he resolutely refuses to offer his patients the alternative of fetal anesthesia in a termination of pregnancy. He correctly guesses that in making an offer of fetal anesthesia, a doctor humanizes a fetus and might make a patient decide against abortion or experience guilt after having the abortion. The result of his political maneuvering is that he is the darling of the rich and famous who wish their abortions to be ultra-confidential. Fitzgerald can accommodate those women who, through indecision or denial, wait until it is late in the pregnancy. In those few cases where the fetus inconveniently escapes the uterus before he can disassemble it, Fitzgerald ensures that the poorly timed delivery does not result in motherhood. It's uncomplicated, the way Fitzgerald likes it—the way Fitzgerald is.

Yes, Fitzgerald is uncomplicated, like most intelligent sociopaths. In truth, he cares not for the patients, the feminists, or the fetuses. What he cares about passionately is Wallace Fitzgerald. If the Supreme Court decided that life begins at conception, Fitzgerald would still find a way to kill the inconvenient little bastards. If, on the other hand, the Court decided that only fetuses with catastrophic anomalies could be aborted, Fitzgerald would find a way to invent and report severe congenital defects in every fetus coming through his door.

Fitzgerald's commitment to the eradication of unwanted pregnancies in the wealthy and powerful is the reason for his late-afternoon foray into Manhattan traffic. The Gunderson Institute, a women's advocacy group, is recognizing his efforts on behalf of women by bestowing upon him their Humanitarian Award. Ostensibly reserved for people who have advanced the cause of disadvantaged women everywhere, the award seems to find its way into the hands of those who have advanced the power agenda of the politically connected. It has been years since Fitzgerald has actually served a poor woman.

Fitzgerald gives his destination to the cabbie and then calls his wife. She didn't make the trip, and that permitted him to visit Cherie. Judith, his wife, knows nothing about Cherie or any of his other liaisons. Fitzgerald met Cherie professionally when she came to him for an abortion. Their intimacy began shortly thereafter. Cherie can't tolerate oral contraceptives or IUDs, and neither she nor Fitzgerald like the inconvenience of barrier contraception. This resulted in two pregnancies, both of which Fitzgerald terminated. Uncomplicated.

After a brief chat with Judith, Fitzgerald hangs up and notices that they are already in slowdown traffic. Fitzgerald checks the driver's ID on the back of the front seat. "Augie, it's been a long time since I've been in a New York taxi where the driver didn't have a turban on his head or reggae on his radio."

"Don't I know it? I'm from Brooklyn, so I only need a work visa to come to Manhattan." I chuckle. "If you're in a hurry, there are a few cut-through alleys that'll save some time."

"Okay, but don't run the meter up. I know these streets."

"Fine by me. I'm not drivin' this cab to get rich. So headin' to the Gunderson Institute? You must be a doctor, right?"

"Exactly. How did you know?"

"A lotta doctors head over there; plus, you've got that doctor look, ya know? So you do abortions?"

Fitzgerald's head snaps up, surprised that a streetwise cabbie would deduce these facts. "Well, we prefer to say 'termination of pregnancy,' but yes, that's what I do."

"Must be pretty satisfyin'. Keeps a lot of brats from cloggin' up the system."

"Well, we tend to think more of the benefit to the woman. An unwanted pregnancy limits her economic and physical freedom, not to mention the stress of a delivery on her body. But yes, reducing the number of babies is a form of population control."

"Especially abortin' all those black babies. I read where nearly half of all black pregnancies in this city get aborted, and nationwide, over one third of all abortions are black babies. Multiply that by the decades we been doin' abortions—man, if those babies had grown up, there would be as many black folks as there are white folks. I bet the Ku Klux Klan really loves you guys." I look out the window and at my side mirrors as the traffic continues to crawl.

"Uh, well, that's not the point."

"That's okay, Doc. The best kind of racism is where you actually get the minority to agree with your genocide."

Fitzgerald doesn't notice the gradual loss of my Brooklyn patois.

"Look, Cabbie, I'm not a racist. I don't claim to care about these fetuses one way or the other, and quite frankly, I don't give a damn about the effect on the population. This conversation is beginning to irritate me. How about you drive and let me work on my acceptance speech?"

"Very well, Doctor." I pull into an alley and drive to the next cross street. It too is clogged with traffic. "We'll pull out here when there is a break in the traffic. It will save a few minutes."

"Fine."

"While we are stopped here anyway, Doctor Fitzgerald, perhaps you could give me your standard speech on fetuses feeling no pain during abortion."

Fitzgerald freezes. He looks up and sees that I have turned to face him with a distinctly hostile gaze. "How do you know my name?"

"You are a famous person. Humor me; do you really think that fetuses feel no pain?"

"What is this? Are you some pro-life idiot who picked me up on purpose just so you could harass me?"

"I guess you could say I'm pro-life, but I'm an angel, not an idiot."

"You are a lunatic is what you are!" Fitzgerald tries the door, but it won't open. Fitzgerald is not accustomed to preemptory treatment and now is exhibiting some panic. "Let me out of this cab right now or you will regret it!"

"I very much doubt that, Doctor. You've caused enough regret in other people's lives, so let's see if there are any regrets in your life."

"I don't have any." Despite his fear, the doctor can still fall back on his sense of privilege and exemption.

"Not yet, but soon." I run my thumb down the side of my nose and adjust my hat. "On the subject of fetal pain, isn't it true that research confirms a stress response consistent with pain in a fetus at least twenty weeks along?"

"I'm not engaging in repartee with a nut job." Fitzgerald tries his phone—no service is available. His forehead is becoming moist with sweat, and he keeps staring at his phone as if willing the signal bars to appear.

"Doctor, isn't it true that you modern, sophisticated pro-abortion types use the same argument about fetal insensitivity to pain that humans used to apply to black folks and crazy folks? You've heard it all, haven't you? Because they are less intelligent and a lesser degree of human, how could they possibly have the same appreciation of pain as a smart white person? Isn't it also true that attributing a capacity for pain to a fetus runs the risk of humanizing it to a degree that the pregnant woman might actually conclude that there is another living being inside her body?"

"I'm not listening." Fitzgerald's fear has taken on a petulance, and now he is rocking back and forth, refusing to make eye contact.

"Then there is the problem of guilt and regret in the woman who has had an abortion. You and your confederates prefer to blame that on the pro-life groups. You claim that the things said by pro-life people induce guilt. In short, the world would be a wonderful place if only everyone would just shut up and agree with you. Aside from the fact that you are wrong, it is insufferable that you patronize these women by implying that any sorrow or conviction they might feel after an abortion is because they are weak willed and easily misled. You simply cannot bear to concede that a strong, mature, independent woman might one day look back and confess that she ended the life of her child."

Silence fills the cab.

"Fitzgerald, you are as silent as—what? Oh yes, as silent as a fetus."

Fitzgerald reaches out to try the door handle again and is surprised that the door seems closer than before. He reaches the other way and is shocked to find that both sides of the cab have encroached and are now pressing firmly against him.

"Comfy, Fitzgerald? Snug as a bug in a rug. Or snug as a fetus in a uterus. Let's try a little experiment. Since we know that environmental factors can influence how a human feels pain, let's see whether the tight confines of a uterus-like enclosure can blunt the sensation of pain."

Fitzgerald erupts in a girlish scream and voids his bladder as there is a rumbling movement of the cab, accompanied by a sucking sound. A large steel rod emerges up from the seat alongside his body. It is topped by a curved blade canted off to one side. The blade rotates inward, and the rod begins to descend downward, bringing the blade down and shearing off Fitzgerald's left arm. Blood splatters everywhere as Fitzgerald's face distorts in a rictus of agony, his mouth open to scream. No sound escapes his lips. The rod extends and retracts, up and down, whittling the doctor's body away, and the suctioning sound increases as the fragments of flesh are sucked into the seat. Soon, nothing remains. Shortly after, I look back at a normal, pristine backseat. In a shimmering moment, the alley is vacant.

After-Action Summary

Angels don't make termination decisions. This human may have been contemplating an activity even more contrary to the will of God than his life had been to that point. I don't know. Was he a good man under the control of a demon? Possibly. Speaking from my experience with humans, there can certainly be a symbiotic relationship in which the human feeds and nurtures the demon to the point where man and demon are indistinguishable. What can God do with such a human? Is this what the Bible calls "hardening of the heart"?

Well, the best example I can give from Scripture is Pharaoh of Moses' time, found in Exodus, chapters 7-14. He was a truly evil man. The Bible refers to God hardening Pharaoh's heart during the plagues. Critics say it was, therefore, God's fault that the Egyptians suffered. Again, this conclusion reflects a puerile assessment of God. God had two purposes at the time: one, to free his chosen people, the Israelites, and two, to demonstrate to them that he was a God of power, fully capable of delivering them.

God didn't have to harden the heart of Pharaoh to the suffering of the Israelites. He simply hardened Pharaoh's heart to the suffering of the Egyptian people and to the begging of his advisers. This hardening of the heart was simply a clouding of a judgment already made evil. The refusal to release the Israelites led to plagues of increasing scope and drama. When God hardened Pharaoh's heart, all he did was make Pharaoh as heartless to the suffering of his own people as he already was to the Israelites. Pharaoh relented after every Egyptian male firstborn, including Pharaoh's own son, died, only to act yet again on the hardness of his heart. In this case, the hardening of the heart simply blocked out the fear that any rational human would have felt (going out to bring back the people who caused all the plagues in the first place does seem a little hazardous), allowing his narcissism to express itself. In prompting Pharaoh to pursue the Israelites with the intent of returning them to slavery, God set the stage for the ultimate display of his power: parting the waters for the Israelites and then destroying their pursuers. So perhaps humans should conclude that the hardening of a human's heart is yet one more way that God tries to get his message across to his beloved children.

Did this display of his power accomplish God's goal? It certainly is memorialized in the most important of Jewish holidays, Passover. On balance, however, the Jews still whined in the wilderness, and their corporate lack of faith kept them out of the Promised Land for a generation of time. Considering that God is working with the human species, he can only expect so much success. The debate about the fairness of God punishing someone, whether a Pharaoh or a Fitzgerald, whose heart God himself has hardened does not edify. Humankind still fails to learn God's intent.

Pharaoh and Fitzgerald, men who embraced lifestyles that included prohibitive spiritual risk, were both men of hardened heart. Was Fitzgerald's termination merely heaven's reaction to abortion? No. The pro-abortion people would love to hear pro-lifers say yes, so they could attack them as judgmental. The hardline Christians would wish it so in order to justify exactly such a judgmental attitude. Every human owes God a death. Some humans give their lives nobly; others squander theirs. Many people's lives are taken from them for the convenience of others. Why should a fetal human be exempt? The termination of a fetal life is one of the prerogatives of free will. The very legality of its practice, along with its Byzantine justifications, is reflective of the health of the society that practices it. As an angel, what bothers me most is the schizophrenia it has caused in America. Consider the following:

> A gynecologist performs an abortion on a twenty-week fetus; the mother is on Medicaid. He then gets in his car and, while driving, is text messaging. Due to inattention, he runs a stoplight and hits a car driven by a woman who is twenty weeks pregnant. The same government that pays him to terminate the first fetus will now charge him with involuntary manslaughter in the death of the second fetus.

This simply means that a fetus is only a human being if the mother wishes it so. Recall the garden of Eden. When Adam's mate (she wasn't called Eve until after the fall) ate the fruit, she did so with the intent of having a knowledge of good and evil equal to God's. Only knowledge. It did not empower her to act like God, and that was not her desire. The American legal system has accorded to women a far greater power than the fruit granted to Eve: the right to decide the validity of a human life. A fetus is not alive unless the pregnant woman says so. If God doesn't punish America for this, he should apologize to Eve.

As a consequence, the American legal system has no definition of when life begins. Is this sophisticated legal thinking? No, it is cowardice of the basest sort. The lawmakers, the judiciary, and the abortion supporters lack the courage and integrity to simply say, "Yes, a fetus is alive, but it is inconvenient and must be killed."

The abortion supporters argue that unwanted children are a drain on society and that abortion reduces the number of criminals and social misfits. That sounds strangely reminiscent of Hitler when he gassed homosexuals and the mentally handicapped, maintaining that it was for the good of society. Because over one-third of abortions are performed on African Americans (according to the CDC, African American abortions constitute 35 to 39 percent of all abortions despite African Americans representing only 14 percent of the entire population), this notion also suggests that unwanted black children would be far more likely than unwanted white children to increase the criminal element. From this angel's perspective, there is no way you can assess current abortion policy in America and not find racism.

Margaret Sanger, the founder of Planned Parenthood, was a virulent racist who spoke and wrote extensively about the need to purify the human race by getting rid of the bad elements, which included blacks. She was a Darwinist who felt that so-called lower classes of humans (Sanger agreed with Darwin that the Negro race was less evolved than the Caucasian race) had less sexual control, stating that an Australian aborigine had only slightly more sexual control than a chimpanzee. While her supporters claim these quotes are taken out of context, the intent behind her words is clearly racist and white supremacist even when put back into context. Adolf Hitler and the Nazis used her writings to justify their eugenics-based destruction of Jews, homosexuals, and other alleged undesirables.

Her supporters have tried to soften these extremist views and revise history to make Sanger appear altruistic. Planned Parenthood certainly claims an altruistic rather than eugenic basis for their provision of abortion. I do not doubt their charitable intent, but the result of the disproportionate aborting of black babies has been to limit the number—and, therefore, the economic and political power—of African Americans.

While I don't claim to know God's plans, I do know that there have been, within this population of aborted children, humans who, had they not been aborted by their fellow man, would have provided advances in cancer research, created programs to relieve human suffering, and given joy through their contributions to heart-stirring literature and music. America's loss is heaven's gain. These little ones are in the bosom of Papa, who wants them all.

There are over fifty thousand adoptions in the USA every year. Increasingly, couples are opting for international adoption. There are many reasons, but two stand out. First, the legal system has made domestic adoption expensive and cumbersome. Second, in the era of open adoption, a couple has no guarantee that a domestic adoption will be defensible if the birth mother changes her mind and wants the baby back. At least an international adoption provides a degree of geographical protection.

In an ideal world, the number of couples seeking to adopt would equal the number of unwanted pregnancies. Your world, as self-conceived, is far from ideal. There is a debate in America regarding the removal of "under God" from the Pledge of Allegiance. As an angel, I am in favor of its removal. If the USA were truly "under God," it would be an altogether different nation. No nation "under God" kills its children.

Chapter 16

Case File M-361-AD

Tis now the very witching time of night,
When churchyards yawn and hell itself
Breathes out
Contagion to this world.

—Shakespeare, *Hamlet*

Moloch is a demon. When he is in the skin, he is fierce, yellow-eyed, and hideous. Walking hunched over, he still towers over most humans. When he flies, his wings sound leathery, creaking and crackling like a sailboat in the wind. In his mercy, God usually blocks such monsters from human view. Moloch's voice is a mix of whispered foghorn and broken glass. He leads a demon crew. Some demons work by invading a human's body, exerting influence over thoughts and feelings. Moloch is not an agent of subtlety; his specialty is havoc and injury. The target of Moloch's crew tonight is a mission group—teenagers bound for Nicaragua to spread the gospel. Moloch's goal is to disrupt or destroy the mission and, if necessary or convenient, to kill.

Moloch is accompanied by his familiar retainers. Belial is a sly, weaselly demon about the size of a small pony. With a body like a gerbil, he might even appear cute and appealing as long as you are upwind of his stench and as long as you cannot see the deadness in his eyes. Romulus and Remus are matching nightmares, like mantises that have stopped praying. Their insectile jaws are replaced by fangs that can slice and rip. Their bodies are encased in a chitinous armor that renders an eerie scuttling click when they move. They are jitter-stepping in anticipation. If their foul mission succeeds, they will perform a ritual victory dance that resembles the capering of drunken madmen.

Accompanying these veteran demons are eight apprentices. Every bit as old as the veterans, these demons have no prior earthly experience. Their function, to this point, has been largely clerical in the dominion of hell. Tonight is a night of upward mobility for them. If necessary, they will leave their current bodies to inhabit the souls of these Christian teenagers and disrupt the mission with jealousy, envy, malice, or lust.

While Satan himself can inhabit a visible body of surpassing beauty, he doesn't waste his aesthetic touch on his working demons. Like the four veterans, the apprentices collectively look like the wardrobe locker of a B-rated horror film. Three look like Notre Dame gargoyles. Three appear like festering corpses, replete with a corresponding fragrance. The remaining two could best be likened to animated cesspools.

"They've finished their commissioning ceremony and will be coming out to board the bus. I'll break the bus down on the way to the airport. For now, spread out, and we'll just follow them." Moloch is calm, almost bored. More accustomed to open spiritual warfare, he views this clandestine guerrilla work as a somewhat junior-varsity endeavor. Nevertheless, the boss's decision is clear, and apprentices must start somewhere, even if the pros have to babysit.

He floats down from the steeple and cuts through the foggy night air, describing a circle around the church parking lot. In his peripheral vision, he sees Romulus flying down toward the bus. Just then, the thump of an impact reaches his ears as he sees Romulus jerk in the air. His abdomen bulges and then explodes forward as a light seems to pass out of him. Romulus folds in the middle and crunches onto the parking lot, his intestines drooling on the tarmac.

"Damn, damn, damn! They're onto us. Deploy, deploy!" Moloch is no longer bored as he scans the night sky, straining his leathery wings to greater speed as he begins evasive maneuvers.

Paulie the angel has just scored a direct hit on Romulus and rockets up into the sky, where Raya and I are waiting. "Hah! Nothin' but net!" Then he looks down at his hands. "Ugh, why don't those guys use regular blood like we do? His insides stink like toxic waste."

I give a short laugh. "You're the one who decided to nail him in the chitlins, Paulie. Now get down to that church and get that congregation praying. That'll give us enough juice to handle these guys by ourselves." Paulie flits down through the church roof. The parents are hugging their children good-bye. Paulie, invisible to the humans, touches Pastor Bryant on the chest. The preacher calls out, "Folks! I don't know what's happening, but we need to get on our knees again right now! Call down some power." The assembled believers, accustomed to their pastor's militant prayerfulness and themselves beginning to feel an oppression, drop and pray. Before he clears the church roof, Paulie feels the supercharging of the believers' prayers. He veers away as Raya and I peel sideways to attack. Belial is gone, as Raya cleaves his skull with the flat of her hand. She hits Remus before he can flee. She grabs both of his feet and then puts a foot into his groin. She pulls with her arms and pushes with her foot, splitting him open from crotch to neck, grimacing in disgust as she drops the carcass to the ground.

The prayers are stoking the angels, and they are almost gleeful as they outmaneuver the demons. The apprentices have never witnessed prayer-powered angels, and their fear overwhelms them. Paulie dispatches two gargoyles by crashing them together like cymbals. They crumble in the air like putrid cookies as Paulie thumps the third gargoyle on the head, driving his skull down into his chest like a reverse jack-in-the-box. Raya, in a fastidious moment, decides against any more actual contact. She dives between the remaining five apprentices and begins to spin. She creates a vortex that captures the hapless demons, shattering them like a trailer park in a tornado.

I have been corralling Moloch, maneuvering him like a sheepdog with a ram. "Come on, Augie—just get it over with."

"Where's your sporting blood, Moloch? I just wanted to give you a chance to watch your crew strut their stuff."

"You couldn't have done it without those prayers."

"Don't I know it? Three angels against twelve demons. Even with ones as stupid as you, we might have had trouble without prayer. If you were as smart as you are ugly, we might have lost. Okay, Moloch, see you later." I snatch Moloch's wings away. Then I snatch the demon's head off. I gag a little as Moloch plops onto the ground, and then I ask Paulie if he has any hand sanitizer.

After-Action Summary

Satan doesn't equip his demons with attractive exteriors. It's all creep chic. He seems constitutionally incapable of creating beauty unless it's for temptation—or, of course, if it involves his own beauty. He is malignant narcissism personified—or demonified, if you prefer. Satan also cannot create; he can only render shabby replicas of God's creations. God created love; Satan gives lust. God created admiration; Satan gives envy. God created joy; Satan gives transient happiness followed by misery. God created conviction; Satan gives guilt.

Satan's demons aren't much better than their boss. They have no snappy names and have to plagiarize from human sources. Thus, we have Moloch and Belial, names borrowed from *Paradise Lost*, and Romulus and Remus from Roman mythology. I even know a pair of demons named Punch and Judy. You don't want to know their physical appearances.

You cannot kill a demon any more than you can kill an angel. The goal in any spiritual warfare is to confound and disrupt. Demons don't normally attack angels. Their goal is to destroy or capture humans. Our goal is prevention. When we effectively disable a demon, as in the action covered in this chapter, he cannot complete his assignment and must return to his home base for repair. Similarly, a sufficiently injured angel is hors de combat and must go back to our repair facility, the zip shop. Angel injury is usually mild, for two reasons. First, a demon's first line of defense is olfactory—they stink when you get close to them and stink worse when you injure them. The odor isn't harmful, but it can ruin an otherwise delightful battle. Second, angels have prayer backup. Human prayer is like an anabolic steroid for an angel. That is why Paulie's first move in our battle was to get the humans delivering up our rocket fuel. It is impossible to overstate the importance of prayer in spiritual warfare. With those parents praying a hedge of protection around their children, three angels against twelve demons was a slam dunk.

Spiritual warfare, as a phenomenon, is an ongoing action. It rarely occurs outside nightclubs, raves, dance halls, or gambling dens. The humans who frequent those establishments are already under the sway of the world and the flesh, and Satan doesn't need to waste demonic resources by tempting people who have already succumbed and actually like the waste dump they are in. Spiritual battles are fought where Satan's control is either tenuous or threatened—mission efforts, outreaches, revivals, church business meetings. To Satan, the Great Commission of carrying the gospel of Christ is a fearful thing, an assault of ultimate good against unalloyed evil.

God has constructed his salvation plan so that angels may on occasion be completely dependent on prayer by humans. Prayer is not worship; it is a petition. Angels hear human prayer and also help convey it to God (Revelation 8:3-4 and Genesis 19:20-21). Because we are often called upon to carry out God's will among his humans, prayer is the fuel for our engines. Could we do God's will all the time and do it with no prayer at all? Yes, but God wants the union of the human, the angelic, and the divine to be relational. Part of a human's maturing is learning the ability to recognize situations in need of prayer. Jesus prayed often to the Father. So should you. As an act of love, I will not revisit quantum physics and how the power of prayer is carried at light speed or faster from one quantum entity (the person praying) to another quantum entity (an angel) providing the instruction for an assignment and the energy to carry that assignment out. Because all life-forms, human and angelic, are in quantum relationship with God, he oversees all the impact that prayer has upon angels. I am glad I don't have that job. If that ain't love . . . A true prayer warrior is coveted by those angels who guard the humans for whom the prayers are made. Look at your congregation, and select the least likely among you: the crippled, the old, the infirm, the shy, those who, on their knees, carry our battle into the fetid belly of the Enemy. The names of your insignificant praying folk are hallowed among the host, both divine and angelic. Before you ask, the answer is yes; even Augie the angel loves his human warriors. A single human on his knees equals ten demons flat on their backs. When you join those seemingly meek friends of yours in prayer, you join us in warfare. The impact of your prayers makes a mockery of the strongest Hollywood superhero. You humans literally have no idea of the power God has placed at your disposal. There is nothing more attractive to an angel than a human with demon scalps on her belt.

Chapter 17

Case File M-64-AD

"**F**ile a flight plan. Right. This afternoon." Reverend Leviticus Lane flicks off his intercom and swivels in his chair to look out his office window at the skyline of Atlanta. He blinks, purses his lips, and then turns again to study his ego wall. He is pictured with the rich and celebrated: here with power brokers; over there with Hollywood stars; and, just a bit farther on, grouped with star athletes. He always has the same expression: bright gray eyes crinkled at the corners, heart-melting, lopsided grin—a visage of joy, enthusiasm, welcome, spontaneity. With a self-effacing smile, he thinks back to how many hours he has practiced that seemingly spontaneous grin in front of a mirror. Practice has paid off, but not without the grinding work of travel, revivals, and setbacks.

Reverend Lane came from a dirt-poor family of believers. Early on, his beautiful singing voice and self-deprecating humor marked him as a young man touched by God to carry his gospel. After a short stint in seminary, he took to the roads, never giving a thought to becoming a pastor for an established congregation. No, evangelism beckoned, and the highway spread its arms to enfold him. The family mortgaged itself to provide a third-hand bus, and he began with tent revivals. Small southern towns embraced him and his wife, Merilee, and they returned the love.

As an interesting twist, Lane began with a revival at night. The next morning, he partnered with a local preacher and held riverbank baptisms, weather and location permitting. His standard line was "Once they are wet, they never forget," and it became his public mantra. The simple folk loved him as an evangelist who went the extra distance with them and got right down in the water with them. He had to purchase a bigger tent. He began to collect the love offerings in trash cans instead of collection plates. He would ask the audience, "Know why I use trash cans instead of plates for the offering? Because they hold more money!" The people laughed and responded with more money. With more money coming in, a large RV was purchased with cash. Tambourines and acoustic guitars were replaced by an organ, a generator, a synthesizer, a complex sound system, and, finally, a quartet of silver-throated gospel ladies.

Lane would sing. Lane would cry. He would growl from deep in his belly like an enraged Kodiak bear and then whisper the invitation to bring their sins to Jesus. The song "Just as I Am" accompanied the altar call, and rarely were the seats more than half full at the end. The podium would be lined with those seeking the Lord's favor or believers seeking to recommit. Reverend Lane would lean over each supplicant, the sweat dripping off his face onto their bowed heads like an intimate baptism, and he would feel the joy of snatching so many souls from the Enemy. He and Merilee and the crew would high-five and congratulate one another for "giving the Devil a headache" that evening. Exhausted and spiritually spent, Lane would go to sleep in the RV while the crew broke down the tent and stowed the instruments. When he awakened, Lane would be at the next stop.

People began to beg for healing, for laying on of hands. Faith healing had not been practiced in his home church, and seminary had not prepared him for it. At first, it felt odd watching folks rolling around in the sawdust, jumping up, speaking in tongues. But even Lane was astonished at the miracles. He would even call back to the local preacher, who would confirm the durable nature of most of these healings.

Frightened at first by his channeling of God's power, Lane became more comfortable and gradually stopped seeking the face of the Lord before the camp meetings. There was so much to do. The tent was replaced by rented auditoriums, and revivals became programs that needed planning, scheduling, and choreography. Larger cities beckoned, and Reverend Lane had to retain a booking agent. His input was needed on incorporating, scheduling, and even investing. To free up his time, Lane would fly commercial while his crew drove between venues. With a few high-profile healings and the conversion of several jaded celebrities, Reverend Lane hit the stratosphere of lucrative evangelism. He established a large home church in Atlanta, paying cash on the barrelhead for all-new construction. The architecture and lavish appointments would have troubled the young Reverend Lane, but the now-experienced evangelist barely noticed them.

Travel is now restricted, and programs are scheduled based exclusively on profit. The Learjet 60 that will soon fly him back home is a recent acquisition of the ministry. Purchased ostensibly for staff travel, it is, in truth, reserved solely for the reverend. Going to visit wealthy and influential people makes private jet travel practically obligatory. There are also visits to a variety of winsome ladies. Although still married to Merilee, Reverend Lane views these ladies as similar to the concubines of David and Solomon—rewards to men upon whom God has conferred a great mantle of responsibility.

Still, there is an itch in a part of his soul that he can't reach, a vague disquiet. Maybe, he hopes, a trip back to the old homeplace will settle him.

The corporate jet delivers him to the local airport, where he keeps a Mercedes coupe that he uses exclusively for his home trips. All his family members had long ago moved into upscale housing in the city and then eventually gone to be with the Lord. Lane, however, has held on to the old homestead.

He gets out of his luxury car and stares at the old house. It's really more of a shotgun shack. He walks around the house and heads down to the river. There is a chilly autumn breeze rattling the few remaining leaves on the trees, and the sycamores on the riverbank trace a skeletal filigree against a gunmetal sky. Reverend Lee shrugs his coat closer against his neck and walks down to his thinkin' rock. This was where the Reverend had proclaimed, "It's best to be sittin' on a rock when you're contemplating the Rock of Ages." He sits down and watches the indecisive current ripple the brown river water past him.

"Glad you came home, Reverend?"

Reverend Lane whips around to find me standing nearby. As usual, I am middle aged and paunchy, and I am wearing a down jacket and an Angels ball cap. "You startled me," he says. "I didn't hear you walk up."

"I hear that a lot. I didn't walk up. Since you're a man of God, I'll just jump right in. My name is Augie, and I'm an angel, and God sent me."

Lane silently studies me. "What's the punch line?"

"No punch line."

"Well . . . Augie, was it? Ah, how long have you been off your medication?"

"Good one, Rev. I thought I could dispense with that 'prove it to me' stuff. I mean, you being so accustomed to channeling God's power to heal the afflicted, I figured one fat old angel wouldn't be a big leap for you."

"Humor me. Show me some angel stuff."

"Okay." I snap my fingers, and the sycamores disappear. I watch while Lane walks over to where the nearest tree had stood. "Rev, I had better make them come back—you know, root system, erosion of the riverbank, all that eco-stuff. Don't want to get in trouble with the Sierra Club. You might want to stand back. Don't want you getting whiplash from a miracle, do we?" With a snap of my fingers, the sycamores return.

"Okay, you're an angel." He pauses. "God sent you here?"

"Yes."

"Why?"

"You tell me."

Lane looks up at the lowering sky, his old farmboy instinct predicting a pending rainstorm. "I don't know. Somehow, some way, everything is all confused. It's like my whole life used to be on color TV. Now it's black and white."

"Like salt that has lost its savor?"

"Yes. I have followed this wonderful path for so many years. God didn't just open doors for me; he ripped them off their hinges. When people think of televangelists, they think of me. When they think of faith healers, they think of me."

"But among your close circle, when they think of adulterers, they think of you. When a congressional subcommittee thinks of abuse of tax-free status for religious organizations, they think of you. When critics of the Christian faith talk about evangelical profiteering, they think of you."

The reverend has the grace to hang his head in shame. He pauses as though to collect his thoughts. "Augie, you really know how to sugarcoat a bitter pill, don't you?"

"Leviticus Lane, you have, in your time, been a good and godly man. Now you are neither. The *Rev* in front of your name used to stand for *Reverend*. Now it stands for *Revenue*." Lane attempts to maintain eye contact but drops his gaze as my conviction bores into him. "You speak of a colorless world, Leviticus. That is your soul sickness. It's provoking you. Your soul is starving and shrinking from a steady diet of worldly garbage. Be grateful that you still have the spiritual integrity to be troubled by what you've done with God's blessing. There are many out there who have been completely corrupted, except for those who were corrupt from the start."

"So what do I do?"

"It's already been done for you. A bit of rough mercy, if you will."

Together, we walk back toward the house. As he rounds the corner of the shack, Lane sees that the Mercedes is gone. Parked in the driveway is a hand-me-down, battered bus with an ancient trailer attached. As his face morphs from surprise to understanding, Reverend Lane sees his wife, Merilee, coming from the house, pulling the door shut. "Come on, Reverend Honey Bunny. I've packed our stuff, and the crew will have the tent up by the time we get there. One-hour trip if we hustle and the bus holds up. Let's go give the Devil a headache." Merilee looks younger, but perhaps that's just the result of a burden having been lifted.

As Merilee hops on the bus, Lane turns to me. "Is everything gone?"

"The Mercedes, the jet, the money, the church, the lady friends. Every recollection by everybody of your overblown ministry. All gone, except in your memory."

Reverend Lane looks down, and a small smile blossoms into his old, unpracticed, lopsided grin. "Augie, there was a man named Bill Bright, founder of Campus Crusade for Christ, who said, 'There's no limit to the amount of money God will give to a man if he doesn't let it stick to his fingers.' Thanks for washing the glue off my hands and for the second chance."

I cock my head back and look at him with one raised eyebrow. "Don't thank me. I voted for you dying in a plane crash, but Papa thought different."

"Well, thank him for me. Better yet, I'll do it myself. He hasn't heard from me in far too long. Meanwhile, I'll implore him to enroll you in angel charm school, if there is such a thing."

"Indeed there is. Know it well. Flunked it twice. Where are you headed, Reverend?"

Reverend Lane, with a spring in his step, heads for the bus and his beloved wife. He turns back and says, "I'm going to give the Devil a headache."

"Attaboy."

After-Action Summary

Televangelism, while a marvelous development, may also have become the new "last refuge of the scoundrel." With any degree of success comes the temptation to look upon the love offerings as personal rewards and the temptation to believe that the messenger trumps the message. Reverend Lane's deterioration was directly proportional to his monetary gain. Success can be a terrible burden to an evangelical human or to a church. In Revelations, Jesus addresses the churches of Asia Minor. The churches for which he reserved his greatest criticism were those that were prosperous and safe (Revelations 3:14). The most effective churches were those under duress. In Matthew 25:15-29, Jesus describes the resources provided to a man's stewards. The one steward who was punished was the one who took the resources entrusted to him and failed to invest those resources for the furtherance of his master's affairs. Simon Magus (Acts 8:9-24) was a magician who became a committed believer yet made a major error in mixing a profit motive into the delivery of the gospel message.

Any church, or any Reverend Lane, must understand that material success, if not redistributed for the expansion of God's kingdom, can become logistical support for the Enemy. In many cases, the diversion of resources is simple narcissism: expensive clothing, homes, vehicles, and lifestyle. This is blatant and, in the case of Reverend Lane, can be reversed if there remains a conscience that God can reach. In the story of the prodigal son, the father ran to greet his returning boy. But first, the son had to experience the internal conviction and turn toward home.

A far more subtle, and therefore potentially more hazardous, redirection of resources occurs seemingly for altruistic reasons. Angels like me have seen many well-intentioned churches embark on expansions: youth centers, dining facilities, athletic facilities. Most American cities have at least a few of these Protestant "Vatican Cities" within their precincts, all of them dedicated to a God who "does not dwell in temples made with hands." (Acts 7:48) There may have been some humans who gazed at a lovely church edifice and fell to their knees, shouting, "What a great building! It makes me believe in God!" But I have never been present for such a conversion event. I am not saying there should never be a building fund or a facility where children may safely gather. But if accomplishing this goal means servicing a debt (thereby subordinating the church to a lender) or if maintenance costs lead to diversion of money from missionary efforts, great care must be taken to avoid a skewing of priorities. After all, which facility is more likely to serve the Great Commission: a fancy dining facility for the congregation or a soup kitchen for the homeless? If in reading this, you would like to chew this angel out, then you might wish to consider that your own church is at just such a crossroads.

Sadly, great intelligence may actually be an impediment to the resolution of such quandaries. Really smart people can construct seemingly rational justifications for choosing nonproductive endeavors for their resources. What is needed is spiritual vision. And by that, I don't mean someone on a committee saying, "The Lord spoke to me last night and said we needed a multicolored fountain outside the front of the sanctuary, just like in Las Vegas." A loving God can bring a Reverend Lane or any church back to his true path. Free will, however, requires that the Reverend Lanes or the church leadership have responsive, yielded spirits. Not all prodigal sons come home, nor do all prodigal churches.

Chapter 18

Case File A-1914-AD

Cry "Havoc!" and let slip the dogs of war,
That this foul deed shall smell above the earth,
With carrion men, groaning for burial.
—Shakespeare, *Julius Caesar*

Europe 1914. The wind is coming from the northwest, and winter storm clouds seem to triumph as the sun makes its suicidal descent to the horizon. Close to the winter solstice and this far north, night is a near-constant companion. A steady drizzle becomes a mix of snow and sleet, immobilizing the humans and bankrupting their spirits—not all spirits, though.

From aloft, Salete scans the battlefield. All appears well. The humans are murdering one another at a record rate. Technology and advances in armaments have enabled mankind to kill in larger numbers and at greater distances. In a development that seems borrowed from the demon horde itself, humans have begun to fly and are dealing death from the sky. Satan must be so proud! Salete is a pragmatic demon. In appearance, he is tall and of skeletal proportion. He is nearly humanoid except for oversized eyes that constantly bulge as though he were the recipient of bad news. His eyelids blink upward, not down. His mouth boasts oversized canine teeth that rasp and sharpen with each jaw movement. His legs are human except that they articulate backward, making him walk like a kangaroo.

Salete is no stranger to large-scale slaughter. This is his favorite endeavor because it permits a certain demon collegiality. Satan controls his demons with fear, envy, and competition. In peacetime, demon crews are broken into sectors, usually corresponding to countries. Salete, for example, is a demon assigned to France. He and his compatriots are in direct competition with the German demons for the harvesting of lost souls in their respective geography.

In war, however, the French demons are rewarded for the deaths of lost souls they accomplish among the German humans and vice versa. War creates a nightmare for the bureaucratic demons in charge of body counts, but Salete keeps a close eye. The Demon Chain of Command is a meritocracy, reward and advancement going to those with the greatest soul harvest. Should an accounting demon make a clerical error on the battlefield, his body is murdered and he is sent back to Central Control, where he will answer for both the tally mistake and for the loss of the body he was issued. Consequently, demon clerks are most careful.

Salete flies over to parlay with his German counterpart, Mundgeruch. This abomination is lizard-like with yellow, seemingly unfocused eyes. Vile mucus dripping from scabrous nostrils, he speaks with a smoky hiss. Incongruously, his lower body is far more human. With a high rump, he walks like a woman wearing spike heels and a constricting skirt. Such mismatched bodies are common among veteran demon spirits who suffer multiple returns to the repair facility for quick patch-up jobs using whatever is available. The angel zip shop has a far better budget. Even under the collegial pall of war, Salete doesn't trust Mundgeruch. More devious and deceitful than any demon Salete has known, Mundgeruch has multiple successful habitations to his credit. He has variously controlled Attila the Hun, Vlad Dracul, and Pope Urban II, who began the Crusades. His grasp of evil is frightening and admirable. Salete prefers to meet Mundgeruch on the ground. Mundgeruch has concave feet that make a sucking sound when he walks. Salete can, therefore, hear him coming. With the colossal mortality of this war, Salete can't afford any trips to the repair facility.

"Things are going well, Salete?"

"Maybe. Too many churches and homes full of those humans praying for these soldiers. It's even worse now that it's getting toward Christmas. Damned Christians! If we're not careful, they will ruin a perfectly good war."

"You call them damned. That's the problem, isn't it? The Christians aren't damned." Mundgeruch stops to clear mud from his arched feet and then continues his sucking walk as he blows filthy mucus from his nostrils. "My other crew leader is coming. Are yours on the way?"

"There they are." The remaining French demon commanders—Poubelle, Morve, and Vomi—fly in and hover as the sole remaining German demon, Dungkopf, comes in from the east, flying low through the combination of mist and snow. Poubelle is bald, thickly muscled, and hunched over, exuding a foul perspiration regardless of temperature. His mouth is a lipless gash with tiny teeth, his viper eyes deep set beneath a protruding brow. He gives out a high, girlish squeal whenever excited or frightened. Other demons tease him by sneaking up and whispering the name Jesus in his ear. At least he is never constipated. "I don't like it, Salete. Our troops, both French and English, are singing carols and pulling out their Bibles."

Dungkopf nods in agreement. He wears a dark floor-length cloak that gives him the appearance of a black friar. His eyes shine with malevolent intensity. He has a lantern jaw with scorbutic gums and broken teeth. Oddly, his body looks like a half-plucked chicken. He says, "Our German humans are decorating their trenches with Christmas ornaments and yelling spiritual greetings across no-man's-land to their enemy."

Morve is lupine in shape and has oversized teeth that keep his lips forced open. He walks around on hind feet with a strut. His lower body is hairless and wrinkled. "We're having no success invading new souls and a lot of trouble holding on to the ones we've got. The garbage in those hymns seems to be unclouding their senses."

"Vomi, how about your sector?"

"Same problem, Boss." Vomi is a fat, cherubic sort, rather like Cupid with rabies. His incongruously dense eyebrows would contradict his baby-smooth skin, except for the widespread leprous sores that he constantly itches or licks. "We're pushing the French and British generals to continue fighting. The middle command officers are becoming obstinate."

"That means they are here, but we don't—Look out!" Mundgeruch's screaming hiss warns the other demons as he takes flight. Poubelle, the last to react, has only one leg off the ground when, with a sickening crunch, he is thrown face forward onto the mud. A flashing light propels his legs over in a somersault. His squeal of fear is cut off as his face digs deeper in the mud, his legs continuing forward, hyperextending his neck until it snaps. The light separates from the convulsing demon and condenses. It's me. "Don't any of you guys ever bathe?" I shout as more angels converge on the demon commanders. Paulie, Raya, Herb, Happy, and Sid deploy to their assignments. The male angels are growling a baritone jungle rhythm—"Just keep prayin', people; just keep prayin'. Just keep prayin', people; just keep prayin'"—as they lock on to their respective targets. Raya, the female, screams a nerve-shattering ululation as she rides Dungkopf to the ground. She grabs his cloak and swings him like a lariat and careens him into the caisson of a howitzer. The wheel collapses, and Dungkopf is crushed beneath the falling cannon.

Raya's partner, Herb, has taken off after Morve. Herb's prayer-powered speed makes short work of the chase as he grabs the demon and rockets straight up into the sky. Herb executes a hammerhead turn and pile-drives Morve's oversized teeth into a concrete revetment. Gagging at the smell, Herb and Raya hurry to help Happy. Happy is moving through the soldiers in the trenches, performing hand exorcisms by reaching in through mouths, nostrils, or ears to grab the inhabiting demons by their throats to effect unpleasant evictions. Herb joins him in this enterprise, while Raya follows behind, stomping the evil spirits that have managed to get back into their demonic bodies after leaving the soldiers. The resulting nose-clogging stink seems to be a preview of the gas warfare that will soon visit these trenches. The soldiers on both sides of no-man's-land begin to exchange season's greetings across the void between the front lines.

Paulie is having trouble with Vomi, who, despite being quite chubby, is highly maneuverable. He has partially disabled one of Paulie's wings. Widening the gap between them, Vomi pulls up to a French captain. If he can get out of his body and inhabit this soldier, Vomi can use his considerable habitation skills to avoid extraction. Just as he is getting ready to make the spirit leap, Vomi is shocked to hear a rifle report and see a hole appear above his navel. Paulie drops the rifle he had grabbed and uses Vomi's shocked immobility to close the distance and grab Vomi by the throat, preventing spirit escape.

"You shot my body!" Vomi accuses. "You shot me! Angels aren't supposed to do that; it's not fair! I'm going to tell." Paulie folds Vomi in the middle and stuffs him, butt first, into a nearby howitzer. He reaches down and pulls the lanyard. The cannon fires with a ground-shaking explosion, and Vomi turns into reeking, dripping confetti.

Salete thinks he has eluded me. Flying at top speed toward the adjoining sector, Salete hopes to lose himself among the other set of demons. Just at his sector's border, Salete stops in midair, shocked to see angels in ascendancy over the demons in that sector as well. As he contemplates his next move, he looks down to see a rope looped around his leg. He traces the rope behind him to a hydrogen-filled observation balloon with an attached piece of smoldering slow fuse. I am backpedaling in the air, grinning at him. "Salete, since your boss is the 'prince of this world,' it's time you fertilized it for him." I dart away just ahead of the exploding hydrogen that splatters Salete across the trenches.

I join the regrouping angels. The sounds of gun and cannon are gone, and dawn is not far away. From both trenches, voices are singing "Silent Night" in unison. Soon, no-man's-land will be filled with soldiers who, ignoring their respective high commands, invoke their own ceasefire to talk, exchange gifts, and join in carol singing. Angelic activity against this magnitude of evil cannot prevail for a prolonged period, but it is enough that the common soldier has an interval to celebrate the birth of his Savior.

I look over at Paulie. "How did it go?"

Paulie grins. "As future generations might say, if you want peace on earth and goodwill toward men, sometimes you just gotta kick some demon butt."

"Raya?"

"The score was cannon one, Dungkopf zero."

I nod my approval. It appears we had a good creep harvest. "Sid, were you able to bust up Mundgeruch?"

"I need to irrigate my sinuses with sewer water to improve the smell. I busted him up pretty badly, but he disappeared inside a German corporal, and I couldn't get him out. Mundgeruch is hard enough normally, but it was like this human was actually protecting him."

I think about that for a moment and then decide we have other concerns more immediate. "We'll have to let him go. Let's partition this sector and hold off the demons at least until midnight. Then it'll be back to individual assignments for all of us." Everyone agrees and gets set to fly off.

"Sid, that German corporal that Mundgeruch went into—what was his name?"

"Some guy named Hitler."

"I suspect we'll be hearing from him. Okay, Sid. Good job. Take off."

After-Action Summary

Believe it or not, from an angel's viewpoint, sickening death tallies are not the worst feature of modern war. The death rate in the world doesn't change when someone schedules a war. It remains one death per person. What horrifies us is the naked, self-serving ambition of the leaders who offer up their youth to the sound of the war tocsin.

In Old Testament times, kings accompanied their troops and put their lives on the line. Kings Saul and David, for example, earned the respect of their armies by being there, in harm's way. Saul and his son died in battle. The last time a Western head of state died in battle was over five hundred years ago (Richard III).

In America, Congress has the constitutional responsibility of declaring war. Despite multiple conflicts, Congress has not declared war since Franklin Roosevelt demanded it of them over seventy years ago. Congressmen have shirked their constitutional responsibility and have alternatively cheered or cursed the soldiers who get committed to hostile action as a result of congressional policies. The only link these human opportunists have to any war is the campaign dollars they receive from arms manufacturers or Department of Defense contractors. Perhaps the Geneva Convention should be amended to require that the chief executive of each nation involved in war, declared or otherwise, be on the front lines. How about the congressional leadership? They can dig the latrines. It is the one military activity closest to their elected job description.

World War I was the last of the old wars and the first of the modern wars. It was the only war that featured both cavalry charges and aerial warfare. Although the Big Bertha howitzer could deliver death at a distance of nine miles, this was the last war where lethal force was predominantly applied by armies within view of one another—fundamentally one man, one rifle, one target. The December 1914 unofficial ceasefire occurred across wide stretches of the western front. In a sacred dereliction of duty, the common soldier on both sides of this conflict paused in his war to honor the Prince of Peace. What did we angels do? We did nothing more than suspend the influence of evil, permitting an inherent goodness to assert itself.

As wars become more impersonal and distant, and as the reasons for war become more abstract, don't expect angels to trump its sterile insanity—not, that is, until Armageddon. Stay tuned.

# Chapter 19

Case File M-763-AD

It's a gorgeous late morning in Los Angeles. The smog level is sublethal, and foot traffic is heavy on Hollywood Boulevard. Tour buses lumber down the street, and tourists are either looking up at the huge Hollywood sign on the hillside, looking down at the cement signatures in front of Mann's Chinese Theater, or looking around the Kodak Theater for actors who only go there to get awards and display fashions on a red carpet.

Ray Strobel looks around for a suitable location. Ray is a street preacher, an evangelist who engages the street visitors in matters of faith. He had formerly chosen his location based on the stars on Hollywood's Walk of Fame, selecting stars who had some association with religion: Mr. Rogers, who was a Presbyterian minister; Mahalia Jackson and Etta James, who were both gospel singers in their time; Tennessee Ernie Ford. Ray had hoped for some added horsepower from his proximity to their stars. Then he'd become concerned that this practice might smack of idolatry, so he had stopped. Besides, it hadn't worked.

Ray Strobel feels he is an unaccomplished evangelist. As somewhat of an apprentice, he accompanied more experienced men and women, observing their casual yet impassioned approaches. Ray has been able to adopt their methods but still freezes up when confrontation or ridicule occurs. Ray falls mute or, worse, stutters. This leads to grins of derision or, more embarrassing, a patronizing smile and a pat on the back. Alone in his apartment, in front of a mirror, Ray is a Saint Paul, a fearless orator, preemptive in debate, unvanquished in rhetoric. On the street, Ray is a wimp. To his knowledge, he has led no one to the Lord in two years of hitting the streets on his days off from work. He continues to show up—not because he enjoys it but because he can't *not* go there. Soon, however, he may leave this work to the more skilled believers and restrict himself to attending church, volunteering with the children's ministry, and, of course, praying.

He sets down his backpack filled with tracts and Bibles. He is ready to start his day. As is his custom, he spreads his arms, closes his eyes, and raises his face to the sun. Tall and lean, with Ichabod Crane-length legs and arms, he has an engaging smile with a shyness that appeals to more ladies than Ray notices. "This is the day that the Lord has—"

A teenage gangsta wannabe mutters, "Stuff it, dude," and his girlfriend giggles.

Not an auspicious start. He looks around to engage someone, make eye contact, and ask, "If you were to die today, do you know where you would go?" Instead, he feels a gentle hand on his shoulder. He turns to see me smiling at him—middle aged, a bit heavy around the middle. My warm green eyes make Ray feel like an admirable person.

"Good morning."

"Hello."

"Name's Augie."

"Mine's Ray." We shake hands.

"Ray, before you get started, do you mind if we visit a little?"

"Not at all." We walk up the street a short distance, and I think, *The way Ray and I are shaped, you put us together and we look like the number ten.*

"Good. I've been around here awhile and have watched you preach. You're pretty good."

"No, I'm not. You must not have seen me when I'm getting my head handed to me by some atheist wiseguy." Ray's rueful expression isn't completely hidden by his self-deprecating smile. He fidgets a little, pulls at his ear like Johnny Carson, and looks at the crowded sidewalk.

"Actually, yeah, I have watched. What's good about you is what you *don't* do during those episodes. What you don't do is get angry and strike back." I move to let a gaggle of teenage girls go by. They cast covert glances at Ray, giggling at his oblivion. "You don't pop back with a bunch of judgmental criticism that ruins your message."

"But the message is already ruined."

"You mean those times that you bow your head and say, 'I'm sorry. I can't argue with you. But I will pray for you'?"

"Yes. Sounds pretty limp." Ray laughs in a Jimmy Stewart manner, pinches his nose, and huffs his breath out.

"Nope. Let's talk a little reality. The first thing is, you aren't necessarily communicating with the one you are talking with."

"Come again?"

"The person that is arguing with you and jacking you up already has his mind made up. Your communication is with the folks observing the argument."

"And I am communicating that I'm a wimp who can't debate."

Again the self-abasing humor, I think. *If the teenage girls were still here, they would be swooning.* "You are communicating that a gospel of love cannot be argued and that you are not meeting anger with anger. You are also offering to pray for the person who is offending you. Sounds fairly Christian to me. People who are used to watching arguments over global warming, illegal aliens, or ecology are used to both sides screaming. What you are is different, in a positive way. I think folks remember that. A lot of folks would like to be able to rise above screaming and rancor. They see you as somehow above all that; it makes them curious about what you have that they don't have. You are a more compelling witness than you realize."

"You're making me feel better. Anything else?"

"Sure. First, Satan doesn't attack you when you're doing what he wants, which is to fail. When he sends one of his trained attack mice to argue with you, it's because he's concerned about what you're doing or who you might influence. So when somebody comes after you, understand that, as Sherlock Holmes would say, the game's afoot."

"Wow. Anything else?" Ray is standing up taller, his shoulders jacked back.

"Of course. As you can tell, I love to talk. When you debate, you have been asking God to give you strength and knowledge. You are asking him to give you what you already have. You get yourself keyed up when you need to be keyed down."

"Keyed down?"

"Yeah. Talk with batting coaches for baseball players or swing coaches for golfers. They will tell you the biggest issue is getting their guys to relax, not to tense up. Messes up their swing mechanics." I mimic my best Jack Nicklaus golf swing. "You try to assemble a thousand facts in your head before a debate the same way a bad golfer tries to remember fifty different things about his swing. Screws him up. Screws you up."

"So what do I do?" The fidgets are getting worse, but in a manner different from before. Now he is excited to get going.

Matthew 10:19 talks about "not worrying about what you will say, that God, through the Holy Spirit, will provide the words." You've been so busy organizing your own speech that you don't give him a chance to help."

"Okay, so I should learn to be happy when someone comes down on me. I need to relax and enjoy myself while God organizes my response." The fidgets give way to a jitterbug rocking back and forth from foot to foot.

Boy, he is pumped! I smile and lean toward him. "Sounds pretty biblical to me. How about we walk a little way up here? I just have a feelin' today is your day."

Ray and I drift closer to the Kodak Theater. Tourists are milling about in groups. Ray knows that a lot of them will listen, but primarily because so-called Jesus freaks are part of the California scene and, like a Universal Studios tour, part of the de rigueur vacation experience. If Ray can connect with one, he considers his effort rewarded.

No sooner than he begins his "This is the day that the Lord has made," Ray hears an overloud voice with an affected Oxford drawl say, "Oh bother! Must we suffer you people everywhere?"

I whisper to Ray, "Bingo. This is the part where you relax and enjoy." Ray feels a calm settling over him as he turns to face the speaker. The man, who looks to be middle aged, is thin and has a bad comb-over and eyes that are heavy lidded as though world weary. His arm is around a much younger woman.

Ray smiles at the couple. "Hi, my name is Ray. Yes, we people are everywhere. Wherever folks need the gospel, you are going to stumble across us. What is your name?"

"Hello, Ray. My name is Matt Diamond." A smug smile crosses his face as he gives a well-rehearsed pause. "Professor Matt Diamond. Sorry to interrupt you, but I've heard this spiel so often that I could give it myself, despite the fact that I believe none of it." Diamond looks down at his companion with an arrogant smile while she adoringly returns his glance. "And this lovely creature is Shasta."

"Nice to meet you both. Professor Diamond, where do you teach?"

"College-level science up in Palo Alto." The nearby tourists who have been listening come nearer at the prospect of a lively discussion.

"Okay, Professor. Well, my basic *spiel* is that God exists; he created the world and then sent his son to prepare people for heaven by cleansing them of sin. All they have to do is admit their sin and accept his gift of salvation." Ray looks over at me, and he can see that I am loving this. Ray looks back at Diamond. "If the message were any harder, I probably wouldn't be able to remember it."

Shasta laughs, which appears to irritate Diamond.

"Where would you like to begin your criticism?" Ray asks.

"Right with page one of your Bible, Ray. Let's cut to the chase. Do you believe the universe is six thousand years old?" Diamond adopts a superior pose, like a gerbil about to pounce on a leaf of lettuce.

"Six thousand years and six days, yes."

"Despite carbon dating, the fossil record, and the fact that some pretty smart people estimate the age of the universe at about fifteen billion years? Your Bible forces you to turn your back on a lot of scientific data." The professor doesn't see the freight train he is about to encounter.

"No, it doesn't."

"Do you mean that you accept the idea of a fifteen-billion-year-old universe?"

"Yes."

Professor Diamond laughs and glances around at his growing audience. "Ray, you can't have it both ways—it's either six thousand years or fifteen billion years. Which is it?"

"Both. First, let's deal with carbon dating. As a science professor, you know the half-life of carbon 14, right?"

"Well, uh..."

"It's fifty-seven hundred years, right? Okay, that means that radiocarbon dating can't be employed at over sixty thousand years. So it doesn't contribute at all to the billions of years of the universe."

"But that still exceeds your six-thousand-year-old universe."

"Only if you make certain assumptions, none of which are supported. You assume a stable passage of time and a stable decay rate of carbon 14. You also have to allow that the nuclear age has introduced carbon 14 into the environment and that the creation of carbon 14 is roughly equal to its decay rate right now."

"So you throw out all the data based on weaknesses in carbon 14?"

"No, I just wanted to demonstrate that at least one of the supporting arguments against creationism is incredibly weak. The biggest issue is the passage of time. Was the passage of time the same for the fifteen billion years of the universe as it is now?"

"Sounds like a creationist's weak excuse for their Bible."

"No, actually, it was Albert Einstein. It's called his theory of time dilation; only, now that it has been proven, it should be called the *law* of time dilation. Of course, Professor, you're familiar with it, yes?"

"Uh, why don't you sum it up for everybody here that is listening?"

"Sure, it's part of the relativity concept. Time doesn't pass equally on things traveling at different speeds. If, for example, you put identical clocks on two—oh, let's say meteorites—traveling through the universe in a straight line but at different speeds, the clocks would register different passages of time. Similarly, say an object is traveling at three-fourths the speed of light and then suddenly slows down to half the speed of light; a clock attached to it would change the way time is recorded. Check with a quantum physicist who works with linear accelerators. Ask him: If he could put a clock on one of those subatomic particles he creates with his smasher, would it record a different rate of time passage? The answer is yes."

Diamond looks skeptical. "What does that have to do with the age of the universe?"

"Simple. At the time of your so-called big bang, which we Christians equate with 'Let there be light,' that is where science and the Bible agree—all that existed, at time zero, was light. It was diverging away from a central point, traveling, of course, at the speed of light. When the first subatomic particles formed, time was going at a different rate than now. I won't go into a long explanation, but the six days of the biblical creation line up with the fifteen billion years of the physical universe with pretty interesting precision."

"Again, it sounds like some Christian high school science teacher's attempt to muddy the water."

"You might want to look at a book called *The Science of God*, by Gerald Schroeder. He lives in Tel Aviv, so he's probably not a Christian. He explains this reconciliation nicely. By the way, he got his PhD from MIT."

"MIT?"

"Yes."

"Massachusetts Institute of Technology?"

"Yes, that MIT."

"oh."

Ray scans the crowd. "Folks, there is a lot more controversy about new universe versus old universe and the day/age theories. I think the important thing to grasp is that anyone who tells you science excludes creation is wrong, poorly educated, and stuck in the physics of Isaac Newton in the eighteenth century. However someone explains the creation of the universe, they must allow for the different speed at which the entire universe was moving early on. It is obligatory if you accept the big bang."

A young man in the crowd says, "You mean the world was traveling superfast compared to now? Maybe dinosaurs got extinct because they, like, you know, flew off of the planet?" People laugh.

"Well, right now, you are standing still, right?" says Ray.

"Right."

"Well, no you're not. The earth spins on its axis at a rate of a thousand miles per hour. It circles the sun at seventy-two thousand miles per hour. Our solar system is rotating around the center of our galaxy at seven hundred twenty miles per hour. You feel none of this, because you are in this cocoon of gravity and atmosphere. If we increased earth's speed to where it was on day one of creation, you wouldn't feel it. Again, my point is, science and creation are perfectly compatible."

Professor Diamond is strangely silent but is now off to the side as younger people pepper Ray with enthusiastic, nonaggressive questions. I sidle up next to Diamond. "I think you got a pretty good answer, Professor."

Diamond gives me a sour look. "I'm still not persuaded."

"Didn't think you would be. Ray just wanted you to stop hiding behind the flimsy excuse of science. What's more important is what he didn't do to you."

"What do you mean?"

"He was gentle with you when you attacked him. He met your argument with a reasonable response that you were unable to refute. After that happened, he didn't scorn you. He also didn't expose you."

"What do you mean 'expose'?"

"Well, you first started out speaking with a fake upper-class drawl, which now appears to be gone. You said you were a college professor in Palo Alto and let everyone fill in the blank—'Oh, he means Stanford University.' In fact, you teach basic science at a community college."

"How do you know that?"

"Trust me. I know it."

"Well, there is nothing wrong with a community college."

"Not at all. The community colleges up there are great. You're the one who seems ashamed, hinting that you were a big gun at a more prestigious university. Believe me—Ray knew it the moment you couldn't keep up with him on Einstein. He didn't try to shame you, which would have been very easy to do. Were the situations reversed, you would have shamed him with glee on your face."

"Why didn't Ray try to shame him?" asks the girlfriend.

"Because people who love God don't act that way. They don't feel like they have to build themselves up by tearing others down. Besides, Ray still wants you in heaven someday."

"Yes, well, thank you. I have a lot to think about," says Professor Diamond.

"We both do," says his girlfriend as they walk away.

I turn back to find Ray talking with a woman. She is in her late twenties, is a little heavy, and has long black hair. She is holding a cigarette, rocking back and forth, exhaling smoke with an audible hiss. "Look, Ray, I'm from New York. I've seen it all. Your science stuff—all well and good. But I've heard it all, seen it all. I'm just not persuaded. Sorry." She shakes her head and looks around at the crowd. Her body language conveys that she knows she is being watched. She is the sassy, no-nonsense Yankee whose world-wise experience sets her apart. She looks back at Ray with a challenge in her eyes.

This time, I smile, because Ray doesn't first glance at me for reassurance. "What is your name?" Ray asks.

"Michelle. Michelle Crandall. New York born and bred."

"So I suspect what you say is true. You're smart, savvy, and you have seen a lot."

"You got that right." Michelle is smoking faster now.

"But I bet there's something you don't know. Something even a smart girl like you is clueless about."

"Yeah? Like what?"

Ray moves closer to her, his eyes arresting her such that the cigarette stops moving, his voice dropping in register, turning soft and compelling. "Let's get away from the science and the talk and the debate. What you don't know—what it is impossible for even a smart person like you to know—is how much this Creator loves you. More than any father or mother has ever loved you; more than any brother or sister has loved you; and more than any lover has loved you. Has anyone ever loved you enough that they would sacrifice their child for you? Let me tell you a secret, Michelle. It's at times like this that I feel weak and foolish and completely inadequate because I can't find words to communicate to you the love that the Creator has for you." Michelle feels the crowd fading, and she seems to be in a soft corridor alone with Ray. His voice resonates inside of her. "He also put into you a capacity to love. You ever feel joy when you hear a baby laughing? A lump in your throat when you see a beautiful sunset? A warmth deep inside you when lovely music stirs you? Guess who put that inside you? Those are just little tastes of the love that God put in you. So my question to you, Michelle, is this: Are you smart enough, strong enough, brave enough, and, yes, even woman enough to permit yourself to feel his love for you? Folks can be skeptical and leery of being fooled, but there is no risk here. Give yourself permission to feel this love, and he will take care of the rest. He doesn't demand your love as part of the deal. He doesn't have to, because you won't be able to keep from falling in love with him. So how about it, Michelle? You start with accepting that Jesus died for you. You accept his sacrifice. Invite him into your heart. Anything that happens after that is between you and God."

Michelle is still in the corridor. She hears herself say, "I didn't have a good experience with my father."

She sees the understanding in Ray's eyes and sees her pain reflected there. "Oh Michelle, I am so sorry. So many people have a bad earthly father, and it makes them bitter about all fathers. They may even blame God for what happened. Let me ask you: Do you like the freedom you have—to come and go, to have your own independent thoughts?"

"Sure I do."

"That's free will. God wants us to be independent in thought and action, not automatons without choices, without the freedom to dream, without the freedom to make those dreams come true. The gift of free will, however, comes with a cost. Too many people abuse free will. Believe me—because he loves you so much, God is sadder than you about what your earthly father must have done to you. Your earthly father will probably not enjoy the reckoning God has in store for him. Meantime, give God a chance to make things right. You don't have to decide right now; you can—"

"No. I understand. I want to do it now."

Ray smiles and bows his head with her and helps her recite the prayer for forgiveness and salvation. I smile as I watch the crowd. Not generally inclined to give humans credit for sensitivity, I am glad to see that they are respectfully quiet. A few Christians have come forward and have bowed their heads along with Ray and Michelle. Ray gives Michelle a tract and a Bible, gets her address so that he can pick her up for his Bible study that evening, and then gives her a hug good-bye.

"Ray, take a break and walk with me a little," I say. Ray falls in, and we head up the street. "You did well."

"Only because you were there to give me confidence."

"You might think you're being modest, but you are actually insulting the Holy Spirit that is in you. What you did was get out of God's way and let him do the work. Sort of like a holy hand puppet."

"I never asked you, Augie. Where are you from? What do you do?"

"Me? I'm an angel."

"I guess this is where I should be surprised or suspicious, but something happened here today that suggests heaven's influence. I prayed for God's help, so I guess I shouldn't be shocked when an angel shows up."

"Good for you, Ray. I'm glad I don't need to do any Las Vegas tricks to prove that I'm an angel. One other thing before I go—Papa knows that you feel you haven't saved any souls and that your despair has been Satan trying to get you to quit. That's why Papa gave you the gift of today. He also authorized me to tell you that over two hundred people have been saved either directly or indirectly as a result of your ministry. Considering the town you work in, that's a pretty fair number. You won't get many immediate conversions like today, but somehow their rarity makes them all the sweeter. Keep up the good work. Good-bye, Ray."

"Good-bye, Augie." Ray watches me walk away and become less substantial with each step until, by the time I get to Mahalia Jackson's star, I am gone.

After-Action Summary

There are many reasons why people don't accept the Lord. One reason is that they haven't heard the Word. That is what the Great Commission is all about: carrying the gospel to all corners of the earth. In America, however, most humans have encountered the message of God and the sacrifice of Jesus Christ. These individuals can be divided into two groups: those who have heard the wrong message and those who have heard it pretty much correctly. Within these two groups are the people who reject the Word of God. Evangelists like Ray seek to correct those who are rejecting an erroneous gospel and to challenge those who reject what they think is correct gospel.

Professor Diamond and Michelle fall into the latter group. They possess head knowledge of the gospel. Professor Diamond's rejection is based on a fear of appearing unsophisticated. Michelle had been rejecting a heavenly father based on abuse she suffered from an earthly father. We should view them separately.

In Diamond's case, the "sophisticated" scientific view, under pressure from secular atheists, is not only prohibited from allowing for a God but also forced to reject intelligent design as the origin of the universe. This produces a schizoid situation. Show a picture of a homemade wagon to a group of six-year-old children, and then show them a picture of an automobile. Ask them which thing required greater skill and intelligence in its creation. They will say the automobile. Show them vehicles of increasing complexity, and they will agree that each level of sophistication requires yet greater skill and intellect. Then show them the space shuttle along with its blueprints. Tell them this immensely complex entity either came about by accident or built itself. See how far you get with persuading them. This is where modern atheistic science finds itself. It would be laughably absurd if it weren't so sad. The truth is that atheists cling to fairy-tale science because it protects them from having to acknowledge a power and authority greater than themselves. Humans. I need a vacation.

Michelle is representative of a wholly different group. These are the humans who have been hurt by some human agency. The worst situation is when the person is small and vulnerable and the abuse is at the hand of an adult who is traditionally tasked with the role of protector. All I can say is that the Michelles of the world could almost feel pity for their abusers if they were permitted to know what is in store for the abuser who never repents, never genuinely seeks forgiveness for those historic sins. If the abuse they inflicted causes someone to reject God, the punishment is unthinkable. Thankfully, God pursues these victims with loving persistence.

Another subgroup is the people who reject a God who could allow bad things to happen. Some of these people have legitimate, profound grief, such as the parent who loses a child to illness. It would seem counterintuitive to run for comfort to a God whom you blame for your sorrow. My angel heart aches for these people. I don't claim to know the mind of God. But recall the death of Lazarus. What was Jesus' response? He wept. He didn't weep because Lazarus was gone. After all, Jesus brought him back. He cried because of the sorrow and grief that death brings upon the people who loved the deceased. The contract, however, that God made with Adam mandated one death per human for the violation of that contract. God doesn't cancel that contract. What he does, however, is replace the lost physical life of an innocent human with an eternal one. He also offers comfort for those who grieve. Humans, in their sorrow, are invited to come to him—to the God who holds their lost loved ones in his hands and wants to reunite them in eternal life. Again, free will allows you to reject it. Why, however, would you? John 4:14 tells us, "[B]ut whoever drinks the water I give him will never thirst again." Your grief is your thirst. God is the only one who can assuage it.

Chapter 20

Case File A-101-BC

Who could have guessed there were so many shades of green? The shadow-dwelling plants are dark green, nearly approaching black. The climbing vines and sun trees have pastel green leaves. A light wind stirs them, and they sway in the midafternoon sun. The shadows are lengthening and seem more somber, as though the forest is donning mourning garments. I pass silently through a quiet forest; birds are witness to my passing—mute as though the music of their song would clash with the solemnity of the moment. This is—or, rather, was—Eden. I have passed the sword-bearing cherub who now guards the Tree of Life. He pointed me this way, and their footprints confirm my direction. I come upon them in a clearing. For the first time, I see humans clothed; God has given them soft animal fur to cover bodies that, in the newness of their circumstance, are a source of a totally new feeling: shame. They sit on opposite sides of the clearing. Adam is facing back, looking at what used to be Eden. The woman, misery in her downcast eyes, casts fleeting glances over at the back of her mate. I fly over to her, making deliberate noise to announce my arrival. "Hello, Angel."

"I am sorry for what you've lost."

"Well, it was only Paradise." She suppresses a sob and buries her face in her hands. "Oh, what have I done to him?" Compared to modern human females I know, the woman is beautiful. She has thick black hair gathered at her neck and tied with a strand of yellow vine. Her face, when not contorted in grief, is smooth, with no hint of the aging process that will begin to carve its designs into her complexion.

"Him? You mean God?"

"No, him." She points to the other side of the clearing, her hand still moist from her tears. "Adam. He was always strong. He never even looked at that tree." She covers her mouth to stifle the sobs.

"Yet here you both are."

"If it had been up to him, he would never have disobeyed. He wasn't tempted by the snake or the fruit. He was tempted by me."

"And now?"

"I don't understand it all. We will feel pain—something I've never had before, except for what I feel now in my chest. We will have to make our food grow instead of having it just be there. It will hurt to have babies. We will also die, but I don't know what that means."

"What *do* you understand?"

"I understand that God will no longer be a constant companion." Tears begin anew. "What is it that I am feeling now?"

"Humans in the future will call it sorrow."

"It feels very bad. If Adam leaves me because of what I have done, I will feel this way all the time. If death makes this feeling stop, I will welcome it."

"He won't leave you. As for God, he is disappointed, yes, but he is still entrusting you with the bearing of his most beloved creation. All humans will trace their origin back to you."

"And they will blame me for this pain, this death, this separation from God."

"No. These mistakes against God will be called sin. This particular occurrence will be referred to as 'the sin of Adam.'"

"But that's wrong! I did it. The blame is mine."

"It's complicated, but perhaps you should feel better because history won't lay the blame at your feet."

The woman is quiet, looking over at Adam. "No," she whispers, shaking her head, her hair an emphatic metronome against her neck. "No, I don't feel better. What will I ever be able to do to make it up to him?"

"Just don't ever stop loving him."

"Angel, that is as easy for me as breathing."

I put an arm around her, kiss her on the forehead, and then walk over to Adam. He is aware of me. In modern times, he would be considered a tall man with the smooth muscles of the aerobic athlete. He wears a wolfskin breechcloth. Unsurprisingly, having been created rather than born, he has no navel on his lower abdomen.

"I have nothing left for you to take. The last angel took everything."

"Not everything, Adam."

He glances around, not quite far enough to see the woman. He darts an anxious look at me. "You don't mean to take her from me, too, do you?"

"You have paid the price for loving her already. She is yours. By the way, she has a name. God did tell you to call her Eve."

Adam considers this and then gives a little smile. "Eve. The name has beauty. I like the way it feels on my tongue."

"Hurting is a new feeling for both of you, but she hurts for you, Adam. More than the loss of Paradise, she hurts and fears the loss of you."

"I already faced that risk. I made my choice. It would be foolish now to reject her." Adam has a resolute expression, but it still seems he is resistant to actually looking at her.

"She is saddened that mankind will come to view this as your error, not hers."

"Her temptation was not the same as mine. She wasn't confronted with choosing between me and God. I had to choose between her and God. I chose her. It might have begun with her. But it was my choice alone."

"Explain it to me."

"There were two trees we were told about. The Tree of Life was never a temptation, because we already had eternal life. The fruit of the Tree of Knowledge of Good and Evil was not for us. It was there, I had thought, to give us a choice to obey or not. To be self-disciplined rather than rely on God to control us. If you eat and gain the knowledge of good and evil, you are sentenced to die. The antidote would be to run to the Tree of Life. Eating its fruit would then give you eternal life, along with knowing evil as well as good. That is why we were expelled from the garden containing the Tree of Life. We have already proven ourselves untrustworthy."

"And the Tree of Knowledge of Good and Evil?"

"It is gone. Now its poison passes on to our children through us. Every child from now on will be born with the knowledge of good and evil, along with the capacity to commit both, embedded in their soul. Thanks to us." He cannot hide the bitterness and self-recrimination. Pain, shame, bitterness—so many new emotional sensations for these two formerly innocent humans.

"You, however, will also pass along the capacity to rise above the evil. Also, everyone will have the capacity to seek God. Every person, in fact, will find a god, whether it be the God of heaven or one of their own invention or an idol provided by the world."

"You comfort me somewhat, Angel. It won't be the life of Paradise, but it will be life with God."

"Don't forget, Adam: God is sad, but he hasn't stopped loving you. He will continue to manifest that love."

Now it is Adam's turn to cry, but they are silent tears, coursing down a face that has never before known grief. "Thank you, Angel."

"You can thank me by continuing to do for Eve what God is doing for you. Look upon her with love, and treat her accordingly."

I step back as Adam turns back to Eve. Her look, fearful and uncertain, turns to joy as he gathers her in his arms. "I truly don't know what is to become of us or where we will go. But whatever we do, we will do it together. Come; let's start this life God has given us."

After-Action Summary

Why does Scripture refer to the loss of Paradise as the 'sin of Adam'? The sin in the garden is the sin of Adam because of the circumstance. Eve was tempted by a cunning demon of surpassing intellect. While he appealed to her acquisitive nature, Satan did not suggest that the choice was the acceptance of something in place of God. Beguiled, she sinned. Adam, however, knew exactly what choice was before him. Scripture records God telling Adam of the consequence of eating this fruit. Eve's information was secondhand. Adam had a choice. On the one hand, he could refuse to eat the fruit and let his loving partner be taken from him, expelled from Paradise, and sentenced to death. He would then have a limitless life in which to grieve. His other option was to value her above his Creator and choose a life where his woman was close and God was distant. He was not beguiled when he made his choice.

Scripture records God telling Adam that, on the very day that he ate of this fruit, he would surely die. Scripture then records that Adam lived over nine hundred years. Atheistic crowing about this seeming contradiction once again ignores Einstein's time dilation. The Bible is a good physics textbook for the receptive mind.

Jesus referred to himself as the last Adam. Both Jesus and Adam were born sinless but had sin ascribed to them. Adam acquired his sin through his own sinful behavior; Jesus assumed the sins of mankind onto his sinless soul. Jesus was also a sort of reverse Adam. Through the first Adam, eternal life was lost. Through Jesus, the reverse Adam, eternal life was restored.

Chapter 21
Case File M-2012-AD

Yusef considers himself to be pious. Unlike so many of his brethren, he has not succumbed to the fleshly temptations of the West. Yusef has never let alcohol pass his lips. He has never allowed a dalliance with Western women and is oddly proud that their near-universal harlotry continues to astound him. It also helps that his health, never great, prevents any vigorous activity. He has been married to one woman for over thirty years and is proud of the seven children she bore him. She dresses in the chaste manner of proper Muslim women, a wardrobe that also covers up the ravages of multiple childbirths and indifferent health care. She doesn't accompany him into the West when he travels on business. While he tells her that this protects her from having contact with infidels, in truth, she would be an embarrassment. Uneducated and inarticulate, she had been an acceptable brood mare for his offspring, but she would confound his worldly sophisticated image. Besides, Yusef believes that business is man's work.

At home, he is a devout Muslim, observing all the pillars of Islam. Away from home, he is two people. On the surface, Yusef is a midlevel banker, gliding through world financial capitals on a river of petrodollars. Yusef doesn't sit in the richly appointed salons and corporate boardrooms but is at the beck and call of those who do. It is into his ears that financial instructions are given and through his computer and phone that transactions are initiated.

All this mobility and proximity to wealth give him international cachet and, more importantly, camouflage for the second Yusef. The second Yusef is a link between the Wahhabist jihad leaders of his homeland and the independent cells of Muslim warriors who reside in the bosom of the Great Satan, America.

With Homeland Security and the NSA becoming ever more vigilant and clever, financial transactions and transfer of instructions via the Internet have become more difficult. Disposable cell phones and encryption programs have become untrustworthy. When orders must be verbal and face-to-face, Yusef is the man. When cash or precious stones must be delivered, Yusef is the man. Yusef has never fired a gun or thrown a grenade. His somewhat precarious health prohibits such violent activity; his common sense forbids it.

He has met only a few foot soldiers. He has occasionally met with leaders of individual terrorist cells but mostly deals with those who coordinate two or more separate groups. Yusef has clean hands, and his knowledge of the results of terrorists' attacks is limited to what he sees on television.

Today, Yusef is somewhat at loose ends. This trip to New York had been for two purposes. The first was to give final instruction to a group preparing a coordinated suicide bombing near the New York Stock Exchange. His second purpose was to see an esteemed cardiac surgeon at Columbia Presbyterian Medical Center. Yusef's heart has been failing over the years, and surgery has become imperative. The slightest exertion leaves him breathless. Medication no longer provides relief.

To his chagrin, Yusef had sat in the surgeon's office for two hours before an apologetic receptionist told him that the surgeon was involved in a trauma case and would be tied up for several more hours. Would the patient like to reschedule? Yusef had grimaced upon learning that the next appointment was two days later. He had left the building, walking slowly. His breathlessness had seemed acutely worse as he walked to the street. In the past, his fastidiousness had prompted him to reject continuous nasal oxygen. Now he would need it. He'd had to lean against a light pole as he hailed a cab.

I had pulled up and, seeing Yusef's obvious distress, jumped out and held the door. Yusef had gasped that he needed to be driven around the corner to the emergency-room entrance. I had suggested that he sit in the cab long enough to catch his breath. Yusef's breath had not slowed.

Then a most 'extraordinary' thing had occurred. I had placed my hand flat on Yusef's chest and said, "Let's give it ten minutes and see how you feel," and then gone around to sit behind the wheel. Yusef had had the most amazing relief of pressure, heaviness, and fatigue. His breathing had slowed, and he'd felt a slow, steady thump in his chest replace the vague fluttering sensation that had been his constant companion for years.

"Still wanna go to the ER?" I had asked.

"N-no. I must admit to suddenly feeling better." Yusef had looked as though he might ask me what I had done, what magic I had conjured with the touch of my hand. Then he'd looked at the crucifix hanging from the rearview mirror and at my ID. *Impossible*, he'd thought. Clearly he had thought better of asking. After all, could a cab-driving Christian infidel named Augie have cured him with a touch? *Absurd.* "Just take me back to my hotel, please." He had supplied the hotel's name, and I'd driven in silence. Yusef had given me a large tip and exited the cab with absolutely no shortness of breath.

The following two days had been a dream come true. Yusef had not needed to sleep propped up on four pillows. His ankles were no longer swollen at the end of the day. He had even walked up two flights of stairs. His legs, unaccustomed to the activity, had rebelled, but he had suffered no breathing difficulty. This was truly a miracle. Allah be praised!

Yusef has come back from a walk around Central Park. He goes to the bathroom to get all his medicines. He has canceled his surgeon's appointment. He will call his cardiologist back home to see what medicines he can stop taking. As he returns to the living room of his suite, he is startled to see two men sitting there—one of them is me.

"Who are you, and what are you doing? Wait a moment—I recognize you. You are the cabbie from the other day. Your name . . . Alonzo?"

"Augie."

"Yes, yes, just so. I recall. But what are you doing here?" Yusef is uneasy, but I and the other man seem friendly and unassuming. We are both dressed in work clothes and wearing baseball caps on our heads. We are much the same age as Yusef.

"This is my friend Paulie. Look, Yusef, I won't beat around the bush. We are here because you are financing and coordinating terrorist activities, and that's not nice."

"You must be joking." Yusef squares his shoulders and is set to go into a prepared denial.

"Nope." I raise a hand and come around to stand close to Yusef. "No time for denials. You have a couple of your suicide idiots ready to blow up themselves and a bunch of innocent folks outside the Stock Exchange in about six minutes."

"I assume you have some proof."

"Yusef, we're not Homeland Security or any other agency."

"Well, what are you?"

"We are angels."

Yusef's eyes bulge as his eyebrows explode skyward. His continental polish vanishes as he juts his jaw out and nearly screams, "Well, of course you are! You Americans and your arrogance! First there is 'America, God shed his grace on thee.' You are almost worse than the Jews with that 'God's chosen people' trash. So now we have Americans claiming to be angels. You have one minute to leave before I call security."

"Speaking of Jews being God's chosen people, what does the Koran say, Yusef?"

"What?" Yusef, now thoroughly confused by the change in subject, sits down on the sofa.

"In the Koran, Sura 3:30, and again in 5:46-47—those verses attest to the truth contained in the Torah. That's the Old Testament, virtually the entirety of which says that the Jews are God's chosen people. Are you telling me that the prophet Mohammed was wrong when he wrote that down?"

"No, you demon!" Yusef explodes off the couch. "How dare you insult the prophet? Jews and Christians have gone astray and left the true faith. That is why we oppose them."

"No, Yusef, that is how you justify murdering them. So you are saying that people who oppose the will of God should be killed?"

"If there is no other way, yes. Allah decides."

"Your terrorists, with your help, will shortly be trying to kill a crowd of people containing widows and orphans. Mohammed made a special point of caring for them, not killing them. How do you reconcile the murder of such people with the will of God?"

"It is not murder! It is jihad!" Yusef controls his trembling and calms himself. In an almost detached way, he notices that his heart is racing but strong and steady. He is not breathless. His lips curl in disdain. The sophisticated veneer has fallen away to reveal the cheap murderer beneath. "I will not continue a discussion with madmen. You must leave."

"You're still ignoring the angel part. Listen to me, Yusef. Your aortic valve was completely shot, and I put my hand on you two days ago. Now your heart is fine, and you feel healthy. That is the act of an angel, not a madman. We are out of time here, and I am not interested in persuading someone as obtuse as you. Paulie, go on into the bedroom." Paulie picks up a vacuum cleaner and trash bags from behind the sofa, walks into the bedroom, and closes the door. I move over next to Yusef, press him back onto the sofa, and sit down beside him.

"Yusef, your boys aren't going to slaughter anyone but themselves in about, oh, one minute." I still have a light, conversational bounce to my voice.

"I do not admit that anyone is my *boy*, but how do you know about this failure?"

"Because I pulled a little switcheroo, and their explosive vests have been, let's say, exchanged."

"Exchanged?"

"Yes. I read in the Koran that the pig is a filthy, unclean, detestable animal. So when your boys press their detonators—which is happening . . . right . . . now!—the small explosive is only spraying them with bacon grease."

Yusef's head retracts in shock. "You have really done this to them?" His voice is nearly a whisper, and he is no longer making denials.

"Yeah, but they won't notice it, because the same small explosive is driving sharpened ham hocks through their hearts. By now, your boys are dead. Everyone else is fine. Do you think those virgins will like it when their heroes show up in paradise smelling like a sausage factory?"

"I do not believe you have done this." Yusef is slowly shaking his head as though to exorcise an ugly reality.

"Well, they sure didn't have their original vests on. Look." I open my jacket to display a Semtex vest. "This is one of their vests.

The other one is under your chair. And will you just look at these things in my hand? My gracious, I do believe they are detonators." Yusef is trembling, suddenly drenched in sweat. He is looking at a face no longer friendly, now only hard and cold.

"Yusef, you aren't a good man, a good Muslim, a good anything. You are an upper-level thug who invites young, inexperienced, misguided people to offer up their lives for your mission. You certainly wouldn't permit any of your own children to be recruited for such lunacy, would you? You have encouraged innocent people to lose their lives in the murder of other innocents. Since you embrace the concept that dying in this so-called holy war is a guarantee of paradise, we are going to give you a chance to personally endorse it. What's that smell? Oh Yusef, you appear to have fouled your pants. That's not very courageous."

"Please . . ."

"By the way, Yusef, when I fixed your heart the other day, I installed an aortic pig valve. You now have part of a filthy animal inside you."

"No!"

I push the detonators.

After-Action Summary

Paulie came in after the explosion and picked up the pieces of me. What he couldn't pick up, he vacuumed up, and he took most of me back to the zip shop. They got me back together pretty well.

You will be disappointed if you are expecting a clarification about Muslims in heaven. Refer to chapter 7, "FAQAAs, Part 3," the section on heaven. I have never been there. I will say that heaven doesn't entertain any Jew, Christian, or Muslim who perverts his or her own faith for the creation of a demonic world order. The world's three major religions differ greatly but stand united in the one thing that matters: the Creator of the universe is a deity of love, mercy, and kindness. Any human who believes that you can frighten, kill, abuse, or regiment other humans into a meaningful relationship with their Creator is the Devil incarnate. Sadly, all three major religions have provided examples of such misanthropy.

I wanted Yusef's final seconds to be appropriately fearful. He feared that pork products in or on his body would make him unacceptable to heaven. Imams from responsible Muslim sects have denied this, since the Koran proscribes only the eating of pork. It is unlikely, however, that Yusef would have believed them. He certainly didn't believe the thoughtful, compassionate Muslim clerics who have condemned terrorist activity. Yusef's rejection by heaven would not be for the unsuitability of his heart valve but, rather, for the blackness in his soul.

Sadly, there are secularists in the Western world who claim to know the root causes of terrorism. They continue to mouth the same vapid prescriptions for eradicating terrorism. What are the root causes? According to them, poverty and ignorance, of course. Chanting this mantra makes the secularists happy because it (1) lets them off the hook, since they have long been in favor of spending someone else's money to correct any and every issue, and (2) puts the blame on rich humans who, as everyone knows, want to keep everybody else poor and stupid. The only problem is that many terrorists come from wealthy nations and from nations that are founding fundamentalist schools throughout and beyond the Muslim world for the purpose of fomenting a "convert the world by terror" ideology. Smart rich terrorist nations don't have problems with poverty and ignorance and they certainly would not permit an American form of education within their borders.

There is only one solution. Thankfully, it is promised. The good news is that Jesus is coming again. The bad news? He won't be coming back to negotiate.

Chapter 22
Case File O-1867-AD

Gideon Schuyler looks at his pocket watch as the ferryboat pulls away from the dock. It has been a full day, and he is feeling tired and a little bit sick. Schuyler is a self-made man. The gladiatorial arena of nineteenth-century New York business is not for the faint of heart. It is no mean accomplishment to survive in it, but to thrive in it, you must be brave, resolute, and ruthless. Schuyler is such a man. He had begun by organizing immigrant families to roll cigars in their tenement homes. He had employed whole families and paid them less than four dollars for a thousand rolled cigars, which he could then sell for over forty dollars. He had then moved into the garment trade. When he had a sufficient number of seamstresses, he'd rented factory space with no heat or running water and expected sixteen-hour work days, giving them Sundays off. If a seamstress was ill or unproductive, he fired her.

Gideon Schuyler has always considered himself a religious man. With his increasing wealth, he has moved his family to Clinton Hill in Brooklyn, where he attends Plymouth Congregational Church. He enjoys the preaching of Reverend Henry Ward Beecher, and during the war, he enthusiastically contributed to the purchase of Beecher Bibles—firearms provided to the citizens of border states who opposed slavery. Schuyler contributed to the formation and outfitting of a volunteer infantry regiment to fight in the War Between the States.

Schuyler supported the abolitionist movement and the Republican Party but was ever a practical man. He maintained a friendship with William "Boss" Tweed of Tammany Hall, who, though a Democrat, was egalitarian in the finances of favoritism. In exchange for a modest kickback, Tweed steered lucrative government contracts to Schuyler. This resulted in mass production of military uniforms that were high in number and very low in quality. The war was good to Gideon Schuyler. It was fought for principles that Schuyler espoused. It made him proud to be so strongly identified with the right people, on the right side of the argument.

He gives his tithe to the church and serves on its council. He can find nothing about Beecher's opinions with which to disagree. In fact, Beecher's lack of sympathy for the working man, while seemingly at odds with his support of emancipation for slaves, provides Schuyler with the religious support that he needs to justify the brutal schedule of his sweat-shop factories in these postwar years. He sees himself as Schuyler the businessman, Schuyler the gladiator, and Schuyler the pious Christian.

He is coming home to Brooklyn from his Manhattan offices. The ferryboat is plunging through unusually heavy waves, whipped by unseasonably cold winds. Schuyler has caught the last ferry of the day, which is nearly empty, but a warm coach will be waiting for him at the dock in Brooklyn Heights. He exits the cabin and walks forward. The cold wind hits him and seems to take his breath away. Suddenly, he feels a crushing pressure in his chest and a throbbing ache that runs up to his jaw. A wave of nausea hits him, and he collapses onto the deck. Solicitous hands loosen his collar. I remove my overcoat, fold it, and place it beneath Schuyler's head. Here, below the railing, we are shielded from the wind. We are alone. His chest pain continues to come in waves. I take a brandy flask from my pocket and pour a little between Schuyler's lips.

"What is happening to me?"

"You are having something the doctors call angina pectoris. Your heart muscles are dying from a lack of blood flow." My voice, for all it portends, seems strangely detached and calm.

"Does this mean I am dying?"

"Yes."

"Oh, the pain! Are you a doctor?"

"No, I am not."

The pain eases up. Schuyler catches a few full breaths, and the turmoil in his chest subsides. "Have you no feelings, man? Aren't you troubled in the least by what you see happening to me here?"

"I see that I'm not the one dying."

The pain is beginning again. "Oh no, it's coming back. Can you do nothing for me?"

"Yes. I am an angel, and I have been sent to be with you in this moment."

The pain eases a bit. "Angel, the next pain is going to take me, isn't it?"

I nod.

"I have been a faithful member of his church, so I will go with a clear conscience." I am silent as the final pain signals the end of Schuyler's life.

"To be absent from the body is to be present with the Lord," I mutter.

Gideon Schuyler opens his eyes, blinks a few times, and sees me again. "I'm not dead."

"Yes, you are."

"But I have fingers, toes—a whole body!"

"That's how things are in the afterlife."

Schuyler looks around. We are in a small room with white walls, ceiling, and floor. It is quiet and snug. "When do I see Jesus?"

"Soon."

"When I see him, should I fall down and worship him?"

"You never did while you were on earth, so why break a lifelong habit just because you're dead?"

"It's all right, Augie. I'll take over. Turn around, Gideon." Schuyler turns around and sees Jesus standing there—no halo, no shimmering lights, no radiant garments. He is of average height. His face, bearing no resemblance to the art of Renaissance fantasy, is stamped with his Hebrew lineage. His eyes have a look of infinite sadness. Schuyler falls to his knees.

"That's a pretty good imitation of reverence, Schuyler. You probably would have hit the ground faster it if had been a dollar bill standing in front of you."

"Augie, please."

"Sorry, Lord Jesus; it just slipped out."

"Gideon, stand up." Schuyler stands, unable to look away from those sorrowful eyes. "Gideon Schuyler, in your life, I never knew you."

"But I tithed, attended church, supported good causes—"

"Yes, but I was always aware of your motives in doing so. The heart that caused your physical death was the same heart that you never gave to me." Jesus turns and walks away, his form seeming to melt into the insubstantial light.

"But, Jesus, isn't there to be a judgment seat—something? Please . . ."

"That was your judgment, Schuyler." Schuyler looks back to see me standing by a door. Outside the door, it is totally dark. "Walk through here."

"Where am I going?"

"Out. When you get outside, an individual named Moloch will escort you. If he's in a good mood, he will leave the lights off so you won't have to see him."

Gideon Schuyler looks down and, sobbing, stumbles through the door. As the door closes, a light flashes on in the hall. The closing door cuts off the beginning of a horrified scream.

"Hmm," I whisper. "Moloch's not in a good mood."

After-Action Summary

> Many will say to me on that day, Lord, Lord, did we not prophecy in your name and in your name drive out demons and perform many miracles? Then I will tell them plainly "I never knew you. Away from me evildoers."
>
> —Matthew 7:21-23

On the surface, Gideon Schuyler was a worthy man: regular church attender and contributor, generous to select humanitarian causes. God, however, does not assess a human's suitability for heaven by the external behavior. He looks into the soul for the motivation. You might recall that the one person Jesus took with him to paradise was the thief on the cross beside him. I think it safe to conclude that humans should not rely on external appearance or behavior to predict salvation.

Let's examine Jesus' encounter with the rich young ruler. This human came to Jesus and asked what good thing he had to do to acquire the guarantee of eternal life. Jesus said that he should keep the commandments. The rich man asked him which ones he should observe. Jesus gave him six commandments: don't murder;

don't commit adultery; don't steal; don't lie; honor your father and mother; and, finally, love your neighbor as yourself. It is interesting to note that Jesus gave him five commandments that were directly from the Ten Commandments, the cornerstone of Jewish law. Those five commandments make the final commandment mentioned by Jesus appear oddly out of place: "Love your neighbor as yourself" (Leviticus 19:18). When the rich man affirmed that he kept all six commandments, Scripture tells us that Jesus felt love for the man and told him to sell all his possessions and give the proceeds to the poor. Hearing this, the young man left. Jesus had exposed that the rich man had not, in fact, kept all six commandments mentioned. Had he loved his neighbor as himself, this final commandment would not have seemed onerous. Jesus had revealed that the rich young man had merely kept those commandments that were not inconvenient.

There is another encounter that causes Christians a bit of confusion. In Matthew 8:21, a disciple asks Jesus if he may "first go and bury my father." Jesus replies, "Let the dead bury their dead." This makes Jesus seem heartless. In fact, it was the tradition of the time that a father was buried by the eldest son. What else did the eldest son do? He inherited. What this man was actually saying to Jesus was "Let me go home and make sure I get my inheritance." Jesus loved these two men but saw beyond their words and actions and into their hearts. Yes, Gideon Schuyler was a church attender, tither, abolitionist, and supporter of worthy causes. He was also an unconscionable war profiteer and sweat-shop owner. More men died in the Civil War from disease than from battle. Adequate clothing could have prevented many of those deaths. By placing profit before reliable clothing for those poor soldiers, Schuyler reasonably placed a certain number of the death tally at his own feet.

It is one thing to be a rich man who ignores the suffering of the poor. It is quite another to be a rich man whose accumulated wealth is taken from the poor. Schuyler's wealth accumulated from paying slave wages and maintaining intolerable working conditions. He then used that wealth in self-serving contributions to causes that were in vogue and that made him appear to be a humanitarian. He found it convenient, for example, to be an abolitionist simply because it was not *his* workforce that was in question. Papa looks at the hearts of his children.

No doubt, the rich young man and Gideon Schuyler felt that eternal life was meant to be merely a perpetuation of the wealthy life they were enjoying on earth. They were wrong. Dead wrong.

Chapter 23

Case File G-12-JC

Matthew 26:36-43

There is a breeze from the south that puts a haze at treetop level, and the odor of burning trash from just outside the Dung Gate spoils an otherwise beautiful night. I'm in the olive grove. I gaze up at the Mount of Olives and then turn around to gaze across the Kidron Valley at the sheer expanse of the east wall of Jerusalem, the temple immediately above. I turn back and see him. He is moving this way, separating from some of his disciples. As I watch, he stretches out on the ground, his hands raised above his head. I move quietly toward him. I glance over and see his friends have already fallen asleep. I wait while he talks to Papa. I can't make out the words, but the tone is tortured, agonized. If I possessed a human heart, it would surely break.

Jesus straightens up and seats himself on a rock, peering through the darkness in my direction.

"Hello, Augie—out rambling again?" His voice is weary but still welcoming.

"No. Papa sent me here to be with you."

"Ah, I should have known." Jesus is distracted, now standing up and pacing around the rock.

"Jesus, what is happening? I know you are planning to save the humans, but we angels have been pretty much in the dark about the plan. I have heard you say you will give your life as a ransom for many, but I still don't understand why or how." It is at moments like this that I feel sorry for Jesus because he has to deal with dense angels like me. I still can't understand where all this is going.

"All right, Augie, you've been around for pretty much the whole mission, so I'll explain." Jesus takes a deep breath and looks up at the night sky. He has been sweating, but the arid breeze has dried his face, leaving a strange, powdery pink substance on his dark skin.

"Augie, how does a person atone for a sin?"

"By giving a sacrifice."

"Yes. Now, how does that person determine the amount of the sacrifice?"

"It's based on the degree of sin. The larger the sin, the larger the sacrifice required."

"Yes. So a small sin is atoned for by something small, like a sparrow or dove. A larger transgression would require, for example, a bull. Is there anything special about each sacrifice?" Jesus seems to have shed the burden of his thoughts, now comfortable in his role of teacher, even to a fool like me.

I nod. "The animal has to be healthy and as close to perfect as possible."

"Any exceptions?"

"Well, yes, I guess so. In the case of murder, for example, the sinner's sacrifice is his own life, whether he be healthy or perfect."

"Right. But except for that . . ."

"The sacrificed animal has to be as nearly perfect as possible."

"Yes. Now, Augie, imagine what kind of sacrifice would be needed to cover all the sins of one man for his entire life."

"Pretty big, pretty perfect animal."

"Now multiply that to cover all the people on earth."

I don't like where this is going. "Jesus . . ." I feel the quivering of my voice, and it seems to run down into my arms. The night seems to be compressing me, and I suddenly wish I could lose my ability to hear.

"Then, Augie, multiply that to cover all the people who will ever live on earth."

"No. No!"

"Yes. To cover all of mankind's sin for all time, it wouldn't be sufficient for a man, even a very good man, to die in atonement."

"Oh Lord . . ."

"How else can man and Papa be reconciled and all mankind be acceptable for heaven? Something divine must be the sacrificial animal in order to satisfy the law."

"So all of this—your living in a human body, your preaching, your miracles. It's all just to . . ." I am having trouble getting my thoughts out through my mouth.

"To satisfy the law. I have told everyone that I came to fulfill the law. What law is more important than man being made acceptable to God?"

I gaze across at the walls of Jerusalem. Just around the corner is the Sheep's Gate, where the sacrificial animals are brought in below the temple. Now I understand. My eyes begin to burn and water.

"How is it going to happen, then?"

"It begins tonight."

"But the people here love you. Look at how they greeted you when you rode into the city."

"That will change. The demons are here. It will not be nice to watch. But, Augie, you must promise me something." Jesus comes close to me, and I feel a comfort despite my fear.

"Yes?" My throat feels too small for my voice, and all I can manage is a whisper.

"No matter what happens, don't intervene. It must happen. Let it happen."

"Will it, at least, be dignified?"

"No. I will be brutalized before my body is killed. I will be in the company of murderers and thieves. I will die with taunts and curses around me."

Just now, I want to leave my body. "Is that what has you troubled tonight, thinking of the pain that is coming?"

"No, Augie. If it were simply physical pain that I had to endure, I would gladly go through it once for each human on earth and for every future human."

"Then there is something troubling you that I can't grasp."

Jesus looks down and nods, tears dropping from his cheeks into the dust. The sorrow that had been on his face while praying to Papa returns. "Augie, at the time of his death, the sacrificial animal carries the burden of the sinner for whom it dies. The animal is sinless but must wear that sin. What will Papa do when he sees me like that?"

Now I am crying as I try to envision the greatest concentration ever of sin placed on the back of the least sinful human being ever.

"He has to turn away from me. You know how Papa feels about even one sin. I will literally be the dirtiest thing he has ever seen."

"But you haven't done anything wrong!"

"Still, he has to reject me, break his link with me. Augie, all my life, I have felt him. I could never tell where I ended and he began." He takes a few breaths as if to control his emotions. "I have never been alone, but I will be. I have never been forsaken, but I will be. I have never felt unloved, but I must be." He now has the saddest smile. "All my life, even when I have been walking, I have always felt as though he had his arms wrapped around me. How cold a child must feel when the warmth of his father's arms is taken away."

Now I know why Papa sent me.

"Jesus, this isn't much, but I have seen a lot of sin in my assignments. Papa doesn't need me to turn away from you. I am going to stay with you. I will leave my body when all this happens, and I'll be as close to you as I can get."

"Thank you, Augie. That will help, because there is something I want you to do after the sacrifice is complete. There is a curtain in the temple I will want you to tear" (Luke 23:45).

"Is it okay if I start calling you Lord Jesus again?"

"Yes, Augie. I love you."

"And I love you, Lord Jesus."

After-Action Summary

The adjective *excruciating* means "out of the cross." Most of the time, humans use this word to define extreme physical suffering (i.e., excruciating pain). The suffering of Jesus on the cross undoubtedly had an enormous physical component. Throughout history, however, many people have suffered even greater physical abuse than the physical suffering of Jesus on the cross, and for longer periods of time. The suffering that Jesus feared, that which made him sweat blood and cry out for his Papa, was not physical. No human has ever had the spiritual bond, the connectedness that Jesus had with his Father. Consequently, no human could adequately grasp the horror of this coming moment. Jesus was accustomed to rejection by humans. Nothing, however, could prepare him for this: to have the Father sever the bond and to view him with disgust in the process.

Christians have, at various times in history, blamed the Jews in general for the crucifixion. These humans have been the victims of poor scholarship. The push for Jesus' death came from politicians and certain citizens who had an agenda. Blaming Jews for the crucifixion would display the same logic as blaming the residents of Maryland for John Wilkes Booth's assassination of Abraham Lincoln. Furthermore, Jesus forgave his killers—how can a human think that Papa would consider it proper for one of his children to continue holding that grudge? Peter, under the power of the Holy Spirit, also pointed out that the Jews had acted in ignorance and that the crucifixion had to occur in order for God to fulfill prophecy (Acts 3:17-18). There are two more Scriptures that humans need to bear in mind: "Give no offense either to Jews, or to Greeks, or to the church of God (1 Corinthians 10:32 NAS), and "Jesus Christ is the same, yesterday, today, and forever" (Hebrews 13:8 NIV).

What was Jesus when he was on earth? A Jew. If Hebrews 13:8 is correct, then Jesus is still Jewish. His heavenly Father is the God of Abraham and the God of Israel. If I were a Christian human, I would think hard about Judaism, since I have essentially been adopted into a Jewish family and my Savior is a nice Jewish boy. The majority, if not all, of the authors inspired by God to write both biblical testaments were Jewish. Virtually all of the early church leaders were Jewish, beginning with Peter. In the early centuries of the church, the Romans considered Christians to simply be Jews who believed the Messiah had already come, the rest being Jews who were still waiting for the Messiah. In AD 132-136, the Jewish Bar Kokhba revolt against Roman authority in Israel led to Rome expelling all Jews from Jerusalem. Although the

Christians did not support the revolt, they were likewise expelled. Rome made no distinction. A Christian was just another Jew.

If Hebrews 13:8 is correct, Jesus continues to love the Jews as he did during his earthly ministry (Matthew 23:37). There have been some humans who have claimed that God replaced the covenant he made with Abraham's descendants and now honors only the covenant made with Christians based on Christ's redemptive blood. Their argument is that persistent sin and faithlessness by the Jews forced God to turn to the Christians. Shame on them! If God broke the Abrahamic covenant with the Jews because of human faithlessness, he could break the covenant of Christ just as easily, and for the same reasons. That would make John 6:37 ("Everyone who the Father has given me shall come to me and whoever will come to me I shall not cast out") merely a breakable vow. God is faithful, even if you are not. Chapter 8 of Hebrews mentions a "new covenant" through Christ. This new covenant, however, clearly replaces the Mosaic covenant (Exodus 19:5-6) and not the Abrahamic covenant (Genesis 15:18-21).

Humans must also bear in mind that it was love, not nails that held Jesus on the cross—love for all people, Jew and Gentile alike. When he returns, will it simply be a matter of Jews saying, "Messiah, welcome," while Christians say, "Messiah, welcome back"? Humans, masters of absurdity.

Chapter 24

Case File M-1413-AD

Robert Kiegler thinks he is alone. He labors at his computer, sifting facts, analyzing trends. He is accustomed to solitary work. In the Byzantine bureaucracy of the federal government, the real work is done by individuals and closed committees. If something occurs in open Congress, open debate, or open committees or can be seen on C-SPAN, it is of no relevance to the progress of the mission. Government activities that are for public consumption are eyewash for the citizens. The electorate requires cajoling because, after all, they elect to office those individuals who might actually impact the mission. That is the drawback to representative government: elected officials are perfectly capable of getting in the way of proper government.

The mission is an abstraction—it has no author, no father, no mother, no guidelines. Yet the bureaucrats have always worked toward its end point with the corporate dedication of ants in a colony. What is the mission? To sustain and expand government. To paraphrase Abraham Lincoln, bureaucrats are here to ensure that government of the bureaucracy, by the bureaucracy, and for the bureaucracy shall not perish from the earth. Ants do not need committee meetings or marching orders. Neither do bureaucrats. They function as one mind when dealing with generic threats to the bureaucracy or individual threats to their particular fiefdom.

Regarding the latter, consider the US Postal Service. If faced with budget cutbacks, they do not reduce midlevel administration, expense accounts, or gratuitous travel for senior staff. No, they immediately pull back the customer service staff in order to create long lines that lead to complaints to the elected bozos from their constituents. The congressmen learn not to propose budget cuts, the threats go away, and the bloat is protected. Bureaucracy doesn't just protect its budget; it protects its prerogatives.

Look at law enforcement. A rapist gets a slap-on-the-wrist jail term. Upon release, the rapist receives a well-deserved beating by the rape victim's father. That father's jail term will be far longer than that of the rapist, and the rapist will also successfully sue in civil court. Why? Because more than rape, the government is concerned about private citizens taking the law into their own hands—even if a human is taking into his own hands a law that was dropped and stepped on by the law enforcers.

Kiegler is a bureaucrat. Unlike many, however, he is totally aware of the purpose and end point of the mission. A graduate of Brown University and the Kennedy School of Government, he has been around long enough to know either how to be in the right place at the right time or how to turn the wrong place into the right place.

Beginning with the Kennedy School concept that all money belongs to the government and only government can decide how much money is out there, either controlled by individuals or in play, Kiegler's goal is to be always close to the in-play money, to help in its control, and, of course, to judiciously sample it. He has benefitted from the Fannie Mae debacle and from the General Motors stock restructuring. Like so many of his fellow Socialist bureaucrats, his first job is to ensure his own financial ascendancy.

Because he is neither a limousine liberal nor a trust fund humanitarian, Kiegler had to amass his own wealth from a series of small golden parachutes accumulated from his various government enterprises. His financial autonomy now established, Kiegler can afford to be altruistic and is devoting himself to the evolution of a Socialist USA that, ignoring the wealth accumulated by Kiegler and his ilk, will target the finances of any citizen of the USA who had the gall to actually earn it.

Kiegler and his friends know that an unhappy electorate is meddlesome. They may slow the progress of government by elitists, but it is too far gone now to halt. The government is the perceived source of too many benefits for too many voters, be they real voters or fraudulent. Still, it makes sense to spread Socialism in baby steps, significant gains buried deep in congressional bills deliberately too large to be read by the congressmen. Congress is never a problem anyway; its members will simply exempt themselves from the unpleasant features of any bill that they inflict on the rest of the country.

The American public thinks that the two-party system pits the Democrats against the Republicans. In truth, the two-party system is the voters against the incumbents and bureaucrats. The Democrat voter is someone who enjoys being lied to by liberal politicians; the Republican voter is someone who enjoys being lied to by conservative politicians.

Kiegler's greatest satisfaction derives from the exorcism of God from government. There was a time when spiritual strength and commitment were perceived as a positive. Thanks to a blend of political correctness and a leftist media, it is now a closet skeleton to have a reverence for God and a commitment to moral absolutes. Kiegler has no problem with religion, just as he has no problem with Santa Claus or the tooth fairy. He is even okay with the moralizing nonsense as long as it is kept out of government and kept out of the way of progressive thinkers.

He works toward the ideal of a Socialist world government, providing for the needs of people clearly incapable of providing for themselves. This will involve insisting on lifestyle changes for people too stupid to manage their own health. Such governance requires two things: First, leadership must consist of visionary, brilliant men and women united by the altruism of the Socialist agenda. Individualism must be allowed only to the extent that it can create taxable wealth or create benefits for mankind, for which the government can easily claim credit. Second, the enforcement and perpetuation of such a government can only be assured by eradicating any concept of an authority higher than the government itself. How can people become dependent upon, and grateful to, a strong government as long as those people also feel a dependency upon, and gratitude to, some deity?

No, the formula is as follows: step 1, separation of church and state, and step 2, church destroyed by state. Once free of the encumbrances of religious ethical absolutism, the state may write its own morality, altering it when and where convenient. The citizens under such a government will no doubt feel relieved for the legal destruction of all guilt-inducing religions. Christianity must be first, but Judaism and Islam are also toxic to government ascendancy.

I walk into Kiegler's waiting room. I am unsurprised to see two demons. Moloch and Belial are at first startled to see me, but they relax after studying me. Standing up slowly, Moloch greets me. "The prayer business must not be doing well, Augie. You look positively weak."

"You're right, Moloch. Not enough people praying for this country. I don't have enough power to get you out of here. I could maybe conjure up some deodorant. It's a good thing humans can't see or smell you. We'd have people trying to get into heaven to save their nostrils instead of their souls."

"Okay, Augie," says Moloch, slouching back down into his chair. He isn't stupid enough to try taking me on, even if I'm not backed up by prayer. "I think you still have plenty of power, even without prayer. Why is that?"

"No rule says an angel can't fight dirty."

"If you're not here to get us out, then why are you here?" Moloch is, as usual, doing the talking. Belial just sits there, picking his nose and studying the product with the eye of a connoisseur.

"Just checking out your guy Kiegler." Humans know a lot about guardian angels but precious little about the existence of guardian demons. Moloch and Belial are functioning in that capacity, watching Kiegler to prevent him from doing anything righteous. Kiegler is so far down the road that there is little risk, but Satan is taking no chances in his bid to consume the American government. "He's never seen you guys, right?"

"That's right. Boss's orders."

"Okay. Well, I'm going to meet Kiegler."

"Wait a minute, Augie." Moloch puffs up his chest and moves closer.

I look calmly at Moloch and quietly say, "Back off, Demon."

Moloch fails to hold my gaze and shuffles back, mumbling, "The boss won't like it if you mess with him."

"Just sit back down and be a good little demon. You might ask Belial if he has a Tic Tac. Just to keep things fair, I'll get Kiegler to come out here where you can keep an eye on me, okay?" I knock on the door, and Kiegler opens it.

"As you can see, sir, it's quite late and my secretary is gone. I am exceedingly busy. May I ask what you are doing here?" Kiegler has a sheaf of papers in one hand and an iPad in the other. His coat is off, and his man-of-the-people look is gone.

"Mr. Kiegler, I have come to meet you. While I don't have bureaucratic credentials equal to yours, I am also a member of a large organization." I cross my arms as he talks to me while keeping his eyes focused on the iPad.

"Your name?"

"Augie's my first name. That'll do."

"And the nature of your business?" Kiegler drops the papers on an end table and starts texting on his keyboard.

"That's a little complicated. Let's first establish my legitimacy." I figure it's time to get his attention, so I give him a list of the numbers and banks of his highly secret offshore accounts. I summarize Kiegler's involvement in three sub-rosa government activities of questionable legality. Kiegler has turned pale and, looking behind him, sits heavily in a chair. The demons, invisible to Kiegler, look on in concern. Even Belial stops harvesting his nasal mucus. Kiegler wipes some perspiration from his face and attempts to compose himself.

"All right, Augie, so you have some pretty damning information about me. I don't suppose you'll tell me what group you're with. It doesn't matter anyway; this is all about leverage. What do you want me to do in order to keep you from exposing what you know?" Kiegler is back together. He is used to the occasional quid pro quo and the occasional threat. He, after all, is a master at using both. This, at least, is a familiar arena. Or so he thinks.

"This is where it goes from a little complicated to a lot complicated, Kiegler. The truth is, I represent a philosophical presence, if you will, that is troubled by your involvement in getting rid of God and replacing his righteousness with your own slippery brand of morality."

"What? Are you from some covert, militant Christian group?"

"No. Think higher."

"Some church?"

"Higher."

"Okay, so you're a nutcase with really good intel on what I and my friends are doing." He shakes his head in dismissal and starts to rise from the chair.

"Actually, you need a more open mind." I raise a finger, and Kiegler's chair rises from the floor, smacking against his half-raised buttocks and propelling him into the air, the chair hovering three feet above the floor. Kiegler gives a little squeak and grips the chair. "I'll spin you around so you'll see there is no special equipment here." I describe a circle with my finger, and the chair rotates slowly all the way around. Kiegler looks at me with shock and fear. "What in God's name are you?"

"In God's name, I'm an angel." I set him down gently. "Kiegler, I assume you are sufficiently persuaded that you don't need further proof of what I am. Would it be okay with you if we at least base a discussion on the assumption that I am an angel and you are a well-educated idiot?"

"Uh, yeah . . . yes. Yes, we can." Kiegler is afraid to get out of the chair but is stretching his neck backward as though his head is trying to escape and leave his body in the room.

"Okay. Kiegler, I'm sorry to tell you that God doesn't cease to exist simply because you and your mentally challenged friends devoutly wish it so. Unfortunately, God doesn't part the seas or lead people around with a pillar of cloud anymore. Because God is subtle, people like you can persuade themselves that he either doesn't exist or does exist but doesn't care about mankind. Because he honors the concept of free will, you perceive him to be an absentee God who has left you here with free license."

"Okay, Augie, since we are having a discussion based on the assumption that you are an angel—"

"And don't forget the assumption that you are a well-educated idiot."

"Ah, right. Well, Angel, what could your God have to complain about? Our goal is to provide food and health care for people who need it. We want to educate the ignorant. We want to eradicate war by uniting the world under a single authority. That all sounds like something God would approve of."

"No, you are looking at the veneer of your goal, Kiegler. As for health care and food, what you really want to do is gain control of it and then dispense it to those people who knuckle under to your authority and surrender that which is precious about themselves—their individuality. You will take every good thing that an individual human can invent and claim it as an entitlement that the government, in its beneficence, will bestow upon the faithful sheep in the electorate. For those who dare to oppose you, it will be the extortionate withholding of everything that a truly free society should make available to every citizen.

"Your education is like the old education of Stalin and Chairman Mao—nothing more than indoctrination. Individualism and attempts at freedom of thought would need to be slapped down. You talk about celebrating diversity, when you only want diversity of appearance and behavior while demanding absolute non-diversity of thought.

"As for one world government and ending war, you will only eradicate war by making sure that no one has anything of value that someone else might consider taking by force. Universal poverty—what a unique concept!

"Of course, there will need to be a ruling class—a group of people who, like yourself, have accumulated wealth by stealing from the people you seek to subjugate. This ruling class will never suffer the health-care or education systems they will ordain for the rest of mankind. Perhaps the saddest issue is that you wish to separate these humans from a God who loves them and then place them under the authority of people who, like yourself, disrespect and despise them."

"Angel, every government that claimed to have God's guidance has been evil or corrupt."

"Kiegler, even Satan can quote Scripture. Those who loudly proclaim God's guidance often work for his opponent. As for the USA, you disappoint me if you believe your own rhetoric—your politicians have apologized for so many righteous actions carried out by the USA that you totalitarians actually believe that the USA has been a bad country. The USA is the only country in all history where the people, not the government or a priestly class, heard the message of Scripture and attempted to act on it. You and your friends are seeking to expunge the one thing that has made America both strong and unique."

"We can achieve even better things for mankind without having people abandon common sense in favor of some vague spiritual quest. Facts are facts, but faith is whatever you want it to be."

"Exactly wrong, Kiegler. In your world, facts are whatever the media and spin doctors proclaim them to be. As for faith being 'whatever you want it to be,' that's exactly what you and your secular humanist friends fear—it can't be taxed, regulated, controlled, or predicted. What you want to do is promote faith in Mother Government alone and destroy all other forms of its expression, just like what was attempted behind the Iron Curtain.

"Look at history, Kiegler, and make a list of all the nations, empires, and civilizations that tried to destroy Judaism or Christianity. None of them—not one—still exists, yet these faiths flourish. You will be joining a group notable for their abject failure in achieving their goal. Speaking of joining a group, you seem to have a lot of diverse organizations joining you in trying to bring down the capitalist society of America."

"Many people have suffered at the hand of American corporate greed, yes, and that makes for a diversity of groups." Kiegler has by now stood up and is attempting to stand tall, but through his trousers, I can see his legs shaking.

"But you haven't met all of your allies, have you?" Moloch and Belial, standing off to the side, are beginning to look nervous. "Kiegler, let's introduce you to a couple of demons whom Satan has detailed to watch over you and all your good works. They have been here, watching you." The demons have looks of horror as they cringe down as if in supplication. I snap my fingers, and the demons become visible. "Meet Moloch and Belial."

Kiegler's head snaps over to the two newly visible presences in the room. He takes a step back, stumbles over the chair, and falls to the floor. Moloch, caught unprepared, tries to mount what he believes to be a smile on his face. The result of his unfamiliarity with these facial muscles distorts his already hideous countenance into a vision beyond the limit of human psychic tolerance. Moloch and Belial, now both angry with me, begin to spit, hiss, and curse. They are silenced by a wail, beginning low and almost panting, rising now and punctuated by grunts, finishing with an earsplitting scream. Kiegler's mind is gone. The end of the scream is the end of Kiegler's verbal communication with the world of the living. His next verbal communication, years hence, will be with the demons of the afterlife.

After-Action Summary

If I do it right, this After-Action Summary should anger just about everybody. While there are certainly outliers in every group, the majority of Americans reside in either the liberal or conservative camp. To both groups, I would point out that the first-century church was not just Socialist but reflected pure Communism.

> All the believers were one in heart and mind. No one claimed that any of his possessions was his own, but

they shared everything they had. With great power the apostles continued to testify to the resurrection of the Lord Jesus, and much grace was upon them all. There was no needy person among them. From time to time those who owned lands or houses sold them, brought the money from the sales and put it at the apostles' feet, and it was distributed to anyone who had need. (Acts 4:32-35 NIV)

Long before the world heard of Karl Marx, Jesus Christ was the first Communist. Angels find that it is here that humans are at their funniest and most inane: liberals want the Socialism without Jesus, and conservatives want Jesus without the Socialism. Neither side is innocent, but the guilt is one of mistrust. With the love of God and his guidance through Jesus Christ, Communism would work because the basis is love, not government coercion. Conservatives tend to trust God but not their fellow man. Liberals tend to distrust their fellow man and resent God. Until Socialism is run by humans who refuse to use it for their own personal gain, it will fail. Can any human name a single Socialist government in history that was so constructed? No, you cannot. Subtracting God from government simply allows his Enemy in by default.

Satan manipulates leaders by persuading them that they deserve the reward of wealth for all the good they do. Karl Marx was an utter fool when he taught that Socialism would evolve into Communism, because he never allowed for the cupidity of people in control and for their enthusiastic response to the blandishments of Satan. What despot or oligarchy ever peacefully surrendered power? The Socialist governments of the world will deteriorate. The moral absolutes of society that the liberals so gleefully tamper with are like the structural steel in reinforced concrete. Your building will get constructed without the steel in the concrete, but don't expect it to last. As the deterioration continues, martial law will become harsher, and no human agency will ever be able to wrest control from the oligarchs. Witness North Korea. That is why Jesus spoke of a second coming. He isn't returning because he wants to; he will return because he must.

I add this little section for those humans who are interested in biblical prophecy, specifically as it relates to the end times. Has it seemed strange to you that the USA is not portrayed in any identifiable way at the time of the war of Gog and Magog against Israel? Indeed, up through Armageddon, the USA is a nonfactor. For Jesus' second coming to occur, Israel must exist and be surrounded by enemies. The USA must be unwilling or unable to come to Israel's aid. From the time of Israel's creation in 1948 until 1978, it could not truly be said that Israel was surrounded by enemies. Although the Yom Kippur War (1973) involved invasion efforts by Israel's neighbors, Israel's salvation was at least partly due to a source that today would seem impossible. One country in the region continued to supply Israel with oil and armaments during this war. That country was Iran. So long as Iran was allied to the USA and, by extension, to Israel, biblical prophecy could not be fulfilled.

President Jimmy Carter helped speed prophecy along by unilaterally and preemptively withdrawing his support from the shah of Iran. The shah's government fell, and the Iran of today is the result. The recent overthrow of Middle East dictators, with the passive approval of the USA, ensures an Islamic fundamentalist movement into the power vacuum. They cannot form coalition governments, since their instinct is to destroy anyone opposed to their ideology.

So for the first time ever, now Israel is truly surrounded by enemies. What of its distant ally, the USA? The current administration of the USA is doing to Israel what the Carter administration did to the shah of Iran: signaling to the rest of the Middle East a gradual withdrawal of patronage.

Why? I don't know a single angel who thought humans capable of a political schizophrenia on the scale of that which is current in the USA. Here is a country rich in energy resources—coal, oil shale, offshore and Alaskan oil, and clean nuclear sources. Yet it insists on acts of economic self-castration, mandating its own dependence on foreign oil, access to which forces the USA to placate nations whose domestic policies regarding women and religious tolerance should horrify any rational human.

Why would America be so self-abusive? Golly, gee, it sure can't be a run-up to Armageddon, can it? After all, humans are too sophisticated to fall for that. Thankfully, God doesn't worry about sophistication.

Chapter 25

Case File A-73-AD

Matthew 26:57-67
John 18:28

He awakens to the early morning sound of carts on the cobblestones, the din of vendors invading even this neighborhood. The sun's heat begins to stir up zephyrs around Mount Zion, which, through his window, bring the mixed fragrances of flowering olive and almond trees. He rises from his pallet and stretches. Caiaphas is young for his position, still straight of posture with a flat stomach and joints free of arthritis. He swaggers over to look out his window at the panorama of Jerusalem. He has a light robe draped on his shoulders against the rapidly fading cool of the night. He sees the temple and knows the early business of Passover sacrifice and ritual is already begun, as the Sabbath ended last evening at sundown. A servant brings a basin of water and a towel so that he can attend to his morning ablutions. Caiaphas indicates the balcony where he will sit and break his fast and then strolls out there as another servant brings out the food.

Ah, yes, he thinks as he settles down to eat. *A wonderful morning, and maybe the first time my anxious stomach will accept a meal.* He eats silently. Then he begins to smile, and the smile becomes a smirking laugh. Why had he been worried? He had pulled it off. He had done it. Caiaphas had choreographed it all, and it had been a thing of beauty. As high priest for over ten years, he has dealt with false messiahs and zealots—never a problem, never a waver, never a doubt. With resolute and consistent skill, he has stopped all these inconveniences with judicious use of fear and torture. When necessary, he has cobbled together charges against these upstarts to compel the Romans to execute them. Caiaphas is a shrewd man. He is of noble birth and a Sadducee, the closest thing to Jewish royalty since the end of the Davidic line of kings. He was politician enough to get Valerius Gratus, the Roman prefect, to appoint him high priest. He is duplicitous enough to balance the interests of Rome, the interests of Israel, and, of course, the interests of Caiaphas.

Then had come that Galilean clodhopper. In a few short years, he had become the talk of Israel. He had started with preaching a bizarre gospel. Then had come the healing miracles. Those hadn't been too wearisome, since most of the pretenders had shills in the audience who could be "miraculously" healed. A quick beating had sufficed to curtail those so-called miracles.

But this Jesus character. Caiaphas frowns at the recollection, and his tender stomach knots up a little. Pharisees and Sadducees had confronted Jesus in debate, trying to catch him up in a blasphemy, a contradiction, or a seditious statement. Each one of them, despite their brilliance and education, had been tied in knots by the genius of this rebel's reasoning. And the insults! It is all very well to insult a Pharisee; Caiaphas himself often indulges in that activity. But to insult a Sadducee, the elite of Israeli society? What is even worse, this Jesus character speaks of an afterlife, a concept that is anathema to a Sadducee. Caiaphas gives up trying to eat and pours himself an extra cup of wine, trying to clear his mind by whispering out loud, "It's over; it's over."

Plots had failed to entrap Jesus, and then, to Caiaphas's horror, had come reports of Jesus having raised a man, Lazarus, from the dead. For a Sadducee, it was bad enough to speak of an afterlife; to actually restore a life after a man had died threatened to confer some legitimacy on this upstart. There had been no question; Jesus had to die. The problem had been how to catch him and then convince the Romans that he was a threat to the empire. Blasphemy and insulting the Sanhedrin were not, to the Romans, capital crimes. Caiaphas had had to be on his mettle to stop this threat to his political stability.

The apprehension of this blasphemer had been simplicity itself. The fool had actually come to Jerusalem for Passover. Had their positions been reversed, Caiaphas would never have been that stupid. He would have concocted some self-serving fiction to justify his absence from an obligatory pilgrimage. But not Jesus, no. This man's arrogance had persuaded him that he could walk around Jerusalem unmolested.

Well, he had come into Caiaphas's territory and quickly learned otherwise. They had paid off a traitor who delivered Jesus into their hands. In the dead of night, to avoid arousing the citizens of the city, Jesus had been brought before a committee of the Sanhedrin, selected for their lack of sympathy with Jesus' message. Caiaphas had been unimpressed. Jesus had been an average-looking Jew and, strangely, had given no evidence of his vaunted debating skills.

Caiaphas had had to struggle to extract a suitable offense, and then he had hit upon the perfect question—he had gotten Jesus to admit that he was the Messiah. Perfect! Caiaphas had torn his clothes at such blasphemy while internally gloating. The very recollection seems to calm him, no doubt helped by the wine. The Messiah was to come from the Davidic line of kings. To suggest a restoration of the Davidic line was invidious to Roman interests; it was a call to rebellion. It was sedition and, as such, punishable by death. After having him beaten, Caiaphas had had Jesus hurried over to Pilate. He himself hadn't accompanied the officials in delivering Jesus to the Romans. Entering a Gentile residence would make him unclean, but Caiaphas was more concerned with distancing himself from this affair. If the Passover crowd in Jerusalem got wind of the trial and turned on the Sanhedrin, Caiaphas wanted to be disassociated from the intrigue. Besides, he had to arrange for some supporters to be outside Pilate's house to incite a beneficial response by the crowd that was sure to gather.

Pilate had vacillated, but a stroke of good fortune had influenced the outcome. Rome had begun a tradition of pardoning, at Passover, a Jewish criminal convicted of a capital crime. Pilate had had two such convicts: Jesus and Barabbas. Caiaphas's men in the crowd, knowing which result was wanted, had screamed for Barabbas to be spared and then had beaten Jesus' supporters. The rest had been simple. Beaten again. Crucified. Dead and buried. Roman soldiers guarded the tomb to prevent Jesus' harebrained followers from any mischief. Well, the rebel was in the ground now, and aside from the inexplicable tearing of the temple's curtain protecting the Holiest of Holies, no disruption had occurred. As Caiaphas had said, it was better for one man to die than for the nation of Israel to perish.

"Good morning, Caiaphas. I love what you've done with the place. Who would think that a humble priest would have your talent for decor? That Nazarene's blood on the steps—it does add a certain flair, don't you think?"

Caiaphas almost drops his wine goblet and barely avoids falling off the porch. "Who are you?"

"I am an angel, and my name is Augie."

Nonplussed, he says, "Uh, angel, you say? What are you doing here? Never mind, I'm calling the guards. How did you get past them?"

"Not a problem for an angel. As to what I'm doing here, that question is odd coming from a man of your arrogance. Who else would get a visit from an angel if not the high priest of Israel?"

"Well, yes, that's so, but I still think you're a madman or demon possessed. A regular citizen doesn't just walk into my house."

"Someone here certainly has a demon. That's for sure." I sigh. "I imagine you will want some proof that I am an angel, right?"

"Yes, indeed." Caiaphas has wrapped the robe about his waist and assumed a supercilious pose.

I twitch my fingers. The wine goblet jumps from Caiaphas's hand and raises upright in the air, once again filled with wine. I move my fingers, and the goblet moves in front of Caiaphas's astonished eyes until it is over his head. I whistle, and the goblet rotates, dumping the wine onto Caiaphas's upturned face. "Sorry. I never claimed to be a dexterous angel. Here." I move both hands, and the water basin rises up and dumps the water on Caiaphas's head. "Oops. Oh well, all clean now."

Caiaphas, still a bit bewildered, doesn't even react when a towel suddenly appears in his hand. He towels himself off. "What kind of a name is Augie?"

"An angelic one. While we're talking about names, does Caiaphas derive from *Keipha*? That means 'a hollowed-out rock.' When your parents named you, did they think your head resembled a hollow rock?"

"For an angel, you're about as insulting as that Jesus character."

"Funny you should mention him. That's why I'm here."

"Yes? He died for blasphemy and rebellion." Now that he is dry, Caiaphas has regained his dignity. He sniffs. "His trial was all done quite properly."

"We won't argue that particular fantasy. I just came to ask you if it ever entered your mind to consider that he might have been telling the truth." I am leaning against the doorframe, enjoying the sun.

"What? Don't be absurd."

"Nice to know that your little bath in wine and water didn't wash away your arrogance. Look, Caiaphas, of all the people in Israel, you are the one man who knows the most about Scripture." Accustomed to, and receptive of, praise, Caiaphas nonetheless looks a bit suspicious. Maybe I have been a little caustic. Jesus keeps telling me I have to work on that.

"Yes, I suppose you could say that." Caiaphas is speaking slowly and enunciating carefully as though looking for an insult.

"Okay. Caiaphas, how many verses foretold a messiah?"

"I don't know."

"Over three hundred," I say.

"That's quite a lot. Surely many of them will not have been fulfilled by Jesus and, thus, would repudiate his claim."

"Find one."

"I beg your pardon?"

"Sorry, I can't use words any smaller. *Find. One.*"

"Well . . ."

"Let me help. Look at Psalm 22. The psalmist declares, 'Scorned by men, and despised by the people.' Jesus got that courtesy of you. Thanks so much for helping fulfill prophecy."

"Now, wait . . ." Caiaphas doesn't like where this conversation is going; his posture has become defensive, and his eyes dart around as if looking for a way to flee.

I continue, "Going on: 'He trusts in the Lord, let him rescue him. Let him deliver him, since he delights in Him.' Didn't your apes in the crowd say that very thing about Jesus? Be sure to thank them for me. They also helped fulfill prophecy."

"Uh . . ." Caiaphas now looks completely undone. He doesn't like other people using Scripture to indict him. He is accustomed to that being *his* prerogative.

"The psalmist goes on to say, 'They pierced my hands and my feet.' Also, 'They divide my garments among them' (NIV). Ah, those Romans! They do know how to throw a great execution. Tell me—did you sneak them a copy of Scripture, or did they fulfill prophecy quite by accident?"

I provide twenty more unambiguous prophecies, and Caiaphas looks more uncertain and haunted. Then Caiaphas brightens. "Wait. Jesus is from Nazareth in Galilee. In Micah, it is written: 'But you, Bethlehem Ephrathah, though you are small among the clans of Judah, out of you will come for me one who will be Ruler over Israel' (NIV). What about that quote? That proves he can't have been the Messiah."

"See there, Caiaphas—I told you that you were the Scripture man."

Caiaphas has a look of relief on his face. He feels he has quashed the debate. He has a mind to be expansive and hospitable to this angel. "Come inside. It's getting hot. Do angels drink wine, by the way? Do let me get you some." Suppressing a satisfied chuckle, he extends his arm, indicating I should precede him back into the coolness of his chamber.

We enter the shade of the room. Over in the corner, I see a man seated comfortably in a chair. He is tall, muscular, and unreasonably handsome, with long, oiled hair held back by a gold circlet. His raiment is a thick indigo garment with light gold cable woven throughout. He greets me with a smug grin. "Having a pleasant day, Augie?"

"I figured you'd be here. You know, we angels all try so hard to like you, but it's difficult for us to be neighborly while we're busy puking."

"What?" says Caiaphas. "Who are you speaking to?" Caiaphas glances around the empty room.

I accept a wine goblet from Caiaphas and then say, "Okay, Caiaphas, let's show you our special guest." I snap my fingers, and suddenly, the seated man becomes visible to Caiaphas.

"Oh my! Another angel?" Caiaphas is again bewildered but has a benign expression on his face.

"No angel wears that particular brand of perfume, Caiaphas. You might call it Eau de Brimstone. Meet Satan."

Satan stands slowly, a grin, slightly predatory, spreading across that handsome face. "Augie, always the funny angel, even when all God's plans are, shall we say, gone to hell."

I hand Satan my goblet of wine and fetch another for myself. Caiaphas is frozen in place, eyes darting between me and Satan.

"Caiaphas, sorry to disappoint you, but that little quote from Micah about the Messiah coming from Bethlehem?"

"Yes?"

"Jesus' father, Joseph, was born in Bethlehem and returned there for that first census called by Caesar Augustus. Jesus was born while Joseph and his wife were in Bethlehem. By the way, Joseph was of the house of David, the house from which the Messiah was prophesied to come."

"You mean . . . ?" whispers Caiaphas.

"There, there, Caiaphas. An honest mistake. Any high priest of all Israel might have made it. Let's just drink a toast, the three of us."

Satan says, "You surely aren't drinking to my triumph, are you? Not thinking of switching sides, hmm?"

Satan really has to find a physical manifestation that doesn't have a smirk on the face, I think. *Makes it hard to drink the wine.* "Become a demon? No offense, but I'd rather become a human, and you already know my opinion of them. Actually, I thought we'd drink a toast to open doors."

Satan looks confused. "Open doors?"

"What?" says Caiaphas.

Just then, the door to Caiaphas's room opens, and I say, "That's door number one." There stands a breathless Roman soldier. He has a slightly smug grin on his face.

"Sorry to interrupt, Lord Caiaphas, but the proconsul dispatched me to advise you that Jesus' body is gone. The stone was rolled away."

I look over at a speechless Satan and can't help crowing, "And that's door number two!"

The messenger is enjoying Caiaphas's shocked discomfort. "Our guards said an angel came and moved the stone from the door. None of Jesus' disciples was anywhere near. We searched the tomb. There is no other way out, and we can't find the body anywhere. The proconsul begs me to advise you that the guards will be disciplined, but this is now your problem. Good day."

The soldier leaves as Caiaphas collapses into a chair. Satan's face contorts in a mask of raging hatred. He is shaking and gasping in his fury. He extends a trembling arm at me and points his finger.

"Don't blame me, Satan. I don't do doors." I have a benign smile on my face. Jesus has pulled Satan's pants down—again.

Pulsing with wrath, Satan growls, "This isn't over, Angel." He vaporizes and is gone.

"Now, what Satan just showed us is a triumph of resolve over intelligence." I pull a chair close to Caiaphas and sit down beside him. I put an arm around the shaken priest. "I'm through joking now, Caiaphas. I only do it while Satan is around, just to irritate him. You have placed yourself in a most difficult situation. History will record that Caiaphas, the one man in Israel most academically qualified to recognize the Messiah, was the very one who had him put to death. Don't bother blaming it on the Romans. We both know you were the instigator. You can take some comfort, however, in realizing that you were only an instrument of God's plan. Salvation couldn't occur without Jesus' death and resurrection. You can take some comfort in one other thing."

"What's that?"

"Satan allowed you to see him in his pretty skin. For your sake, I'm glad he wasn't in the embodiment that reflects his heart. I doubt even an angel could have preserved your sanity in that case."

"So what happens now?"

"What happens now? The beginning happens now. It is all a bit new to me as well, so I have to check in with my superiors about my next assignment. In a way, you are lucky, Caiaphas. A lot of folks will only come to the realization of Jesus as Lord of all after they draw their last breath. You have a lot of breath remaining. I am sure your men reported that, while on the cross, Jesus asked his Father to 'forgive them, for they know not what they do.' He wasn't just referring to the soldiers. He was including you, Priest. He has asked his Father, God in heaven, to forgive his son's murderers. You have a choice to make, Caiaphas. Accept him or not. You must give up that which is familiar in order to grasp that which is divine. The only thing riding on it is your eternal life—something that you Sadducees don't believe in."

As my body evanesces, Caiaphas shouts, "But what do I do now?"

"Choose well, Caiaphas; choose well."

After-Action Summary

Caiaphas was my first experience with a human after Jesus' resurrection. In many ways, Caiaphas was a prototype for the millions of humans I have encountered in the nearly two ensuing millennia. As for Caiaphas, he was a garden-variety narcissist of boring hypocrisy. He was the type of man who, if you went to his house to ask if anyone there was sick, would take his own temperature and, finding it normal, would report to you that everyone was healthy. When applied to politics, this attitude persuades the person to conclude that the health of his nation is ineluctably tied to the preservation of his own power and position. Americans must love this sort of person; they elect so many of them to high office.

Because Jesus was a threat to him, Caiaphas's first and only consideration was to destroy him. While espousing a religion that prophesied a messiah and while purportedly representing a people who sought the freedom that would be brought by a messiah, Caiaphas gave no thought to the possibility that Jesus was a fulfillment of Scripture. It has been my repetitive experience with humans that sound intelligence is no guarantee of revelation knowledge. In fact, it may be an impediment, for the possessor normally rejects faith as a valid means to enlightenment. Since "without faith, it is impossible to please God" (Hebrews 11:6), such smart guys are at a distinct disadvantage.

The Roman occupation was a prerequisite to the spread of the gospel. It was the presence of an occupation force that prompted Israel's receptivity to a messiah. It was the *pax romana*—the peace and stability brought to the known world by Roman dominance—that allowed Jews to come to Jerusalem for Passover and return home with the gospel message. The glory of God has been best manifest to the children of Israel when they are oppressed. Indeed, two major holidays—Passover (covered in Exodus) and Purim (covered in Esther)—celebrate deliverances that occurred when the Jews were in foreign captivity. How appropriate that God's greatest redemptive act—salvation through Jesus—occurred when Israel itself was captive to a foreign power.

Caiaphas was granted forgiveness and a life of sufficient duration to repent and accept Christ as Savior. Scripture indicates he did not. How about you? When Jesus asked his Father to forgive those who were killing him, he was including you. Yes, you with this book in your hands. All humans are accessories to the murder of the Son of God. Can you free yourself from the constraints of intellectual myopia and reach with your heart for that which is divine? Or, like Caiaphas, will you end up vying for the title of Smartest Man in Hell?

Chapter 26

Case File A-23-AD

He steps out of the barn. The morning is beautiful, and the sun is removing the modest chill of night. He bids goodbye to the shepherds who came in the early morning to worship his son. Worship. They said an angel of the Lord had come to announce this special birth last night. Special birth! The baby had been born in a stinking hovel with no one but his father to attend the mother. Joseph kneels, tossing pebbles on the ground as he hears Mary cooing to the baby.

Were Joseph a weeping man, this would be an appropriate moment. He had moved to Nazareth years ago, seeking work. He had fallen in love with Mary, and they had pledged to marry. Then had come the confession of pregnancy. He and Mary had not been intimate, so Joseph had known he was not the father. Mary had told him the story of the angel explaining that this child had been conceived by something called the Holy Spirit. Joseph is a simple man and not much given to complex spiritual issues, but he simply had not believed her. How could he? After Mary's announcement, his options had been to follow through with the marriage or to announce his rejection of her, the latter option certain to destroy her reputation and make her an outcast. Had he chosen the latter option, Joseph would have been viewed sympathetically as an innocent man misled by a vixen. There was only one problem: Joseph loved her. He had been hurt and angry, but her smile still made his heart sing. One night, in his dreams, an angel had confirmed Mary's story. Joseph had married her.

On the one hand, Joseph had been glad, because he now had a confirmed explanation of the pregnancy. On the other hand, however, what had the angel actually known about what he was asking of Joseph? When Mary's pregnancy had become obvious, even the dumbest country boy in the backwoods community of Nazareth had been able to do the calculations and know that Mary was carrying a child conceived out of wedlock, a bastard.

In this community, marriage after conception doesn't erase the stigma. Instead of viewing him sympathetically, they scorn Joseph. Those who think him the father view him as a beast that has taken advantage of this poor girl. Most of Mary's family feel this way, only not strongly enough to keep from shunning her. Those who think Joseph is not the father view him with a laughing contempt and whisper insults about marrying a woman impregnated by another man. The story of a heavenly impregnation goes nowhere in this narrow-minded world. Joseph is from Bethlehem and has no family nearby to support him. Proximity doesn't mean much, though, because Mary's nearby family has shunned her. On her side, Mary has only her cousin Elizabeth's support. Elizabeth doesn't live nearby, however, and has been confined since she is far along in her own pregnancy.

This ill treatment was why Joseph and his wife had traveled alone through a dangerous land. No one traveled alone on these roads unless he was mad or being shunned. They had gone first to Jerusalem for the Feast of Tabernacles, and no one from Galilee had accompanied them. Joseph had kept them over, figuring that the child should be born away from the nattering world of Nazareth, and the census requirement that he return to his hometown of Bethlehem, not far from Jerusalem, had been a convenient excuse.

He had been saddened to find, upon reaching Bethlehem, that word of the pregnancy had preceded them via others returning for the census. His family would not take them in. Bethlehem had been crowded because of the census, but there still should have been room somewhere. Everyone who had turned him away had exhibited a clipped, unfriendly manner. The man who'd let them use his barn had been sympathetic but clearly worried someone would find out he had been kind to this couple.

Joseph had helped to deliver his own child. This task was not a man's work, and now he was ceremonially unclean. Soon, when Mary was recovered, they would return to Nazareth and more community slander.

"How is the proud father?"

Startled, Joseph jumps up and spins around. I am standing there, leaning against the barn, a piece of hay dangling from my mouth. "Who are you? I didn't hear you come up," Joseph demands.

"I just got here. I am pretty light on my feet. I thought I'd come by and say hello."

"You must have run into the shepherds, and they told you their story. My son is inside the barn." Joseph points his finger at the door and moves as though to walk away.

"I didn't come to see him. I already know him. He and I go back a long way. I really came to see you."

Joseph is confused. "What do you mean by 'go back a long way'? He was just born."

"I knew him before that. I'm an angel. Name's Augie." I figure that after a night like this and the previous angel visit, Joseph won't be too shocked at my admission. I am correct.

"Right. Another angel. Where were you last night when I needed help with Mary? Or for that matter, where have the angels been while our families and so-called friends turned their backs on us?"

"I'll apologize if it will make any difference. You know enough Scripture to understand that most people whom the Lord selects for a special task end up suffering for it."

"Well, Angel, I am not a smart man. I'm not equipped to do God's work. I surely can't raise a son to be a prophet or whatever."

"He won't be a prophet. He is the Messiah, the one whom all the prophets spoke about."

"Messiah? There have been a lot of them around lately. This child is going to be another one of them, a pretender?"

"Angels don't announce pretenders. Jesus is the true Messiah. Satan just threw the pretenders out there to muddy the water. As for your suitability to be the earthly father to the Messiah, God doesn't need your ability, only your availability."

Joseph looks down and sighs deeply. "All right. So what happens from here?"

"Well, you'll be happy to learn that you won't be going back to Galilee until Jesus is considerably older. You won't have to face the gossip for a while." I hunker down and trace a few lines in the dirt while Joseph looks on abstractedly.

"Why won't we be going back?"

"Another angel will come and tell you where to go, when to go, and why. You won't like the reason why, but it will all work out."

"What do I do until then?" Joseph seems to have become compliant, or he is just exhausted with all the changes in his life. His voice is a monotone, and he has a thousand-mile stare.

"Your relatives from around here will be coming by. They will fall in love with Jesus and with Mary. You will stay here and work alongside them for a few years until it's time to go."

"But we'll get back to Galilee eventually?"

"Yes, because you are a loving husband, and you know Mary will need her family as she raises Jesus and all the other children you will have by her. Her family will also come to love Jesus."

"So I will get to be a real father someday?"

"You already are—perhaps the most real father that ever lived. Certainly the most important in history, even more so than Abraham. God has trusted *you* to raise his son."

"His son? When the angel said *Holy Spirit*, I didn't think . . ."

"His son. The only human ever so loved that God would count him as his son. Can you imagine the love and trust that God is placing in you?" I know that Joseph is having a hard time assimilating all of this information. Even I am having trouble fitting it all into my head.

Joseph is silent, shaken by the immensity of my words. "So what happens after we get back to Galilee?"

"You will raise your son. The rumors will continue, and they will be a burden to your family. Angels, believe it or not, don't have advance knowledge of things to come. I can only relate what I was told."

"Tell me what you can, Angel."

"Come on over here. Let's sit." I sit on a low stone wall, and Joseph joins me. "Joseph, you will die before Jesus begins his ministry."

"Ah."

"He will preach and perform miracles. He will give prophecies, even though he is not a prophet. His end will not be pleasant."

Joseph looks down. "But he's so . . . little. I can't imagine him grown, much less becoming the man you describe. From what you say, at least I won't live to see his end." Joseph seems to take a small measure of comfort from that and makes full eye contact with me.

"His ministry will result in the redemption of the children of Israel and more beyond that. More Scripture will be written about him and added to the Torah. His mother, Mary, will be revered. Some communities of faith will even worship her. You, however, will be largely ignored in those Scriptures and in the years to come. Jesus will be the Son of God, not the son of Joseph. In history, you will simply be regarded as a carpenter who raised his son to be a carpenter."

"What's a carpenter?"

"Someone who works in wood."

"Not much wood around here. I'm a stonemason."

"When his story is told in other languages, it will be easier to call him a carpenter."

"So people will forget me?"

"Yes, almost completely."

Joseph is nodding his head in comprehension. "And for now, I will raise a son who will face a sad ending?"

"Yes, a sad ending, but it is not given to me to know it fully."

"We will still have to live with our townsfolk questioning his conception?"

"That particular controversy will continue for thousands of years. It will always be brought into doubt by men who desperately want there to have been no Messiah."

"That sounds a bit foolish."

"No argument there."

"So all that you are telling me: I will raise God's son as my own, suffer the gossip of ignorant people, die early, and be forgotten. Am I understanding you correctly?"

"Yes. No human in current Scripture or Scripture yet to be written will ever have as important a job yet be so totally unheralded."

"Well, Angel, my mind cannot grasp all that you say."

"Nevertheless, it is what I am told about your future. What do you plan to do with this Son of God?"

Joseph stands up as he hears the baby crying. "Please forgive me, Augie. My wife and son need me." Joseph goes back toward the barn. He turns. "What do I plan to do with this Son of God, Augie? I plan to love him." He goes into the filthy barn.

I wait until I hear Jesus' cries become gurgles of happiness as Joseph sings to his son and cuddles him against his neck. I smile and fade into the morning sun.

After-Action Summary

Much is said of the maternal instinct, almost nothing about a paternal instinct. Yet human men will frequently risk, and lose, their lives to save or protect children who are not even their own. Even though this instinct is a God-given trait, still, I applaud those human men who are so motivated. The man who raises a man-child not of his own begetting is a man after God's heart and, much like Joseph, equally forgettable to this world. I was blunt with Joseph about the future. His acceptance and courage confirmed for me what Papa already knew: Joseph was the perfect man for this role.

Scripture isn't clear on the precise time of the Christmas story, but none of the uncertainty impugns either the accuracy of Scripture or the validity of the salvation message. Shepherds do not graze their animals at night in winter, when all the grass is dead. So Christ's birth did not occur in December, when the grass around Bethlehem would have all been dead. Joseph and Mary observed the pilgrimage holidays as noted elsewhere in Scripture (Luke 2:41), and the Feast of Tabernacles is a pilgrimage holiday. It falls in the autumn, after the harvest and partly in celebration of it. Joseph accomplished two goals by his pilgrimage to Jerusalem and his attendance at the census in nearby Bethlehem.

Humans should recall that Jesus was born into a society of pharisaical judgment. Levitical law was distorted and expanded, visited upon the children of Israel by a smug, self-righteous clergy. Recall how the Pharisees accused Jesus' disciples of working on a Sabbath because they plucked grains of wheat to eat as they walked along (Matthew 12:1-2). Such a judgmental attitude has a trickle-down effect that creates judgment among the regular citizens. In order for Jesus to be rejected in his own hometown at the start of his ministry (Matthew 13:54-58), God had to orchestrate a stigma that attached to the family. Considering that Nazareth was a backwoods location in a backward Roman province (John 1:46: "Nazareth! Can anything good come from there?"), simply being from a working-class family was not a sufficient negative for people to question Jesus' suitability as a prophet, much less the Messiah. Look at how modern unbelievers scoff at the virgin birth. Is there any reason to assume these judgmental Galileans would have been any more accepting or forgiving? Even the Romans, under Augustus, had made laws dealing harshly with anyone appearing to act outside of strict marital behavior.

So why was I sent to Joseph at this time? I suspect God thought it only fair that Joseph know a little of what was in store. By his own admission, Joseph was a simple man—simple but deep and honest. He knew he was inadequate to raise the Son of God. Consider how the men whom God commissioned for great things responded to God's call; read the words of Moses, Gideon, and Isaiah. They all first expressed self-doubt and inadequacy. But Joseph did know how to love a child, and that is what he did. Joseph was taken from his physical life before Jesus' death on the cross, and that was God's mercy. Mary survived Jesus' crucifixion. Joseph's tender heart would have been destroyed.

What may a human father take from the story of Joseph? The answer is simple: raise your children as though they were children of God, for that is, after all, what they are. If you perceive children as merely byproducts of your biologic function, you will completely miss the wonder and, indeed, the majesty of their true origin. You will miss the enormity of the trust that God places in you to raise his child.

The degree to which Joseph is a forgotten man in this earthly world is the degree to which he is revered and celebrated among the host of heaven. When Paul yearned to hear the words "Well done, good and faithful servant," he was hoping to hear the same words that had greeted Joseph when he was taking his first breath of eternal life. And thus it should be among you, the earthly fathers of heaven's children. What will the host of heaven think of your work as a father to a child of God?

Chapter 27

Case File M-7243-AD

Cindy looks out of the bedroom window. Daffodils and azaleas add pastel splashes to the vivid green grass of midspring. Dogwood blossoms sway in a light breeze. Will today be the day? She looks over at Joey. He's on an air bed, slumbering through the subtle hum of the pump. It has been a year of lasts: last Halloween, last Christmas, last snowstorm, and, now, last springtime. Joey is seven years old. Nine months ago, he had developed a vague ache that the family had attributed to growing pains. When it had begun to affect his walking, they had gone to the doctor. Joey had been diagnosed with something called osteogenic sarcoma, a cancer of the bone.

Cindy could recall the helpless fear. A mother would attack hell itself with a bucket of spit if she saw a visible threat to her child, but this stealth terrorist of cancer . . . She had been devastated by the amputation of Joey's right leg and then encouraged by the hope of chemotherapy. Devastation had returned when Joey's little body simply couldn't tolerate the medication. He had nearly died from a pneumonia that overwhelmed an immune system weakened by the chemicals. Reducing the dose had merely slowed the progressive march of the cancer.

Joey is now home to die. Hospice has been supporting the whole family throughout the last months, but it can't last much longer. His frail body just can't endure much more.

Cindy has no more tears. She can't cuddle her child because of the pain. The narcotics and the air bed keep him comfortable, but he resides in twilight awareness. He occasionally twitches like a sleeping puppy, but he now has a beautiful smile on his face. How strange. She walks over to stand beside him and traces his smile with the tip of her finger. He awakens at her touch.

"Hi, Mommy."

"Hi, sweetheart."

"Please don't cry, Mommy. I'm not hurting today." This is the worst part—Joey trying to comfort his inconsolable mommy. That smile of his can still turn her heart into a puddle in the middle of her chest.

"I'm glad, sweetest boy. You know that it hurts Mommy's heart when her little boy hurts."

"Can you see her, Mommy?"

"See who, sweetheart?"

"The angel." Joey points over his head. "Right there. She's real pretty but not as pretty as you, Mommy." Cindy looks where Joey is pointing. Nothing. Just then, the bedroom door opens, and I walk in. Cindy has been expecting a hospice nurse and is surprised at my appearance—a little rumpled, not terribly professional.

"Hello, Cindy. Hiya, Joey."

"Are you with hospice?" asks Cindy.

"Not exactly." I give her my most wonderful smile, my green eyes seeming to dance and sparkle above rosy cheeks.

"You're another angel," whispers Joey, a look of wonder on his face.

"This is a smart boy you have here, Mommy. Yes, I'm an angel. My name is Augie."

Cindy feels fear grip her heart. "Is it time? Have you come to take him?"

"Soon, but not just yet. Papa sent me on this special assignment."

"Papa?"

"God. Actually, Jesus calls him Papa, so we call him Papa. He invites you to call him Papa as well."

Cindy has a mixture of grief, confusion, and enlightenment on her face. "What special assignment did Papa send you down for?"

"You."

"Me?"

"Papa knows what it's like for a parent to have to stand by and watch their child lose his life; after all, that's what he did with Jesus. Papa hates that every human must die, and the fancy arguments about Original Sin don't give any comfort to a mother like you. Papa has to deal with the result of this fallen world, but his heart breaks especially for the folks left behind when a young one dies. Someone like you."

"Then why is he taking Joey? Why can't he just leave him here with me?"

"I don't pretend to understand Papa's mind, but I know we shouldn't worry too much about Joey—that kid is going to love where he is going. Come to the window with me for a second."

As I stand up and Cindy walks to the window with me, Joey asks, "Will it hurt when I die?"

"No, son. For you, it's going to be like slipping into a bathtub full of warm water. You can even pee in the tub. Papa won't mind."

Joey giggles at the thought.

"Cindy, look out there." Cindy looks out the window and is stunned by the vision. Children by the hundreds—no, the thousands—are there, looking back at her with happy smiles.

She sees boys and girls in varied period clothing: some with rich Italian Renaissance fashion, others in Victorian school dress, a child of the Ottoman Empire, a cluster of children with yellow Stars of David on their shirts, a child in the garments of American Southern slavery. Some children hold dolls, others hold a hoop and stick, and others ride penny-farthing bicycles. "Papa had them dress in the clothes of their physical time on earth, just so you'll see that every child, from all times, is here. You've heard the phrase 'No child left behind'? That phrase applies better to heaven than to any human endeavor on this earth. Come on back over." I sit Cindy back down next to Joey, where she takes his hand. The light behind his eyes is dimming.

"I love you, Mommy."

"And I will love you forever, my sweetest boy." The tears are coming again but not the sobbing. Cindy now knows that Joey will be among a host of loving children.

I lean over and whisper to her, "Watch." I wave my hand. "Cindy, meet the angel Joey told you about earlier. Her name is Raya." Suddenly, Cindy sees that Joey has been cradled not by his air bed but by a female angel of surpassing beauty with the softest smile. Joey's head is against her breast. With her free hand, Raya reaches out to touch Cindy's cheek. The mother, the child, and the angel have now become one, a continuous circle. Joey's breath eases out with a sigh through smiling lips. Raya glimmers and then fades slowly away. Joey's body is still on the bed.

"I know you don't want to let go of his hand, Mommy, but come back to the window again for just a second." Cindy comes to the window and sees her Joey being greeted by the children and hugged by the older ones. He has two strong legs, and the haggard look of the past year is gone from his face. He turns around to look at his mommy. He blows her a kiss and then turns, laughing, to join the others at play. Then, as Raya did, the children glimmer and fade, blending into the springtime flowers.

"Cindy, you saw it just like it is. Joey already has a new, perfect heavenly body. Papa wanted you to know that. This body on the bed—well, you can do whatever it is that humans do with vacant bodies. Just remember that it's now a shell, and the thing worth cherishing about your son is alive and well. Raya accompanied him, and he is in the very best of safekeeping, waiting for his mommy to show up."

"Thank you, Augie." She sits down and gathers Joey up, free to embrace the little body that will now feel no pain at her touch.

"No, thank Papa. I don't know why he chose you, but I think he wants you to be his witness on earth. Write a book, give talks, and work through hospice. Tell all the parents the truth of what you've seen."

"Will Joey miss me? Will he remember me?"

"He won't exactly miss you, because that suggests a degree of pain. He won't have any pain. He will certainly remember you. What he will feel is anticipation—kind of a happy excitement at the thought that you will be showing up someday."

"I will still miss him, still cry. Is that ungrateful to God?"

"No, Cindy. Scripture tells you, in Thessalonians, that Christians 'don't grieve like those who have no hope.' Your grief is proportionate to the joy and love you felt for this child, this gift of God. Grief isn't anger at God for taking back his gift. In a way, grief is a sacrificial tribute to the God who provided you with the gift of Joey in the first place. God feels that grief and will transform it into limitless joy one day. Meanwhile"—I kiss my fingers and place them on Cindy's forehead—"Raya and I are here for you, as close as a prayer. Trust me; from now on, when you stand, you will cast a double shadow from now until eternity."

After-Action Summary

I teased Raya about Joey saying his mommy was prettier than Raya. After she stuck her tongue out at me, Raya got a little solemn and said, "That's the only thing about being human that I wish I could experience—being a mother, having a creation spring from my own body. It's an intimacy that is unknowable to male humans and to angels. When the Scriptures talk about man and woman both being of God's nature, maybe that's the part of God that he gave to women. Only God and female humans have the experience of something separating from their being and becoming fully human, fully loved. Augie, what's wrong? You've never been this quiet."

"In truth, Raya, I don't know. Something has churned me up."

Raya is looking at me with a smile on her face and tears in her eyes. "Augie, turn around," she whispers.

I turn, and there is Jesus. His smile alone, if humans could see him, would have people knocking down the gates of heaven, demanding entry. I am so glad that I am in the skin so that I can actually *feel* his presence.

"Augie, you have been changing. You gave a pledge to Cindy that you would be with her—something I have never seen you do before. Raya, do you think Augie is ready?"

"I think so, Lord."

Jesus touches two fingers to his lips and then presses his fingers against my chest. I feel his eyes and his fingers on me, in me, and around me as a thrill of warmth shudders through me. "Augie, you were well on your way. I am merely speeding up the process. You are now—"

"Filled with the love of mankind," I finish for him.

Jesus' smile becomes delighted laughter, and Raya joins him. "Oh Augie! How I love you! And how I love that you now love my creation. Raya and Sid and others here have come to this point, each in their own time. This is your time. I promise you that your visits to earth will never be the same. Where are you going first?"

"With your permission, Lord, back to Cindy. She still needs to grieve, and I am going back to go cry with her."

Jesus smiles again. "I expected nothing less. Are you going with him, Raya?"

"I wouldn't miss it for the world, Lord."

Chapter 28

Case File M-7244-AD

There is a claustrophobic heaviness to the low clouds over the city. Icy rain sheets down onto the high buildings, advertising signs and architectural details blurring like a postmodern painting. The cold and damp intrude beneath umbrellas and upturned collars, compelling pedestrians toward any available shelter. The sun is rare and renegade in this season. Vehicles are driven cautiously; low gear and four-wheel drive are improbably necessary on urban streets made dangerous by black ice.

This time of year is difficult for humans. The holidays are gone, taking with them all their nostalgic pleasure. The days are short, and the weather sentences many people to lengthy incarcerations indoors with that most unpleasant of cell mates: themselves. It is both the worst of times and the winter of discontent.

This time of year, with all its cold and dark, is rocket fuel for any existing human depression. Grief is magnified, sorrow and loss becoming transcendent in the human soul. Minor sadness becomes misery on steroids. Emergency rooms see double the number of suicide attempts, and psychiatric facilities admit double the number of patients with suicidal thoughts. Psychiatrists begin to second-guess their choice of specialty. It appears that all humanity is infected.

But not quite everyone is afflicted. Cindy seems immune to this contagion, despite having more than the average human's quota of mourning. It has been three years of human time since she buried the flesh body of her son, Joey. She still has her moments of crying and aching nostalgia that make a person want to conjure a lost loved one from the empty air. His birthdays are, and will probably always be, hard for her. But there is no anger, no vitriolic mantra repeated endlessly against a heartless God. Cindy has met many such people and has even had some success in exorcising their bitterness.

I should mention that it has also been three years since Jesus filled me with the true love of humanity in much the same way Papa fills humans with the Holy Spirit. And just like humans, I didn't realize it had ever been absent until it was given. My bosses have pretty much left me with Cindy. Except for the odd quickie assignment elsewhere in time or place, usually when Cindy is in peaceful sleep, I am here. Raya has checked up on me, but not so much lately. I suspect that Jesus had a word with my immediate superiors and my assignment to Cindy is pretty much stable. She has a supportive husband, also a believer, but his faith is junior varsity compared to Cindy's.

So why am I here? I think Jesus wants me to learn from Cindy. Jesus, the man, permitted me to see him at his very best and at his weakest. I have also seen Cindy at her weakest and at her finest. I have held her head as grief shook her like a lantern in an earthquake; her sobs were so deep they seemed to emanate from the ground beneath her and explode out of her to batter the air around us. I know she wanted to die. First, she wished to stop the pain. After that, she wanted to die so that she could be with

Joey. Now she has learned that there is work yet to be done. And brother, has she done it! Even though my initial suggestion to her included joining hospice, it was spontaneous advice without prior thought. Having been a nurse herself, Cindy took that ball and ran. At first, I checked with Raya, my angel buddy, concerned that Cindy was hiding herself in busywork to avoid her own grief. Raya's mouth smiled as if to say, "Welcome, Augie," but her eyes had a "You're an idiot, Augie" look in them. She reassured me that Cindy's work was cathartic, therapeutic, and, far more important, godly. I hate it when Raya catches me out like that.

Cindy has worked with families of dying children. She knows when to talk with them and knows when to simply cry with them. Blonde, robust, and now eight months pregnant, Cindy is a bundle of power, a solar flare in a maternity suit. Depending on the need of the family, she can explode into a room like a supernova or seem to merely grow into a room like a silken sunrise. Her touch is light, and her love is palpable. So a human is teaching an angel how to love humanity. I hope she is proud of me. I don't do much. Sometimes I am there in spirit form and sometimes in the skin, following her around like an intern.

I think I'm going to be called away soon. Because I sometimes think my assignment is more for me than for Cindy (don't forget: I flunked angel charm school—twice), it's harder for me to reckon an end point to the job. Cindy will occasionally give me a quiet smile, and I think she knows something that I don't know. Yes, I love humans, but human females can still make me crazy.

We are leaving the hospital, and it has been a good day. The child whose family Cindy has been helping will be leaving the hospital in remission, which is always a happy, albeit temporary, state of relief. We enter the elevator. I am in the skin today, wearing my usual dapper attire of khakis, a windbreaker, an Angels ball cap, and running shoes. (Ninety percent of humans who wear running shoes don't run. Since 90 percent of humans can't be wrong, I don't run either.) The elevator stalls on the second floor. The doors open to let folks in, but the alarm rings, and the doors won't close.

Everybody grumbles good-naturedly as we get off and head down the hall. Everybody else takes the stairs down the one flight to the lobby level. Cindy protests that she can take the stairs. I, however, have become a hoverer and forbid it. What? Here I am, an angel, and I'm fretting over her and not stopping to talk it over with Jesus. My mind plays a little trick: since there are no psychiatrists in the angelic workforce, maybe I need an out-of-network consultation with a human shrink. That would be another story for the zip shop.

Anyway, we walk down the long corridor. To get to the next bank of elevators, we must pass through the adult cancer ward. Long before we reach the room, we hear shrill screaming and cursing coming from the patient in there. As we get near the room, a harried nurse comes out, taking deep breaths and putting her hands over her face. For a while, the screaming stops, as though the nurse had been the cause of the tirade.

"Tough night, Linda?" Cindy asks. She has spent so much time in this hospital that she is acquainted with all the nurses, even those on adult wards. Cindy puts a comforting hand on Linda's shoulder.

"Lord, Cindy, I stopped smoking ten years ago, but I've never had a nicotine craving like I have right now." Linda purses her lips and leans against the wall. "Well, you are hospice, and Mrs. Hearst is well known to you folks."

Cindy nods.

"So I'm betraying no confidences. She was a sweet old lady until the dementia turned her into this screaming witch. The dementia was part of a cancer syndrome, but they didn't put two and two together before she had driven her family off and the cancer was terminal. She is here to die, because she lost her apartment and the family won't take her in. It's so sad, but she makes it nearly impossible to stay kind when she's flaying you alive. I don't know, Cindy. I admire your faith and everything, but this kind of garbage makes it impossible for me to believe in a loving God. She didn't deserve what her family has done, even though I almost understand them."

Cindy nods her understanding just as the ranting begins again. She walks past Linda into the room. Linda gives me a "What the heck?" look and follows her in. So do I.

Mrs. Hearst is in full cry; her eyes unfocused, and only the curse words are intelligible. She looks at the two nurses without seeing them, continuing to roll her shoulders and bellow. She appears to be in her eighties. Her hospital gown is falling off one shoulder, exposing part of a wrinkled breast. Her hair is short, gray, dirty, and spiked from the pressure of her pillow. The seams in her face are deep, like convolutions on the surface of the brain. She has no teeth, and the screaming provides all nearby surfaces with a liberal coating of saliva. Her bedclothes are strewn about the floor. The air is redolent of urine, feces, and the sickly sweet breath of the near dead.

"Augie, talk to her." Cindy is totally calm.

"Who, me?" I don't know why I am in this room. I have no assignment here, and my bosses sent no instructions regarding this old woman.

Cindy looks at me with her usual smile. "Unless you have a miniature Augie in your pocket, yes, I mean you."

"But, Cindy, what can I say?" I am feeling a trifle desperate here. "I don't know how to handle her. I haven't been briefed."

"If you don't try, Augie, I'm going to ask Papa to make my water break right here and right now, and you can handle the delivery."

I gripe that the Bible must say something about humans not messing with angels. Then I remember where Jacob wrestled with an angel (Genesis 32:24-30), and I figure I'll be better off talking with Mrs. Hearst. I don't want the crowd back at the zip shop to find out that I wrestled with a pregnant human, especially if she beat me.

I look at Linda. I whisper, "What's her first name?"

Linda whispers back, "Elizabeth."

I take a chance. Softly, I say, "Hello, Lizzie."

The screaming stops. The woman turns to look at me, straight on with focused eyes. There is absolute silence. Then, slowly, her shoulders rise in delight, and she reaches out to me. "Daddy, it's you! You've come back!" The years seem to drop from her face and her demeanor. She still has a deep, ominous rumbling in each breath, but somehow she has become younger—much younger. "Daddy, come and sit with me." She scoots up toward the head of the bed, giving me room. She is bouncing on the bed, just like the child she has become. I look at Cindy, and she nods, smiling. Linda's incredulous face must be a mirror of my own, but I'm beginning to get a glimmer of understanding. *Why no guardian angels in the room? Hmmm.* I sit down and take her hand.

"Lizzie, you know that Daddy missed you."

She gazes at me with such love that if I'd had a human heart, it would have burst. "I know, Daddy. I know."

I am beginning to understand what Cindy, despite being only human, must have known. You might say Cindy *divined* it. A little angel humor there. "Lizzie, Daddy is so sorry that he was gone for so long."

Even without teeth, her smile is beautiful, and her speech is perfectly clear. "That's okay, Daddy. I'm just glad you're here." She leans her old, wizened head against my shoulder. Then, abruptly, she pulls away and looks at me. She seems a little uncertain, but mostly, she is a little coquette who is preparing to wrap Daddy around her finger. "You're not leaving me again, are you?"

"Never in this world, my love. If I go anywhere, Lizzie goes with Daddy."

She has the satisfied look of a benign tyrant who has gotten her way. "Daddy, I'm a little tired. Will you lie down next to me? Just until I go to sleep?"

I look at Linda. So undone by what she is seeing, she only shrugs. "Sure thing, sweetheart. Just like we used to do." I lie down on the bed, inhaling the odor of urine and feces. "Come on down and cuddle up." I raise my arm in invitation.

She gives a giggle and settles in, spooning up against my chest. Her hair tickles my chin; it smells of body odor and, vaguely, of corrupted, dying tissue. "There," she says. "Daddy, curl my hair around your fingers, like you used to do."

I don't mind the oil and particles of food in her hair as I twirl it around my fingers and massage her scalp. "Lizzie, it's been so long since I've been here. I bet you've had another birthday since I was here."

"Silly Daddy, yes, I am five years old." She snuggles further into the hollow of my arm. "Daddy, where have you been so long?"

"I was getting a house ready for us to move into. Mommy is already there, waiting for us."

"Can we go real soon?"

Linda is beginning to cry. Cindy's eyes are moist, but that halogen smile is as bright as ever.

"You bet, Lizzie—whenever you're ready."

"Maybe just a little nap; then we can go. Daddy?"

"Yes, my perfect princess?"

She gives a contented sigh. "It's been so long since you called me your princess." Her breathing is becoming labored, and I can feel, through her ribcage, that her heart rhythm is becoming irregular. "Will you sing me that lullaby that you always used to sing to me?"

I kiss her cheek and begin to sing softly, just above a whisper. "Hush, little baby, don't you cry. Papa's gonna sing you a lullaby..."

She, indeed, has shed the burden of years and become a child in my arms. This must be how her heavenly Papa has always seen her. I have always been limited—the angel who sees humans as they physically are, not as Jesus and Papa see them. And Raya. And Cindy. Lizzie's deeper breathing signals sleep, then shortens, and, finally, ceases altogether.

Linda is crying openly now, looking down as I embrace and kiss this smelly old woman. I don't know how Linda is going to handle what comes next. I look over at Cindy. No guardian angels. She knows. She smiles. "Good-bye, Augie."

I gather up Lizzie Hearst's spirit as I depart, and my physical body fades from view. Lizzie's spirit now is a weightless burden of joy that is the best of girl and woman as I prepare to take her home to Papa. I hear Cindy laughing and saying to a stunned Linda, "Isn't that just like a man? Disappearing whenever there is work to be done. Come on. While I help you with this stuff, I'll explain about Augie and angels and, yeah, maybe we can talk about your faith."

Before you ask questions about my arrival, the answers are yes and no. Yes, Jesus was there. And no, he wasn't the least surprised to see me.

After-Action Summary

Papa has used humans for a variety of tasks, but Cindy being a tutor to an angel is beyond strange. Yes, I will probably tell the story back at the zip shop. I'm excited about my new assignments.

Cindy doesn't need me anymore. I wonder how soon it was after Joey died that she stopped needing me and began to mold me. I may go back for an occasional dose of her humanity from time to time. I expect I may even pass angel charm school, if needed.

I am focusing more on the loss of a child by a parent or sibling, because it is so profound, but what I learned applies to all similar levels of grief. Cindy showed me what humans have to overcome when they lose someone. An unbelieving world wants you to think that there is no God or, if there is, that he took your loved one away. The world considers anger at God to be an acceptable alternative to having no belief in God. Nonbelievers don't mind as long as your grief contains no loving faith in God. What Cindy learned was that God didn't take Joey away; he took him *back*. There is a difference. The same God who gave this exquisite gift that provided joy has now taken it back, and it is in safekeeping until he takes *you* back. No matter how much a human loves another human, you must confess that he or she is safer out of this world than in it. Some humans say the USA, for example, is going to hell. Not so. The USA is turning the whole country into a theme park with the name Hell on the front gate. Americans are simply enjoying themselves to death.

Cindy learned that there are several ways to help people who are in the midst of such grief. For the acutely grieving, there are no words and no enlightening. You cry with them and bear their sorrow with them. It is afterward that you can turn their hearts to the true nature of God in the midst of this tragedy. As I have said before, for nonbelievers, physical death is an arbitrary end point; this notion is as flawed and erroneous as the humans who believe it.

Human commentators have broken grief into stages: denial, anger, bargaining, grief, and acceptance. Many humans get hung up at or before the anger and grief. Some will acknowledge God but be angry with him for doing something beyond their comprehension. I think some humans end up this way because they never learned gratitude in the first place, never acknowledged that God was the source of this small person who engendered so much adoration in their hearts. If a person truly understands that the child belonged to God before birth and that God continues that possession while entrusting the child to the parents for safekeeping, that knowledge brings a sense of calm and gratefulness.

Some humans take a rebellious course. When freed from its cosmetic rationalization, their thinking sounds like this: "Okay, God, you broke my heart, and I am going to get even with you by deciding to stop believing in your existence. So there!" While I don't doubt the true depth of their despair, I wonder at their power of reason. Going to someone like this for spiritual enlightenment would be like a woman seeking marital advice from Henry VIII.

Anyone who thinks that acceptance is the end stage of dealing with grief must not have met Cindy. For Christians, there is a sixth stage, that of transcendence. When you live in the certainty of an eventual eternity in the company of your lost beloved, you experience a joy that demands its own duplication. The joy is its own clarion, prompting the possessor to seek out those still grief-stricken and to coax them into the same state of grace. Is it hard? Yes. Actually, without God's help, it is impossible. Remember when Jesus made his mission statement in the synagogue at the start of his ministry? In Luke 4:18-19, he referred to proclaiming freedom for the prisoners and release of the oppressed. Not all imprisonment and oppression are physical. Release from grief for humans was on Jesus' mind when he began his ministry.

And Lizzie Hearst? What better release? Papa cleared away all the rage and confusion of her later years. He didn't return her to a rational, mature human—someone who would have been aware that her adult family was no longer around. Papa carried her back to the innocence of her childhood, when her love was unguarded and her joy of life unbounded. As I have said before, Jesus told humans that unless you become like children, you cannot enter his kingdom. Lizzie Hearst, at the end of her physical life, became a top-notch candidate to live in one of Papa's many mansions.

Chapter 29

Debrief

My bosses have reviewed my complete work, this *magnum augius*, and they were a bit smug. Being human, you have never seen a smug cherub. You don't want to. Normally, each of the four faces looks like an IRS auditor. Add smugness to the expression, and you have something like an effervescent Moloch. The true purpose of this work was to "bring Augie to maturity." Now I am tasked with a debrief: What have I learned in this exercise, and what, for humans, are the salient points? For that, we consult the After-Action Summaries.

- The soul is the part of a human that Papa values. It has always been a waveform, never a particle. Your body, the vehicle that you drive during your physical time on earth, is only important in that you keep it holy (set apart) and in good working order. There are no trade-ins (except in the case of angels). Yes, your body is a collection of quarks—immutable particles of God's essence from just after the "Let there be Light" moment (also known as the big bang)—but their value doesn't approach that of your soul. Your quarks are recyclable. Your soul is not. Don't confuse the two.

- Modern science confirms the accuracy of the Bible. Much of what I put in here is a bit dense, for which I apologize. It is sufficient for you to know that the atheist who bases his atheism on science is to be pitied for his poor scholarship.
- Angels answer to God, not man. Some of us (now me included) love mankind, but there are still avengers. Even if faith didn't demand it, common sense dictates that a human is better off on our side.
- Avoid conventional wisdom in regard to issues of faith. The problem with conventional wisdom is that it is always conventional; rarely is it wise.
- The Trinity is perfectly consistent with modern science. No miracle in Scripture violates the laws of Papa's universe, laws so poorly understood by humans.
- Heaven and hell exist. Current human perceptions are comedic and ridiculous. Like the image of the Devil and the pitchfork, they are buffoonery, disguising the true grandeur of heaven and the true evil of Satan and his hell. By the way, a little extra that was not in the book: Satan doesn't live in hell—not in the human sense of *now*. Only human souls who rejected God in their physical life are enjoying hell in the afterlife as a consequence of that conscious decision. Satan will be consigned to hell only after Jesus returns to earth. That is when hell becomes a really fun place—forever.
- Jesus didn't come to make bad people behave. He came to make dead humans live. Viewed from the outside, a life of sinful indulgence is more than offensive to God. It is also

unhealthy. It is also boring and repetitive, like a child who eats only jelly beans.
- Entry into heaven is based not on reward but on a set of beliefs and behaviors; the beliefs make those behaviors both possible and genuine. You may achieve some semblance of heaven as a result of your own goodness, but your heaven will not be the heaven of the Bible; rather, it will be a heaven as humanly created and as arbitrary and inadequate as your own code of ethics. This has been made unambiguously clear, so you can't cry foul after it's too late.
- Free will permits you to walk away from Papa, but you live with the consequences. For those people who pull away from Papa (or for those who call themselves Christians but push people away from his church), there are greater and worse consequences. Before I wrote this book, I disliked campus atheists, for example. Now I merely fear for them.
- Forgiveness and gratitude are the spiritual equivalents of bathing and brushing your teeth. You can get away without them, but soon enough, another perceptive human is going to notice the unpleasant odor of your soul.
- There is spiritual warfare—white hats against black hats. The human mind, despite all the video games and movies it has created, has yet to approach these creatures' reality. In comparison, computer-animated fantasy is a pallid, anemic substitute. Even my poor word descriptions are wholly inadequate to capture the ugliness and evil of a demon, such as Moloch—and what hotties the angels are.
- God loves humans. There should be one thousand bullet points repeating this. I cannot explain his love and won't try. His love is as transcendent as his wisdom and his power. This love animates all his interactions with

humanity. Some human theologians like to emphasize God's righteousness and judgment over his love. Is he more judgmental than loving, or more loving than judgmental? On this question, I can only refer you to the instinct of a human father: if he didn't love his child, he would not demand good behavior. But because God's love persists during bad behavior, this angel concludes that for Papa, love trumps judgment. That should be more than a relief to you. It is an invitation. Come on.

+ Now put down this book, and go out and get some exercise. Tuck your shirt in, treat your body with respect. Oh, and while you are at it, fall in love with your Creator, your Papa. He can't bless you if you keep getting in his way. Allow yourself to feel his love. Then hang on to your hat.

About the Author

Dennis Garvin is a physician, husband, father, and grandfather. Most importantly, he is a lately arrived Christian, coming to the Lord at age 38. He lives in Roanoke, Virginia with his wife, Nancy. Children and grandchildren live nearby. Dr. Garvin has not, to his knowledge, either treated or operated upon an angel. Chances are he would have remembered Augie.

The author was a committed atheist until age 38 when, with the Lord's help, he got rid of the blinders in front of his eyes and found that science, surprisingly, supported God, the Bible, and the mission of Christ. He has studied quantum physics and Einstein's theories. He applies those features of these disciplines that are generally accepted and applies their implications to the Christian faith. The idea of Augie and 'Case Files of an Angle' was a gift from God.